# Timeless Pull

Luna Hope

Published by Luna Hope, 2024.

This is a work of fiction. Similarities to real people, places, or events are entirely coincidental.

TIMELESS PULL

**First edition. October 27, 2024.**

Copyright © 2024 Luna Hope.

ISBN: 979-8227301277

Written by Luna Hope.

# Chapter 1: "Falling for the Best Friend's Brother"

The air was thick with the scent of blooming honeysuckle, a fragrance I had come to associate with lazy summer afternoons spent on the porch with Cassie, sipping lemonade and plotting our next grand adventure. But today felt different. Today, the sun hung lower in the sky, casting long shadows across the grass, and my heart thudded a rhythm of anticipation that had nothing to do with childhood games. As I leaned against the fence, the old wood creaked softly beneath my fingers, and I resisted the urge to twist a loose slat, a habit I had formed during our endless hours of idle chatter.

Then he appeared. Ethan stepped out of the sleek sedan, his presence commanding, a stark contrast to the youthful boy I remembered. I had spent countless nights dreaming of his return, but nothing prepared me for the reality of seeing him again. His dark hair was tousled by the wind, and the sharp lines of his jaw caught the sunlight in a way that made my breath hitch. Dressed in a fitted gray T-shirt and jeans that seemed to hug him just right, he exuded an effortless charm that made my pulse quicken. It felt as if the world had tilted on its axis, shifting my perception of him from the protective older brother to something infinitely more complicated.

I could feel my cheeks heat as he turned toward our house, his deep brown eyes scanning the yard until they landed on me. There was a moment of recognition, a flicker of something unspoken passing between us before he broke into a smile that could have melted glaciers. "Hey, you! Long time no see!" His voice was rich and inviting, like dark chocolate, and I fought the urge to swoon.

"Ethan! You're back!" My voice was a bit too high-pitched, betraying the tumult of feelings swirling within me. I pushed off the fence, shoving my hands into the pockets of my shorts, trying to appear nonchalant despite the surge of emotions I could hardly contain. "Did you bring me a city souvenir? A hipster coffee mug, perhaps?"

He chuckled, the sound rumbling like distant thunder, and I felt a flutter of giddiness. "I figured you'd have enough mugs by now. You know, with the way you hoard them."

I feigned offense, crossing my arms dramatically. "I'll have you know that my mug collection is an art form. Each one tells a story."

"Right. And what story does the 'World's Best Cat Mom' mug tell?"

"Hey! Don't knock my feline pride!" I laughed, unable to suppress the warmth blooming in my chest. The banter felt familiar yet charged, each quip laden with the possibility of something more.

He stepped closer, the late afternoon light catching the golden flecks in his eyes. "You still have that crazy cat, then?"

"Of course! And she's been waiting for you. She's convinced you're her long-lost brother."

Ethan shook his head, a playful grin dancing on his lips. "I can't believe you still have that little monster. Is she still terrorizing the neighborhood?"

I sighed dramatically. "Only when she's feeling particularly ambitious. I think she dreams of world domination."

"Good to know some things never change." He leaned against the fence, mirroring my earlier pose, and I felt the distance between us dissolve like sugar in warm tea.

As we exchanged memories, my thoughts drifted back to the late nights spent whispering secrets and dreams under the stars. Ethan was the one who taught me how to ride a bike, his hands steadying me until I found my balance. And now, he was here, a magnetic force pulling me into an uncharted territory of my own feelings. The thought was both thrilling and terrifying, like standing at the edge of a diving board, wondering if I would soar or plunge into icy depths.

"So, what's the plan for your grand return?" I asked, trying to keep my tone light even as my heart raced. "Are you going to abandon us for city life again?"

He shrugged, the movement effortlessly casual. "I might hang around for a while. I needed a break from the hustle. Evergreen Creek has a certain charm I forgot about."

I leaned in, intrigued. "Charm, huh? Is that code for 'I miss the peace and quiet'?"

"Maybe," he admitted, a shadow of seriousness crossing his face. "Or maybe I missed the people who make it feel like home."

A shiver of delight coursed through me, leaving me breathless. I wanted to press further, to peel back the layers of his thoughts, but the moment hung suspended, thick with unspoken possibilities. Just then, Cassie burst through the front door, her laughter echoing like music through the warm air.

"Ethan!" She flew into his arms, the two of them enveloped in an embrace that spoke of shared childhoods and bonds that time couldn't sever. I stood back, a bittersweet pang in my chest, half exhilarated and half envious.

As they separated, Cassie's eyes sparkled with mischief. "I see you found my best friend!"

"Not just your best friend," Ethan replied, glancing at me, a flicker of something unnameable passing between us again. "But maybe something more."

I held my breath, a sudden rush of warmth spreading through me. Cassie's grin widened as she caught the subtle tension in the air. "Oh, this is going to be fun."

The two of them shared a knowing look that set my heart racing. In that moment, I realized I was standing on the precipice of a summer that promised to be anything but ordinary, where the boundaries of friendship and desire blurred into something dangerously beautiful. The thrill of possibility swirled around me, igniting a spark of hope that perhaps this time, with Ethan back in my life, everything would change.

As Cassie pulled Ethan into an exuberant embrace, I stood frozen, acutely aware of the light breeze that fluttered my sundress, teasing me with the faintest promise of something unexpected. The laughter that spilled from them felt like music, buoyant and effervescent, yet I couldn't shake the feeling of being an outsider in a moment that belonged to them. I brushed a stray hair from my face, catching Ethan's eye, and the spark of recognition flared anew, igniting something deeper within me.

"Welcome back, you city slicker!" Cassie teased, stepping back to scrutinize him. "Did the bright lights and fancy coffee shops change you? Or do you still have that tragic taste in music?"

"Tragic?" Ethan arched an eyebrow, a playful challenge lacing his tone. "Have you heard your own Spotify playlist? I was just trying to broaden my horizons."

"Broadening your horizons? Please, I think you just picked up some pretentiousness along with your artisanal coffee." Cassie rolled her eyes dramatically, and they both dissolved into laughter, the kind that ripples through the air and wraps around you like a warm blanket.

Eager to rejoin the banter, I interjected. "Don't worry, Ethan. I can help you purge that pretentiousness. One day at a time."

"Oh really? Is that your new career path? Professional pretentiousness removal?" His smirk ignited a thrill of competition within me.

"Absolutely! The first step is breaking out the old iPod and banishing those 'cultured' playlists to the dark corners of the internet."

He grinned, a spark of mischief in his eyes. "Challenge accepted. But I have a feeling it's going to be a long, painful journey."

As we bantered back and forth, I felt the tension in the air shift, becoming less about casual jabs and more about something electric—an unspoken chemistry weaving through our words. Cassie watched us, her smile widening, clearly relishing the scene.

"So, what's your grand plan for the summer, Ethan? Besides enduring my lovely company?"

"I thought I might help with the landscaping," he replied, his gaze sliding toward the overgrown garden that sprawled in a riot of wildflowers and weeds. "It could use some love. Besides, I've got a whole summer to explore what Evergreen has to offer."

"Landscaping? You're going to be one of those guys?" I laughed, picturing Ethan wielding a shovel instead of a briefcase. "You know, when you were a kid, you claimed to be allergic to hard work. Have you grown out of it, or are we just waiting for the inevitable meltdown?"

"Hey, I've changed!" he protested, his hands raised defensively. "The city has toughened me up. I can handle a bit of dirt."

"Sure, but I'll believe it when I see you weeding without whining."

"Challenge accepted," he shot back, a playful glint in his eyes.

The laughter faded into comfortable silence, the three of us standing together in the warm sunlight. The soft rustle of leaves whispered secrets above us, and the world felt impossibly right. Yet beneath the surface, my heart raced with a strange mixture of excitement and anxiety.

Later that evening, the sun dipped below the horizon, painting the sky with strokes of pink and gold as I stood in my kitchen, preparing a dinner I hoped would impress. I hummed to myself, the sound mingling with the scent of garlic and herbs simmering on the stove. My phone buzzed on the counter, and I grabbed it, expecting a text from Cassie, but instead, it was a message from Ethan.

Hope you're not planning a five-star dinner. I'm only here for the takeout.

I couldn't help but chuckle, shaking my head at his audacity. Takeout? What do you think I am, some city girl who can't boil water?

His response was swift. That's a bold claim, my friend. Prove it.

I took a deep breath, a spark of playful determination igniting within me. Fine. Come over in thirty minutes. But I'm holding you to a taste test.

The anticipation crackled in the air as I finished setting the table, placing bright plates adorned with a sunflower pattern at each spot. I carefully arranged a bouquet of wildflowers, freshly picked from the garden, in the center. With each moment that ticked by, the kitchen filled with a heady blend of spices and my nervous excitement.

When the doorbell rang, I jumped, heart racing as I wiped my hands on a dishtowel and opened the door. There he stood, a tall silhouette against the fading light, his hair tousled as if he had just come in from a whirlwind adventure. "Is this where I get to critique your culinary skills?"

"Only if you want to end up with something in your lap," I replied, stepping aside to let him in. "And if you're not prepared for the reality that takeout might have been the wiser choice."

Ethan surveyed the kitchen, a smirk playing on his lips. "Looks like you've put in quite a bit of effort. Are you sure you're not secretly a gourmet chef?"

I shot him a look, half-serious and half-teasing. "I'll have you know that I'm not afraid to get my hands dirty in the kitchen. I can even chop vegetables without losing a finger."

"Impressive. But can you manage a soufflé?"

"Only if you want to eat it off the floor."

He laughed, a sound that sent a thrill through me. "I'll take my chances."

Dinner unfolded like a delicate dance, the conversation flowing effortlessly as we navigated topics ranging from embarrassing high school memories to the most ridiculous things Cassie had ever done. With each shared story, the bond between us grew, threaded with a mixture of nostalgia and a newfound spark that sent electricity coursing through my veins.

"So, what's it like living in the city?" I asked, leaning forward with genuine curiosity.

"It's... fast. Exciting, but exhausting. Sometimes I miss the quiet of this place," he admitted, his gaze momentarily drifting toward the window, as if searching for a memory in the dusk. "It's hard to breathe sometimes. Too many people, too much noise."

"Ever consider staying here for good?"

Ethan's eyes locked onto mine, a flicker of something unnameable flashing between us. "I think about it more than I'd like to admit."

Before I could respond, Cassie burst in, her energy a whirlwind. "Did I miss the 'let's reminisce about our childhood' party?" She plopped down at the table, a plate piled high with food in her hands.

Ethan and I exchanged glances, both suppressing laughter as we tried to keep our conversation light, but the air was thick with unsaid words, the tension palpable. I couldn't help but wonder what would unfold as the summer stretched before us, a canvas yet to be painted with our shared memories and perhaps something more.

The warmth of the summer evening wrapped around us as we shared dinner, Cassie's animated chatter weaving seamlessly into the comfortable rhythm between Ethan and me. With each laugh, each story from our childhood, the lingering tension crackled like electricity in the air. I couldn't help but steal glances at Ethan, watching the way his eyes sparkled with humor, the way his laughter echoed through the kitchen, making me feel as though the walls were closing in just to keep our little bubble safe.

"So, what's the latest gossip in the big city?" Cassie asked, plopping a piece of grilled chicken onto her plate. "Is everyone still obsessed with avocado toast, or has that trend finally passed?"

Ethan chuckled, a low, rich sound that sent a delightful shiver down my spine. "Oh, it's worse than ever. I'm pretty sure I saw a café offering avocado toast topped with edible gold leaf last week. Because why not, right?"

"Wow," I said, rolling my eyes in mock disbelief. "That's one way to ensure it's too fancy to eat. Who has gold leaf just lying around?"

"Apparently, city folks do," he replied, his eyes glinting with mischief. "It's the latest craze, I think. Next thing you know, they'll start charging for the air you breathe."

Cassie snorted as she tried to swallow her laughter. "You know, I'd almost consider moving to the city if it meant eating avocado toast like royalty."

Ethan shook his head, chuckling. "You'd be broke in a week. Not to mention perpetually hungry when you see the prices."

As we continued our playful repartee, the kitchen seemed to fade into the background, the scent of roasted vegetables and simmering sauces mingling with the sound of laughter and nostalgia. But beneath the lighthearted banter, I sensed a shifting undercurrent—a pull toward something deeper. Ethan's gaze lingered on me a moment too long, and I caught my breath, feeling the gravity of the moment wrap around us both like a well-worn quilt, soft and familiar yet charged with potential.

Once dinner was finished, Cassie excused herself to the living room, declaring she needed to catch up on her favorite reality show. The invitation to stay felt unspoken, the silence settling comfortably between Ethan and me. I began clearing the table, the rhythmic clattering of plates and utensils providing an odd kind of distraction from the quiet tension hanging in the air.

"Do you need any help with that?" Ethan asked, stepping closer as I stacked the dishes.

"Nope! I've got this," I replied cheerfully, though my heart was pounding. "I'm perfectly capable of handling a few plates. If I can tackle the intricacies of my high school math homework, I can certainly handle this."

"High school math? Now you're just showing off," he teased, leaning against the counter. "What was your biggest struggle? Fractions? Geometry? Or was it just trying to keep your head from spinning while learning how to factor?"

I paused, turning to face him fully, the playful banter giving way to a more serious tone. "Honestly? It was probably learning how to divide my time between school, friends, and my overwhelming love for animals. You should see my cat; she demands attention like a small, furry diva."

"Diva? I can only imagine the demands she makes," he said, a smirk playing at the corners of his lips. "Does she demand avocado toast?"

"She has a very sophisticated palate, thank you very much." I laughed, feeling the atmosphere warm between us again. "No avocado toast, though. Just plain tuna—no golden leaf involved."

Ethan leaned closer, his gaze locking onto mine with an intensity that made my breath hitch. "I'd take the tuna. At least it's honest."

The moment felt charged, electric, and suddenly the familiar surroundings faded away, leaving just us suspended in time. I could feel my heart thumping in my chest, each beat echoing in the silence, urging me to say something. I didn't know what that something was, but the urge to break the spell hung heavily in the air.

"Uh, speaking of honesty..." I began, my words stumbling over the weight of what I wanted to convey. "I've missed this—us. It feels different now, doesn't it?"

His expression shifted, a flicker of surprise mixed with understanding. "Yeah, it does," he said quietly. "It feels... I don't know, like we're standing at the edge of something we don't quite know how to navigate."

I swallowed hard, my heart pounding against my ribcage. The vulnerability in his voice resonated with my own uncertainty. "Exactly. Like there's something unspoken between us."

He stepped even closer, the warmth radiating from him almost palpable. "Maybe we're just scared to find out what that is."

Just then, Cassie's laughter erupted from the living room, pulling us back from the precipice of our moment. I blinked, shaking off the weight of the conversation as if it were a heavy blanket that I couldn't bear.

"Right! I should probably—" I began, stepping back as if retreating from a battlefield of emotions. "I should check on Cassie."

But Ethan reached out, his hand wrapping around my wrist with a gentle firmness that made my pulse quicken. "Wait."

I turned back to him, our gazes locking again, the world narrowing down to just the two of us. "What?"

"I don't want to rush this. But I need you to know—"

A loud crash echoed from the living room, cutting through the tension like a knife. "Cassie!" I shouted, my heart leaping into my throat as I pulled away and darted down the hallway. Ethan followed close behind, our earlier moment forgotten as we rushed into the chaos.

In the living room, Cassie was on the floor, her eyes wide as she stared at the remains of a shattered vase that had toppled off the coffee table. "I swear I didn't touch it!" she exclaimed, hands raised in defense as if she were a child caught with her hand in the cookie jar.

I knelt beside her, heart racing for entirely different reasons now. "What happened?"

"I just got too excited about the show!" Cassie replied, gesturing wildly, nearly knocking over a lamp in the process. "But look! It's a sign we need to throw a party to celebrate Ethan's return!"

I shot Ethan a glance, half amused and half exasperated, but before I could say anything, the doorbell rang. My heart skipped again. "Now who could that be?"

Cassie sprang up, brushing herself off as she headed for the door. Ethan and I exchanged bewildered looks, the earlier conversation hanging in the air like the shards of the broken vase.

"Should I get that?" Cassie called over her shoulder.

"Uh, yeah!" I replied, my heart pounding not just from the surprise but from the potential twists of the evening. "Just—don't open it too wide!"

But the moment she swung the door open, I was unprepared for the figure standing on the porch. It was an old friend of Ethan's, someone I never expected to see. "Ethan! I was hoping to find you here!"

The tension snapped back into focus, the uncharted territory we had been exploring suddenly overshadowed by the arrival of this unexpected guest.

Ethan's expression shifted, surprise mingling with something else—something guarded, as if he had been caught off guard in a moment he wasn't quite ready to share. I felt the air thicken, the tension twisting and coiling around us like a vine, and suddenly, everything felt very precarious.

"Can we talk?" the stranger asked, stepping inside with an air of urgency that sent a shiver down my spine. I glanced at Ethan, who had gone pale, his gaze flickering to me with an unreadable expression.

"What's going on?" I murmured, suddenly feeling as if I were standing on the edge of a precipice, the ground crumbling beneath my feet.

But as the door closed behind them, sealing our little world off from the rest of Evergreen Creek, I realized this summer might hold secrets I was completely unprepared for. The air crackled with uncertainty, and I had a sinking feeling that the summer of possibilities was about to spiral into something far more complicated than I had ever anticipated.

# Chapter 2: "The Unexpected Reunion"

The town was buzzing with excitement, an electric current weaving through the air like a long-forgotten melody. Rumors swirled like autumn leaves, carrying whispers of Ethan's return. It had been years since he'd left, chasing dreams as wild as the wind that rattled through the trees, and I never thought I'd see him again. Yet here I was, staring into the mirror, trying to tame the wild strands of hair that seemed to have taken on a life of their own. The scent of roasted chicken and herbs wafted through the open windows of Cassie's home, an invitation laced with nostalgia and hope.

As I stepped over the threshold, laughter cascaded around me, a warm embrace that fought against the chill of the evening. The walls of the living room were adorned with photographs that danced in the flickering light, moments captured in time—smiles, hugs, celebrations. I could almost hear the echoes of our childhood, where we'd played hide and seek and shared secrets, each day a little adventure etched into our memories.

Cassie was flitting about, her bright red hair a halo against the backdrop of the cozy room. She was a whirlwind of enthusiasm, her laughter punctuating the air like music. "You made it!" she exclaimed, wrapping me in a hug that momentarily stole my breath. Her warmth was a reminder of simpler times when our biggest worries revolved around school lunches and Saturday morning cartoons.

"Wouldn't miss it for the world," I managed, though the knot in my stomach threatened to unravel my cheerful facade. I searched the room for Ethan, a pulse of anticipation thrumming beneath my skin. It felt like standing at the edge of a cliff, staring into the unknown, my heart racing in exhilaration and fear.

And then, there he was. He moved through the crowd with a grace that was both familiar and foreign, a fleeting shadow of the boy I once knew. The air seemed to thicken as our eyes met, the world around us dimming into a soft blur. Ethan had always had that effect on me, like gravity pulling at my very core. His smile, slow and genuine, broke through the din, igniting something deep inside me—a spark that whispered of long-lost possibilities.

"Still scared of the dark, little neighbor?" His voice rumbled across the room, playful and teasing, yet somehow intimate. It felt like stepping into a favorite song, one I hadn't realized I'd missed until that very moment.

I rolled my eyes, a habit I had perfected over the years. "Only if it's your kind of dark," I shot back, the playful banter flowing effortlessly between us, as though the years had melted away. The crowd faded into a soft hum, and it was just the two of us, locked in this unexpected reunion.

"Is that a challenge?" he quipped, taking a step closer, his eyes sparkling with mischief. The space between us felt charged, filled with unspoken words and lingering glances.

"Maybe," I replied, my heart racing as I leaned into the banter, the thrill of our dynamic rekindling old flames. Cassie was flitting around, busy with the details of her dinner, but I could feel her eyes darting between us, her excitement bubbling beneath the surface.

The evening progressed with the warmth of friendship and a hint of something more, laughter threading through our conversations. We settled at the dining table, a feast of color and flavor laid out before us. The roasted chicken glistened under the soft light, alongside an array of vegetables that seemed to reflect the autumn hues outside.

"So, Ethan," I ventured, attempting to steer the conversation into deeper waters, "what brought you back after all this time?"

He leaned back in his chair, a thoughtful expression crossing his face. "I realized I missed the simplicity of it all. The open skies, the familiar faces... I think I needed a reminder of where I came from."

His gaze flickered to me, holding a weight that made my breath hitch. "And some things are worth coming back for."

The sincerity in his tone sent ripples through my heart, setting off a cascade of emotions I had buried deep. Cassie chimed in, eager to steer the conversation back to lighter topics, sharing stories of our town's latest escapades. Laughter erupted around the table, an effervescent blend of nostalgia and joy, but beneath it all, the undercurrents of something unresolved pulsed between Ethan and me.

As dinner progressed, the evening light shifted outside, painting the room in soft shades of gold and crimson. Each moment felt layered, filled with laughter and unacknowledged tension, creating a rich tapestry that enveloped us. I could sense Ethan's gaze on me, a steady warmth that anchored me amidst the swirling emotions.

"I heard you started your own business," he said, his tone casual but his interest palpable. "That's impressive."

I shrugged, trying to play it cool. "It's just a little freelance design work. Nothing to write home about."

"Just a little?" He raised an eyebrow, a smirk playing on his lips. "I saw your website. It's anything but little."

I felt a flush creep up my cheeks. "Okay, maybe it's a bit more than that," I conceded, but the spark in his eyes fueled my confidence. "It's been a labor of love."

"Clearly," he replied, his voice low, the weight of his compliment wrapping around me like a cozy blanket on a chilly night.

As dessert was served—an impossibly decadent chocolate cake—Cassie began recounting stories from our childhood, her laughter echoing like music. Each tale drew us closer, weaving a web of shared experiences that blurred the lines between the past and the present.

But amid the sweetness of nostalgia, a gnawing question lingered in the back of my mind. What did Ethan's return really mean? Would he stay, or was this just another fleeting moment, like the delicate frosting atop the cake? I stole a glance at him, wondering if he sensed my apprehension.

The cake melted in my mouth, rich and velvety, but the sweetness couldn't mask the uncertainty brewing within me. Ethan's laughter mingled with Cassie's, a symphony that tugged at my heart, yet a part of me remained anchored in doubt. The night unfolded around us, filled with the warmth of reunion, yet I couldn't shake the feeling that this was only the beginning of something far more complicated than I had anticipated.

"Scared? I prefer to think of it as having a healthy respect for the unknown," I retorted, crossing my arms defiantly. The playful glint in Ethan's eyes made it impossible to maintain any semblance of seriousness. This was the same boy who'd chased away my childhood fears with stories of brave knights and monsters that turned out to be shadows. I hadn't realized until that moment just how much I had missed his teasing presence, the way he always seemed to know just how to nudge me out of my comfort zone.

We found ourselves gravitating toward the back porch, where the scent of the nearby lilac bush mingled with the cool evening air, creating a momentary bubble of privacy away from the joyous chaos inside. The stars blinked overhead, timidly appearing as the last rays of sunlight retreated. I leaned against the railing, the wood warm under my fingers, as Ethan slid into the space beside me, his posture relaxed yet charged with unspoken words.

"It's good to be back," he said, his gaze fixed on the horizon where the sky met the earth, a thoughtful expression crossing his face. "There's something about this place... it's like a memory that hasn't faded, no matter how far I've wandered."

"Is that why you returned?" I asked, trying to sound casual while my heart threatened to leap out of my chest. "To revisit the past?"

"Partly." He turned his head slightly, his profile catching the moonlight, revealing the familiar features that had haunted my dreams for years. "But I think I needed to figure out what the past means to me now."

Before I could respond, Cassie's voice called us back inside, slicing through the moment like a well-timed punchline. "You two! Come on, it's time for dessert! And I made sure it's the chocolate kind, just like you love."

"Chocolate, eh?" I winked at Ethan. "Looks like I'll have to share with you if you're still as sweet-toothed as I remember."

He chuckled, the sound low and rich. "Just don't expect me to share my slice."

With that, we returned to the lively atmosphere of the dining room, laughter weaving through the air like an intricate tapestry. Cassie had outdone herself; the chocolate cake was a masterpiece, its layers stacked high and glossy, inviting us to dig in. As we each took our first bites, I could see Ethan's eyes widen in delight, the boyish joy rekindling in the depths of his gaze.

"This is incredible!" he declared, glancing at Cassie, who beamed with pride. "If I knew home was going to be this delicious, I would've returned sooner."

"Next time, I'll make a double batch just for you," Cassie teased, her eyes sparkling. "But seriously, it's about time you came home. We've missed you around here. Haven't we, everyone?"

The collective murmur of agreement from the table made my heart swell, yet it was a bittersweet feeling. For all the excitement, a sense of foreboding loomed like storm clouds on the horizon. I couldn't shake the feeling that the reunion wasn't just a homecoming; it was a reckoning.

As the conversation flowed, I found myself gravitating toward Ethan again, slipping into our old rhythm. "So, what's the plan now that you're back?" I asked, curious yet cautious, wanting to peel back the layers of his return without sounding too invasive.

He leaned in, his voice dropping to a conspiratorial whisper. "I think I might start a new project. Something involving local art and community engagement. I've got ideas, but they're still... maturing, I suppose."

"Art? You? I remember the time you painted a mural on the side of the school, and it looked like an explosion of spaghetti."

His laughter rang out, vibrant and infectious. "Hey, I was a child prodigy with a can of spray paint! You have to admit, it was an ambitious vision."

"Ambitious? More like ambitious and a little reckless."

We both laughed, but beneath the humor, I sensed an undercurrent of something more serious. What if this project was more than just art? What if it represented a chance for him to redefine himself in a town that had once been his everything?

The dinner wound down, and as people began to stand and stretch, I caught Ethan's eye once more. "Can I walk you home?" he asked, his tone casual but there was a depth that hinted at something more.

"Sure," I replied, trying to sound nonchalant. "But be prepared; my house is only slightly less chaotic than this one."

As we stepped out into the cool night air, the laughter from Cassie's house faded behind us, leaving a comforting silence enveloping us like a well-worn blanket. The stars overhead twinkled mischievously, casting silver light on the path ahead, illuminating our footsteps as we walked side by side.

"You know," Ethan said, breaking the silence, "I've thought about this moment a lot. The part where I come back and we catch up. It never quite matched what I envisioned."

"Why? Did you picture us reenacting some kind of cheesy rom-com?" I teased, but my heart thudded in anticipation.

He shot me a sideways glance, the corner of his mouth quirking up. "Maybe. But I thought it would feel different, you know? More... definitive?"

"Definitive how?"

His expression shifted, becoming serious as he stopped to face me. "I thought coming back would mean clarity. But honestly? It's all just a bit overwhelming."

I couldn't help but admire the vulnerability in his gaze. "Overwhelming how?"

"I guess I thought I'd know exactly what I wanted, but being back here... it's stirring up old feelings I didn't expect."

The air between us thickened, charged with unspoken possibilities. I wanted to reach out, to grasp his hand and guide him through the emotional maze he seemed lost in. "Sometimes the past has a way of complicating the present," I offered gently.

He nodded, a flicker of understanding passing between us. "And sometimes it's a reminder of what we've always wanted."

The words hung in the air, heavy with implications. Just then, a distant hoot of an owl broke the tension, and I couldn't help but smile, the sound reminiscent of our childhood, when we used to make up stories about enchanted forests and secret kingdoms.

"Are you going to stay for a while?" I ventured, my heart racing at the thought. "I mean, for good?"

Ethan paused, his eyes searching mine, and for a fleeting moment, the world around us fell away. "I want to. I really do."

The honesty in his voice ignited a spark of hope within me, but as he turned to continue our walk, I couldn't shake the feeling that this was just the beginning of a much deeper story, one that neither of us fully understood yet. The night was still young, but the promise of what lay ahead felt like a rollercoaster poised to plunge into the unknown, and I was more than ready for the ride.

The cool evening air wrapped around us like a shroud as Ethan and I walked side by side, our footsteps echoing softly on the cracked pavement. The familiar sights of our neighborhood—the gnarled oak tree at the corner, the old church steeple silhouetted against the night sky—had taken on a different hue, their outlines softened by the glow of streetlamps. Each detail sparked nostalgia, memories swirling like autumn leaves, but tonight they felt charged with potential, as if the very ground beneath us was pregnant with unspoken possibilities.

"What's your plan for tomorrow?" I asked, trying to sound casual while my heart raced, hoping to keep the conversation flowing. "More hometown sightseeing? A trip to the coffee shop?"

He smiled, a hint of mischief dancing in his eyes. "Actually, I thought I might visit the old haunt—the lake. You know, where we used to spend lazy afternoons pretending to fish?"

"Ah yes, the legendary fishing trips where you caught precisely nothing and I caught the sunburn," I replied, chuckling. "That was your strategy, right? Lure me into sunbathing while you sat in the shade?"

Ethan feigned innocence. "Hey, I was providing moral support. Fishing is an art, and I was merely the canvas."

We both laughed, and for a moment, the weight of the evening lifted. But as the laughter faded, a new tension crept in, a silent question hovering between us. Why did he want to revisit the lake? What was it about our shared history that seemed to draw him back, like a moth to a flame?

"I might join you at the lake tomorrow," I suggested, trying to sound breezy, though my pulse quickened at the idea of spending time alone with him. "You know, for old time's sake."

"Are you sure? I wouldn't want to interrupt your busy schedule of... whatever it is you do now," he replied, his tone teasing yet genuine.

"Oh, you know," I replied, pretending to be grandiose, "just saving the world one design project at a time."

He chuckled, the sound reverberating through the cool night air. "Well, maybe saving the world can wait for a little bit. I'd love to catch up. Just us, the water, and the stars."

His words hung in the air like a promise, sending shivers of excitement down my spine. I nodded, my heart dancing at the thought, but a nagging voice in the back of my mind cautioned me. What if spending more time with Ethan reignited feelings I thought I had buried?

As we reached the front of my house, the porch light flickered on, casting a warm glow on the steps. I hesitated for a moment, feeling the weight of the night and the charged atmosphere between us. "Well, here we are. Home sweet home."

Ethan leaned against the railing, his eyes locked onto mine, a smirk playing on his lips. "Home. Funny how one little word can carry so much meaning."

"Yeah," I replied, feeling the weight of his gaze. "Sometimes it feels like home is a place we create rather than just a physical location."

"Like this place, right?" He gestured around, and his eyes sparkled with mischief. "I mean, it's clearly a palace."

I rolled my eyes, but laughter bubbled up nonetheless. "If by 'palace' you mean a cozy little house that occasionally resembles a tornado aftermath, then yes, absolutely."

He stepped a little closer, the space between us diminishing. "You should see the house I rented. It's more of a haunted castle, complete with creaky floors and a yard that looks like it hasn't been tended to since the last ice age."

I couldn't help but laugh at the mental image. "That sounds perfect for your artistic temperament. Who wouldn't want a spooky backdrop for inspiration?"

He paused, his expression shifting, becoming more serious. "You know, I've been thinking about how important it is to embrace the chaos. It's where the best ideas come from, right?"

"Right," I replied, my heart racing as he leaned in slightly, the intensity of his gaze locking me in place. "Sometimes chaos is just a sign that something new is about to happen."

He nodded slowly, as if considering my words. "That's a beautiful way to put it. Maybe we're both still figuring out how to navigate our own chaos."

Just then, the door swung open behind me, and Cassie's voice broke the moment. "Hey, you two! I was just about to head to bed, but if you're planning to share deep secrets about your chaotic lives, at least take it inside. The neighbors might think you're plotting something!"

Ethan chuckled and straightened up, his playful demeanor returning. "Wouldn't want to give them any ideas," he replied, shooting me a conspiratorial glance.

I felt a spark of disappointment at the interruption but quickly brushed it aside. "Well, it was good talking to you. I'll see you tomorrow at the lake?"

"Definitely," he said, his voice a mix of certainty and anticipation. "I'm looking forward to it."

With that, I stepped inside, my heart still racing from the intensity of our conversation. The cozy warmth of the living room enveloped me, but the air felt thick with unspoken words. Cassie was busy tidying up the remnants of dinner, humming softly to herself, unaware of the storm of emotions swirling within me.

As I perched on the edge of the couch, I couldn't help but replay our conversation. Ethan's return felt like an unexpected whirlwind, and I was caught in its embrace, swept up in feelings I thought had settled into the past.

"Are you okay?" Cassie asked, glancing over her shoulder. "You seem a bit dazed. Did the cake have a secret ingredient I didn't know about?"

I forced a smile, trying to mask my turmoil. "Just thinking about tomorrow. The lake and all that... you know, nostalgia."

She paused, her brow furrowing with concern. "You sure that's all it is? You two seemed pretty intense out there."

"Intense? Us?" I feigned innocence, but my heart thudded. "We were just reminiscing, that's all."

"Uh-huh. If reminiscing includes that level of eye contact, I'd call it something else."

I shot her a mock glare, though I felt the heat rising in my cheeks. "Okay, okay, maybe there was some... tension."

Cassie's eyes sparkled with mischief. "Ooh, I love a good love story. But seriously, you need to figure out what you want. You don't want to be stuck in the past, especially if he's planning to stay."

"I know," I replied, the weight of her words settling like a stone in my stomach. "But what if the past is all I want?"

As I climbed into bed that night, my mind raced, the uncertainty clawing at me like a persistent itch. The quiet of my room felt oppressive, every creak of the old house echoing my racing thoughts. I tossed and turned, unable to shake the feeling that tomorrow could change everything.

Just as I began to drift off, my phone buzzed on the nightstand. I reached for it, heart quickening as I saw Ethan's name flashing on the screen.

Can't wait for tomorrow. I have something to tell you.

A jolt of adrenaline shot through me. What could he possibly have to say? My pulse raced as I stared at the message, a mix of excitement and dread swirling within me.

I typed back, my fingers trembling slightly. What is it?

But there was no immediate reply. Instead, an unsettling silence enveloped me, thickening the air around me like fog. I lay there, heart pounding, feeling as though the ground was shifting beneath me.

What could Ethan have to tell me? The possibilities danced in my mind, some exhilarating and others terrifying. I closed my eyes, willing myself to sleep, but the uncertainty loomed larger than ever, a shadow creeping closer, wrapping itself around my thoughts as the darkness outside deepened.

And just when I thought I might finally drift off, the unmistakable sound of glass shattering from the direction of Cassie's kitchen shattered the night's stillness, sending shockwaves of fear coursing through me.

# Chapter 3: "A Change in Dynamics"

The air in the Montgomery household was thick with the scent of freshly baked bread, its warmth wrapping around me like a soft embrace. I often found myself there, drawn in by the chaotic yet comforting rhythm of their lives. Cassie had become my safe harbor—a sanctuary where laughter and love wove seamlessly into the fabric of each day. The house itself, with its inviting beige walls and mismatched furniture, felt alive, almost like a character in its own right, full of stories waiting to be told.

One afternoon, while Cassie stirred a bubbling pot of tomato sauce, I perched on the edge of the counter, swinging my legs like a child. The rhythmic clinking of spoons and the sizzle of vegetables danced around us, providing a familiar backdrop to our chatter. Cassie's laughter rang out, bright and infectious, cutting through the mundane like a bright sunbeam piercing through thick clouds.

"Can you believe Mr. Thompson actually thought he could assign us a ten-page essay on The Great Gatsby? Does he think we have nothing better to do?" she huffed, rolling her eyes dramatically.

I couldn't help but chuckle.

"Right? As if he's never heard of SparkNotes," I quipped back, raising an eyebrow as I adopted a mock-serious tone. "Next, he'll be expecting us to write sonnets about the symbolism of green lights."

Cassie threw a spoonful of flour at me, her eyes sparkling with mischief. "You know, I might just do that! I can see it now: Oh, green light, you tantalizing beacon of unattainable dreams!"

We dissolved into laughter, and just as the sound faded, the door creaked open. Ethan strolled in, shaking off the rain like a large, wet dog, his hair tousled and his jeans slightly damp. His presence filled the room with a quiet magnetism that seemed to shift the air around us, making my heart race for reasons I wasn't quite ready to acknowledge.

"Hey, what's all this ruckus?" he asked, grinning as he took off his jacket, revealing a faded band T-shirt that clung to his lean frame. There was something effortlessly charming about him, something that made my stomach flip in ways I'd thought I'd outgrown.

"Just discussing the finer points of literary analysis," Cassie said, her tone dripping with sarcasm. "You know, the stuff that gets us through the endless hours of high school boredom."

"Ah, yes, the plight of modern academia." Ethan leaned against the doorway, his arms crossed. "Are you two going to form a book club? Because if it involves wearing pajamas and eating snacks, I'm in."

"Only if you promise to share your infamous nachos," I shot back, tilting my head, trying to read his expression. Our eyes locked for a brief moment, and I felt a flutter of something electrifying—a spark that sent a shiver down my spine.

Ethan's laughter broke the spell. "Deal. But only if you promise to keep your literary critiques to a minimum. I'm not sure I can handle both Shakespeare and nacho cheese at the same time."

The conversation flowed effortlessly, each exchange punctuated by playful jabs and teasing. But beneath the surface of our camaraderie, a tension brewed, unspoken and potent, like the storm clouds gathering outside. I could feel it in the air, thick and heavy, electrifying every shared glance, every lingering touch.

That evening, with rain pattering against the window and the scent of herbs wafting through the air, we decided to watch a movie. Cassie chose a romantic comedy that had us rolling our eyes more than laughing, but it was the kind of easy laughter that felt like home. As we settled into the worn couch, I found myself sandwiched between the two of them, the couch cushions softening my worries as I sunk deeper into the warmth of the moment.

Ethan tossed a popcorn kernel at my head. "Hey, don't hog all the good snacks!"

I retaliated by grabbing the bowl and holding it above my head, a grin spreading across my face. "You want it? Come and get it!"

As he lunged forward, his fingers brushed against mine, and that touch sent a jolt through me, awakening something deep and dormant. It was a fleeting moment, barely enough to register in the grand scheme of things, but it ignited a wildfire of emotions I had kept carefully contained. I could feel my cheeks flush as I pulled my hand back, trying to act casual, but the air crackled between us, palpable and undeniable.

"Careful, or you might just start a food fight," Cassie teased, oblivious to the sudden tension that enveloped the room. I shot her a grateful look, silently thanking her for the distraction, even as I struggled to find my breath.

Ethan's eyes were intense as they searched mine, his playful demeanor shifting slightly. "You know, if you wanted to hog the popcorn, you could have just asked," he said, his voice low and teasing, but there was an edge to it—a challenge that sent my heart racing.

I opened my mouth to respond, but the words caught in my throat. What could I say? "I wasn't hogging it; I was just..."

"Just what?" he pressed, a smirk playing on his lips.

And suddenly, I found myself wanting to tell him everything. I wanted to confess the swell of feelings that were spiraling inside me, feelings I had tried so hard to suppress. But I couldn't. Not now. Not when everything felt so beautifully complicated, as though we were all characters in a story that had yet to unfold fully.

The movie played on, but the plot faded into the background, overshadowed by the tension weaving itself through our interactions, a delicate thread binding us together in ways I couldn't yet understand. I leaned back against the couch, my heart racing, the rain tapping a soft rhythm against the window, as if it too was waiting for something to change, to shift, to explode into something more.

As the weeks slipped by, the Montgomery household transformed into my second home, a refuge wrapped in the familiar warmth of friendship and shared secrets. Each evening spent there added another layer to the tapestry of my life, weaving together laughter, the clatter of dishes, and the sweet sound of Cassie's voice, rich with the kind of joy that can only come from a life well-lived. Ethan was the variable in our equation, a magnetic force that pulled me closer, and the tension simmering between us crackled like static electricity, palpable in the spaces between words.

One Saturday afternoon, the sky hung heavy with clouds, a low hum of thunder rumbling in the distance. Cassie had been buzzing with excitement about an upcoming school event, and her energy was infectious. I sat on the floor of their cozy den, surrounded by cushions and scattered magazines, as she animatedly described her plans for a group project that, to be honest, sounded more like an excuse for a party than an academic endeavor.

"Imagine it!" she exclaimed, her eyes shining. "We can do a pop-up café! We'll serve cookies and punch, and I'll wear a cute apron. It'll be the talk of the school!"

"Why not go full throttle and add a live band?" I teased, raising an eyebrow. "Nothing says 'school project' like a rock concert in the cafeteria."

Cassie laughed, her infectious giggle echoing off the walls. "And risk getting detention? I'll save the concert for my senior year. Besides, who would actually listen to me? You saw my last karaoke performance."

"Yeah, but I thought 'Livin' on a Prayer' was meant to be a duet," I shot back, unable to resist the playful jab.

We fell into a rhythm, our banter flowing like the rain outside, each drop a reminder of the changing dynamics that simmered beneath the surface. Yet, even amidst our laughter, I could feel Ethan's gaze lingering on me from across the room. He was sprawled on the couch, one arm draped casually over the back, his expression a mix of amusement and something more intense that made my heart flutter unpredictably.

"Hey, you two," he finally interjected, a playful smirk dancing on his lips. "Why don't you leave the planning to the professionals? I mean, clearly, I'm the only one here with a knack for culinary arts."

"Culinary arts?" I feigned disbelief, crossing my arms. "You mean your signature microwave popcorn and the occasional sandwich?"

Ethan leaned forward, a gleam of mischief in his eyes. "Hey, don't knock my sandwich-making skills. They've won several awards in my kitchen. Best Presentation, Most Likely to Satisfy Late-Night Cravings..."

"Most Likely to Be Eaten in Five Minutes Flat," I added, my smile widening.

He chuckled, and the tension between us shifted, almost imperceptibly, into something charged with possibility. I couldn't help but wonder if this playful repartee was just a cover for the deeper feelings swirling beneath, a way to mask the heart-pounding moments we had begun to share.

The rain intensified outside, drumming a steady rhythm against the windows, and as the light dimmed, casting soft shadows across the room, we decided to move our impromptu planning session to the kitchen. I followed Cassie, excitement bubbling inside me as I anticipated what might unfold next.

Once in the kitchen, I pulled out a chair and perched on it, watching as Cassie rifled through the cabinets. "So, what's next on the agenda, Chef Cassie?"

"Let's see what we can whip up for inspiration," she replied, a glint in her eye as she pulled out a bag of flour and a bowl.

"You're not seriously planning to bake, are you? Flour explosions aren't exactly conducive to planning a party," I teased.

"Oh, come on! Where's your sense of adventure?" she shot back, flour flying as she began mixing ingredients. "Besides, we can call it research. Who doesn't love cookies?"

"Fair point," I conceded, enjoying the way her enthusiasm filled the space.

Meanwhile, Ethan hovered nearby, a mischievous grin on his face as he leaned against the counter. "I'll be the taste tester. I'm very qualified in that department."

"Of course you are," I replied, rolling my eyes, but my heart fluttered again at the idea of him standing so close. "Someone has to ensure the quality of the snacks. God forbid we serve anything subpar at our 'pop-up café.'"

Cassie turned to me, flour dusting her cheeks, her expression earnest. "You should help too, you know. Make it a team effort. I can't do this without my right-hand woman!"

The warmth of her words settled in my chest, reminding me of how far we'd come since those awkward first days of school. I jumped off the chair, ready to join the chaos, mixing and rolling dough while the banter flowed freely. The kitchen filled with laughter, and the comforting scent of baking cookies began to envelop us, but through it all, I felt Ethan's presence like a magnetic field—pulling me in, testing my resolve.

As the cookies baked, we returned to the living room, and Cassie flicked through channels until she landed on a game show, its bright lights and enthusiastic hosts offering a stark contrast to our cozy chaos. We sprawled across the couch, Ethan's arm brushing against mine, sending yet another wave of warmth cascading through me. I tried to focus on the TV, but my thoughts kept drifting to the electric moments we shared, the fleeting touches, the lingering glances that held so much unsaid.

"Okay, so if you were on this show, what would your strategy be?" Cassie asked, breaking the spell, eyes sparkling with excitement.

"I'd probably just try to charm my way through the questions," I said, leaning back and tossing my hair over my shoulder dramatically. "I mean, who doesn't love a little charisma? It's basically my secret weapon."

Ethan rolled his eyes playfully. "You mean your weapon of mass distraction. I'd be the one actually answering the questions. Charisma only gets you so far."

"Oh, please," I countered, a smirk creeping onto my face. "Charisma can take you to the top! Just look at the Kardashians."

Ethan laughed, the sound rich and full. "Okay, but you also need to know the difference between a Kardashian and an actual genius. You might want to brush up on that for your pop-up café planning."

The banter danced between us like a fragile thread, thickening with each exchange. Just as I was about to respond, the oven timer beeped, cutting through our playful war of words. Cassie jumped up to retrieve the cookies, and I watched, my heart in my throat, as she opened the oven door, the sweet aroma flooding the room.

But when she pulled out the tray, a couple of cookies had melted together, forming an amorphous blob that looked more like a cookie monster's disaster than a baked treat.

"Well, at least it's an avant-garde interpretation of cookie art," I said, stifling laughter as Cassie stared at her creation, wide-eyed.

Ethan couldn't contain himself. "Wow, that's some creative baking there. You've officially revolutionized the cookie world!"

"Shut up!" Cassie shot back, but the grin on her face betrayed her amusement.

In that moment, laughter filled the air, yet the chemistry between Ethan and me pulsed beneath the surface, a silent agreement lingering in the space between our shared joy. I couldn't shake the feeling that something monumental was shifting within our trio, a transformation that was both exhilarating and terrifying, promising possibilities that felt just out of reach but tantalizingly close.

As we shared the cookies, each bite a sweet blend of laughter and camaraderie, I couldn't help but wonder if we were standing on the precipice of something new—something thrilling and beautifully unpredictable.

The cookies turned out to be an unintentional masterpiece, a delightful disaster that we sampled while sprawled across the couch, our laughter mingling with the sweet, gooey aroma still wafting from the kitchen. Cassie, with her flour-dusted cheeks and infectious enthusiasm, had declared them "unique," and we each took turns claiming the most oddly shaped pieces as our favorites.

"I think this one is clearly the best," I said, holding up a lopsided monstrosity that had somehow fused with its neighbor. "Look at the way it embodies the spirit of chaos. It's a metaphor for life!"

"Or just a sign that we should stick to pre-made cookie dough," Ethan countered, picking at the edges with mock disdain before taking a bite. "But I'll admit, it's surprisingly... delightful."

"See? Culinary genius over here!" Cassie exclaimed, a victorious grin spreading across her face as she took a bite of her creation. "You were all doubters before, but now look who's eating crow—err, cookies!"

As the three of us lounged in that warm haze of camaraderie, the movie's background chatter faded into white noise, and I felt an undeniable connection pulsing through the room, crackling like the electric energy before a summer storm. Ethan's laughter hung in the air, drawing me closer to him, my heart racing at the possibility of crossing an invisible line that seemed to grow thinner with each shared moment.

"Let's make a pact," Ethan said suddenly, leaning forward, his expression turning serious. "Every Saturday, we'll bake something together. No matter how ridiculous it turns out, we'll own it."

"Only if I get to choose the recipe next time," I replied, fighting the urge to let the moment linger and become something more. "Something that's not likely to end up as a dessert disaster."

Ethan's eyes sparkled, and for a heartbeat, the world around us faded into the background. "Deal. But I warn you, my culinary skills are like my karaoke skills—at best, entertaining."

Cassie chimed in with mock indignation, "We should all stick to our strengths! I'll plan the parties, you'll cook, and Harper... well, you can be the taste tester. Sound fair?"

"Hey, I can plan too! I have skills, you know," I protested, unable to suppress a smile.

"Oh, we know, we know," Ethan added, his tone teasing yet genuine. "Your skill for making popcorn seems unparalleled. You should take that on the road."

Before I could retort, my phone buzzed on the coffee table, drawing my attention away from the laughter swirling around us. I glanced at the screen to find a message from my mom, and I felt a wave of unease wash over me. It wasn't the first time I'd received a message like this—a reminder of the reality waiting for me outside this warm bubble of friendship and laughter.

"Hey, I need to take this. Be right back," I said, standing up and walking toward the hallway, my heart racing. The moment felt like an anchor trying to drag me back to a world I was desperate to escape.

As I stepped into the quieter hallway, I opened the message, my fingers trembling slightly as I read the words. My mom wanted to talk—again—about my future, about college applications, about responsibilities that felt suffocating. I could hear the muffled sound of laughter from the living room, a reminder of what I was about to leave behind, and I hesitated. I knew this conversation would be heavy; it always was.

"Harper? Everything okay?" Cassie's voice pulled me from my thoughts, and I turned to see her leaning against the doorframe, concern etched on her face.

"Yeah, just a little message from my mom," I replied, forcing a smile that didn't quite reach my eyes. "You know how it is."

"Want to talk about it?" she asked, her voice softening, but I shook my head.

"No, it's just the usual. You know how they can be." I attempted to deflect, not wanting to dampen the mood any further. "Let's get back to the cookies. I'm sure Ethan is eating all the good ones without us!"

Cassie's eyes narrowed slightly, but she didn't push. Instead, she nodded and followed me back into the living room. Ethan was half-reclined on the couch, grinning like the Cheshire Cat, crumbs dusting his chin. "I saved you both the best ones! They're right here."

I let out a laugh, grateful for the way he effortlessly lightened the atmosphere. But even as we returned to our easy banter, the weight of my reality loomed just outside the door.

We continued chatting and joking, but the sense of impending change lingered like an uninvited guest, watching from the corner of the room. I couldn't help but steal glances at Ethan, who seemed to sense the shift, his gaze intense yet inquisitive. There was something about the way he looked at me, a silent understanding that felt as though he was waiting for me to take a leap into unknown territory.

As the evening wore on, I caught myself lost in thoughts of what lay ahead. College applications, family expectations, the suffocating pressure to conform—it all felt heavier than I could articulate. The three of us sat there, absorbed in our moment, yet the truth hovered unspoken: we were standing on the edge of something new, and I couldn't shake the feeling that our dynamic was about to shift irrevocably.

Suddenly, a loud crash echoed from the kitchen, drawing our attention. Cassie jumped up, her eyes wide with alarm. "What was that?"

Ethan and I exchanged worried glances before rushing to the kitchen. The sight that greeted us was chaos: the flour bag had toppled over, covering the floor in a thick white dust cloud. It was as if a snowstorm had hit in the middle of summer, and there stood Cassie, flailing her arms as if trying to clear the air.

"Oh no! It's a flour avalanche!" she exclaimed, trying to stifle her laughter as she slipped slightly on the powdery surface.

I doubled over with laughter, but Ethan's eyes were locked onto mine, and for a fleeting moment, all the chaos faded into the background. There was an intensity in his gaze, a connection that felt deeper than friendship, and I suddenly realized how vulnerable we all were, each standing on the precipice of change.

Before I could process it, a knock echoed from the front door, shattering the moment. My heart raced as I exchanged a confused look with Ethan. Who could it be at this hour?

"I'll get it," Cassie said, brushing off the flour from her hands and heading toward the door. I felt a knot tightening in my stomach, a premonition of something I couldn't quite grasp.

Ethan leaned closer, his voice barely above a whisper. "You okay?"

I nodded, but the doubt lingered in my mind, twisting like a vine. There was something in the air, something ominous, and as Cassie opened the door, I held my breath, waiting for whatever might come next to reveal itself.

The figure standing on the doorstep was silhouetted against the porch light, shrouded in shadows. I couldn't make out any features, but a feeling of dread washed over me, making my pulse quicken. What had we invited into our bubble of laughter and warmth? And more importantly, what would it mean for us as friends, and for the uncharted territory I had been tiptoeing around with Ethan?

"Um, can I help you?" Cassie's voice quivered slightly, the cheerful bravado from moments ago faltering.

And just like that, the air thickened with uncertainty, the laughter of the day melting away, leaving only questions that hung in the space between us, waiting for answers that could change everything.

# Chapter 4: "Caught in the Act"

The evening air was thick with the sweet aroma of fried dough and caramelized apples, mingling with the laughter that danced from stall to stall. Lanterns twinkled overhead, illuminating the faces of festival-goers, their excitement palpable as the carousel spun in a blur of vibrant colors. I had never seen our small town so alive, so vibrant, as it was that night, and yet all of that faded into the background as I stood beneath the soft glow of lights, captivated by Ethan.

He leaned closer, his breath warm and sweet like the cinnamon sugar that coated the funnel cakes. My heart raced, a wild creature caged beneath my ribs, as the moment stretched into something electric. Ethan's eyes, a deep shade of hazel, sparkled with mischief and an intensity that made my skin prickle with awareness. We were huddled at the edge of the fair, the world spinning in a whirlwind of laughter and music, but in this small pocket of time, it was just the two of us.

"So, what's your big dream?" he asked, a teasing smile playing on his lips. His dark hair fell into his eyes, and I wanted nothing more than to brush it aside, to touch him. "You can't just hang around here forever, right?"

I hesitated, the weight of my secret pressing heavily on my chest. Ethan was the kind of person who made everything seem possible—his laughter was infectious, his confidence unwavering. I admired him, had for as long as I could remember, but to admit that now felt terrifying. Would he laugh? Would he dismiss my feelings as childish, a fleeting crush?

Gathering courage, I met his gaze. "Actually, I've always wanted to travel," I confessed, my voice barely above a whisper. "To see the world, experience everything it has to offer. But you know how it is here—everyone expects you to settle down, get a job, live a quiet life."

His expression shifted slightly, curiosity flickering in his eyes. "And what's wrong with that? I mean, don't get me wrong, I love this place. But there's a whole world out there, waiting to be explored."

"Exactly!" I breathed, enthusiasm bubbling to the surface. "I want to stand on a cliff in Ireland, see the Northern Lights in Alaska, walk the streets of Paris. I want to live stories worth telling."

"Then go," he urged, the sincerity in his tone wrapping around my heart like a warm embrace. "You're smart, capable. You could do it. You don't have to wait for anyone's permission."

Our faces were so close now, the heat radiating from his body intertwining with the night air. My mind raced, caught in a web of hope and fear. The space between us was electric, the tension so thick it could be cut with a knife. I dared to lean in, my breath catching as our lips hovered mere inches apart. All I could think about was how right this felt, how everything in me screamed to close that gap.

But just as I was about to take that leap, laughter broke through the moment like a sudden chill. Cassie appeared, her blond curls bouncing with every step, her arms loaded with snacks. "Guess who's back with goodies!" she announced, her voice bright and carefree. I froze, my heart plummeting into my stomach.

"Hey, Cass," I stammered, stepping back, suddenly aware of how ridiculous we must look, suspended in that near-kiss moment. I could feel my cheeks burning as embarrassment flooded my system. I could only hope she hadn't noticed the way Ethan and I had been leaning into each other, our secrets laid bare.

Cassie dropped the bags at our feet and grinned, her eyes sparkling with the joy of the festival. "You two look like you were having a serious discussion. What were you talking about?" Her playful tone felt like a spotlight shining on us, and I desperately searched for a way to deflect her curiosity.

"Just dreaming about the future," I replied, forcing a laugh that sounded more like a strangled croak. "You know, like the usual stuff."

Ethan shot me a sideways glance, a hint of amusement in his eyes that made my stomach flutter. "Yeah, nothing major. Just a casual chat about how we're going to conquer the world."

"Right! Just casual world domination," Cassie said, rolling her eyes, blissfully unaware of the pulse of tension still lingering in the air. "Let's just focus on conquering these snacks first."

As she rummaged through the bags, my heart raced, still caught in the throes of what could have been. I stole a glance at Ethan, whose expression was unreadable now. Had I ruined everything? That near moment felt like a fragile dream, now shattered by the mundane chatter of festival life. I could feel the weight of the unspoken hanging between us, thick and oppressive.

"What do you want first?" Cassie asked, her voice full of enthusiasm. "I got caramel apples, corn dogs, and—oh, my favorite—deep-fried Oreos!"

"Let's start with the Oreos," Ethan said, his grin returning, and I felt a pang of relief wash over me. Maybe it wasn't too late. Maybe this wasn't the end. I tried to push down the fear coiling in my gut, the worry that I had blown my chance to tell Ethan how I felt.

But as we settled into our festival fun, a new kind of tension crept in. It wasn't just about the unspoken moment that had slipped away. There was something else—an undercurrent of challenge in the air that hinted at possibilities I hadn't dared to consider. I was caught between two worlds: one where I could stay in my comfortable bubble, dreaming of adventures while holding onto my crush from afar, and another where I could leap into the unknown and explore the depths of my feelings for Ethan, even if it meant risking everything I had known.

As the night wore on, laughter and music enveloped us, yet I could hardly focus on anything beyond the delicious chaos of emotions swirling in my mind. I wondered what it would take to break the barrier between us, to turn dreams into reality. The festival danced around us, but all I could see was Ethan—so close, yet still so far away.

The festival's energy swirled around us, but I felt suspended in a bubble of my own making. The sounds of laughter, the clanging of carnival games, and the upbeat melodies floating through the air faded into a distant hum. All I could focus on was the space between Ethan and me, a tightrope walk over a yawning chasm of uncertainty. Cassie busily indulged in the assortment of snacks she had retrieved, completely oblivious to the tempest brewing just beneath the surface of my heart.

"Here, try one of these!" Cassie exclaimed, thrusting a deep-fried Oreo in my direction with all the excitement of a child presenting a prize. "You have to experience the culinary wonders of our local fair."

I took the treat, my fingers brushing against hers for just a moment longer than necessary, and a thrill shot through me. It was a small, electric connection, but it sparked something—like a flickering flame that ignited my hopes and fears all at once. Ethan grabbed one as well, his hand lightly grazing mine, and for a brief second, I thought he might say something to bridge the awkwardness that had enveloped us since Cassie's arrival.

Instead, he turned to Cassie, his voice light and teasing. "So, did you find anything healthy in those bags? Maybe a kale chip or two?" His teasing tone was playful, but there was an underlying seriousness to his gaze when it flicked back to me. I couldn't help but wonder if he was still pondering our near-kiss.

"Healthy? At a fair? Are you kidding?" Cassie laughed, her laughter infectious, and I felt myself relaxing slightly. "This is a place for indulgence. Besides, I'm pretty sure calories don't count when you're having fun, right?"

Ethan chuckled, and in that moment, my heart tugged at me like a persistent little child, demanding attention. The way his laughter danced in the air felt familiar yet tantalizingly new, weaving a tapestry of feelings I struggled to unravel. With Cassie beside us, the heaviness of unspoken words lingered, a tightrope walk across shifting sands.

As we wandered further into the festival, colorful stalls dotted the fairground, and each one felt like a small window into someone's joy. The vibrant colors of the booths were mirrored in the smiles of people enjoying their evening—couples cuddled close, friends jostled for position at game stalls, and children squealed with delight as they chased each other, their laughter mingling with the cheerful music playing from nearby speakers.

"Let's do something fun!" Cassie declared, dragging us toward the ring toss. The game stood tall and proud, its bright colors flashing under the lights like promises of victory. "I bet I can win us something cute!"

Ethan and I exchanged a glance, his eyebrows raised in playful disbelief. "You mean, if you can aim straight? Last time I checked, your throwing skills were questionable at best."

Cassie rolled her eyes, unfazed. "Challenge accepted! You two just wait and see." With a grin, she stepped up to the line, determination radiating from her. I admired her confidence, but a tiny part of me wished for a moment alone with Ethan again—an opportunity to explore what had barely begun to blossom between us.

As Cassie focused on the game, I leaned closer to Ethan, a whirlwind of thoughts swirling in my mind. "So, how do you feel about Cassie being so... enthusiastic?"

He smirked, his hazel eyes glinting with mischief. "I think it's adorable. Plus, it gives us a chance to witness her epic fails firsthand. It's entertainment and a free show all at once."

"You're awful," I shot back, trying to keep my voice light despite the surge of warmth in my chest. "But I have to admit, she does have a certain charm when she's on a mission."

Before he could respond, Cassie let out an exaggerated shout, her ring narrowly missing the peg she aimed for. "Darn it! Okay, that one didn't count. Watch this." She pulled back her arm again, determination written across her face.

As she lined up for her next throw, I felt Ethan's shoulder brush against mine. My breath caught, and I turned to find him already looking at me. In that shared glance, I felt a wave of vulnerability wash over me, revealing layers of emotions I had tried so hard to conceal. "What if I said I was thinking about taking a leap?" I murmured, my heart pounding.

"What kind of leap?" he asked, his voice low, curiosity piqued.

"Traveling. Leaving. Following my dreams," I replied, the weight of my words both liberating and terrifying. "I want to see the world. Maybe even to take a chance on the unknown."

Ethan's gaze intensified, and the teasing spark in his eyes shifted to something deeper. "You should. You have to, actually. I can't imagine you cooped up here forever." His sincerity wrapped around my heart like a lifeline. "You deserve more than this town, more than the ordinary."

His words sent a shiver of longing through me, and before I could second-guess myself, I leaned closer, heart racing. "What if I went? Would you miss me?"

There was a pause, heavy and charged, as his gaze searched mine. "I'd miss you more than you know. You make the ordinary feel extraordinary."

Before I could respond, Cassie interrupted again, triumphantly holding up a plush bear she had snagged from the ring toss. "See? I told you I'd win! Look how cute he is!" She placed it triumphantly between us, oblivious to the electric moment that had just flickered between Ethan and me.

"Very impressive, oh great ring toss champion," Ethan said, amusement dancing in his eyes as he ruffled her hair. Cassie beamed, and for a moment, the tension dissipated, replaced by the warmth of friendship and laughter. But in the back of my mind, the question lingered: what would it take for Ethan and me to step beyond friendship and into something more?

As we continued through the festival, weaving between stalls and bumping into familiar faces, I couldn't shake the feeling that I was standing on the precipice of something significant. Every glance, every accidental brush of our hands, every moment filled with laughter carried the potential for change. But lurking beneath the surface was a fear that threatened to hold me back. What if I leapt, only to fall?

The festival lights twinkled above, a kaleidoscope of colors dancing through the evening sky, and I felt my heart pulse with a wild hope. In that moment, beneath the laughter and the music, I realized that perhaps the most significant journey I could embark on wasn't just one of travel. It was the journey of stepping into my own life, embracing both the thrill and the uncertainty that came with it, all while wondering if Ethan would be there to join me on this unexpected adventure.

The lively din of the festival continued around us, each shout of delight from a passing child or the sizzling sounds of snacks frying momentarily distracting me from the whirlwind of emotions spiraling within. Cassie's victorious grin from her ring toss triumph faded into the background, a mere shadow compared to the intensity brewing just between Ethan and me. He stood there, the plush bear still nestled between us, an absurd token of a fleeting triumph and yet a poignant reminder of the evening's potential.

"Okay, bear man," Cassie announced, her hands on her hips, "now you owe me for the plushie. I expect my favorite drink in return." She nudged Ethan, her playful demeanor a contrast to the tension I felt crackling in the air.

"What would you like?" he asked, glancing at me before turning his attention back to her. I tried to suppress a smile as I pictured Cassie holding out for something ridiculously extravagant—maybe a unicorn smoothie or a neon-colored slushy that glowed under the festival lights.

"An iced coffee, extra whipped cream, please. My treat for winning the bear," she said, clearly pleased with her victorious bargaining.

"Deal," Ethan replied, his voice light as he started toward the nearby coffee stand, leaving me alone for a moment. My heart sank slightly as he walked away, the brief connection we had shared feeling like a fragile whisper on the wind.

"Hey, while you're at it," Cassie called after him, "make it two! I could use a little caffeine boost to fuel my evening. You know how hard it is to celebrate your win without the right amount of sugar."

"Sure thing!" he called back, his laughter trailing behind him like a melody. I turned my gaze back to Cassie, trying to suppress my swirling thoughts. "You're incorrigible, you know that?"

"Only when I need to be," she replied, her eyes sparkling with mischief. "And you're going to love this bear, trust me."

I tried to focus on the bear, its fabric soft and the stitching surprisingly well done. "I'm sure it's very huggable," I remarked, attempting to keep my mood light. "But really, I think it's just a distraction."

She tilted her head, a knowing smile spreading across her face. "A distraction from what? The fact that you were about to kiss the guy you've been mooning over for ages?"

I blinked, momentarily caught off guard. "What? Mooning? I was just—"

"Admit it," she interrupted, holding her hands up like a referee. "You two were this close to making fireworks happen right before I showed up."

"I wasn't mooning," I insisted, trying to feign innocence while warmth flooded my cheeks. "It was just a moment."

"Right. Just a moment that would have led to a much longer moment if I hadn't graced you both with my presence. Lucky for you, I have impeccable timing."

"Lucky indeed," I said dryly, shaking my head, but there was no hiding my smile. Cassie's knack for turning tension into laughter was a gift I had grown to appreciate, even when it felt like a betrayal of my romantic aspirations.

Just then, Ethan returned, two iced coffees in hand, the sweet aroma wafting toward us. "Here you go, ladies. Extra whipped cream, just like you ordered." He presented them with a flourish, and Cassie beamed as she took one, her earlier victory now fully celebrated with the sugary reward.

"You know me too well," she said, taking a generous sip. "And what about you? Any caffeine left in yours to share the excitement of the evening?"

"I might have just enough," Ethan replied, winking at me. My heart fluttered at his playful expression, the earlier heaviness lifting slightly.

"Let's go check out the Ferris wheel!" Cassie suggested, leading the way. The massive structure loomed in the distance, its colorful lights twinkling like stars against the night sky, a beacon of thrill and anticipation. "I need to see how high I can get before I scream."

"Let's go then," Ethan said, falling in step beside me, our shoulders brushing. I felt that familiar warmth again, a comfort in the simple act of walking together.

As we approached the Ferris wheel, I could see families and friends climbing into the pods, laughter ringing out as they ascended into the night sky. "Are you scared of heights?" Ethan asked, his voice low, just for me.

"A little," I admitted, glancing up at the towering ride. "But I think the view will be worth it."

"It always is," he replied, his eyes sparkling. "Life is about taking risks, right?"

I nodded, feeling a rush of excitement mixed with anxiety. The ride began to sway slightly, and Cassie skipped ahead to secure our seats. The prospect of being so high up was daunting, yet exhilarating. As we climbed aboard, I could feel the flutter of anticipation in my stomach.

"Just imagine all the sights," Cassie said, securing herself into her seat with a playful grin. "If we go up high enough, maybe we'll see our town in a whole new light!"

Ethan sat next to me, our knees almost touching, the warmth radiating between us making my heart race. "Ready to conquer your fear of heights?" he teased, leaning in just a fraction closer.

"I'll manage," I replied, attempting to sound brave, but my voice wavered slightly. As the ride began to move, the ground dropped away beneath us, and I clutched the safety bar, the world stretching out below in a mesmerizing panorama.

"See? Not so bad," Ethan said, his eyes focused on the view rather than my panicking heart. "Look at the lights! It's like a dream."

I glanced out, the town twinkling beneath us, but it was hard to concentrate when his presence was so potent beside me. "You're right," I replied, forcing a smile. "It's beautiful."

As we reached the top, the ride paused, and I felt the breath hitch in my throat. The horizon spread wide, the festival lights mingling with the stars above, creating a symphony of colors and shadows. But just as I began to appreciate the moment, I felt a shift in the air, an unease that prickled at my skin.

"Hey, look!" Cassie pointed down below, her voice full of excitement. "That's where we started!"

Ethan turned to me, his expression earnest. "What's on your mind?" he asked, his voice soft and steady. "You seem a little lost."

I swallowed hard, the words I wanted to say lodged in my throat. "It's just... it's beautiful up here. Everything feels different, like we're in our own little world."

"Sometimes it takes a change of perspective to see things clearly," he said, and in that moment, I felt the tension between us shift again, this time heavier, charged with unspoken truths.

As we began to descend, the thrill of the ride dulled by the weight of our conversation, I felt a flutter of panic. This was my chance to leap into the unknown—to tell him how I truly felt, to reveal my hopes for more than just friendship. I opened my mouth, ready to speak, but a sudden jolt interrupted me. The ride came to an abrupt halt, swaying slightly as I felt a jarring sensation beneath us.

"Uh, what's happening?" Cassie's laughter turned to concern. "Are we stuck?"

Before I could even process her words, a sharp clanging echoed through the night air, and the lights below flickered ominously. My heart raced, panic coursing through my veins. We were suspended high above the ground, trapped in a moment that felt like a dream and a nightmare all at once.

Ethan's hand found mine, fingers intertwining, grounding me in the chaos of uncertainty. "We're okay," he said, his voice steady, but I could see the worry creeping into his eyes.

"Is this part of the ride?" Cassie asked, her voice tinged with apprehension. "I really don't like this!"

The sudden stop sent my mind spiraling. The laughter and music faded away, leaving an unsettling silence that loomed over us like a storm. I could feel Ethan's grip tighten around my hand, and for a fleeting moment, I was torn between the fear of our precarious situation and the warmth of his touch, the connection we had forged in stolen glances and unspoken promises.

Just as I turned to say something—anything—that might ease the mounting tension, a loud crack reverberated from the machinery below, sending a ripple of fear through me. My heart raced, and in that instant, everything changed. The world spun out of control, and I knew that whatever happened next would alter the course of this night forever.

# Chapter 5: "The Confrontation"

The air was thick with the scent of summer, a blend of sun-warmed wood and the distant promise of rain. Cassie and I sat on her porch, the rhythmic creak of the swing beneath us matching the quick tempo of my thoughts. The stars flickered like forgotten wishes scattered across the deep indigo sky, but they offered little comfort. A familiar tension hummed in the silence, electric and unsettling, curling around my heart with a grip that felt almost malicious.

"Come on, spill it," Cassie urged, her gaze sharp and penetrating. She leaned forward, the fabric of her sundress fluttering slightly in the night breeze, her hair cascading like a wild waterfall over her shoulders. It was moments like this, when her protective instincts kicked in, that reminded me why I cherished our friendship. She could smell my turmoil like a wolf sniffing out prey, and I was cornered, left with no option but to confess.

I glanced down, my fingers fiddling nervously with the edge of the porch railing, where the wood was worn smooth from years of restless hands. "It's about Ethan," I finally blurted out, the words feeling like a lead weight tumbling from my mouth. Saying his name ignited a spark in my chest—one that should have felt comforting but instead danced dangerously close to the flames of regret.

Cassie's expression shifted, and the air thickened with unspoken thoughts. "What about Ethan?" she asked, her tone slipping into a guarded inquiry. Her eyes, usually filled with mischief, clouded with a blend of concern and fear. I could see the gears turning in her mind, the protective sister readying for battle against any threat to her family.

My heart raced. "I think...I think my feelings for him have changed," I managed, each word a pebble tossed into the vastness of the universe, hoping for a ripple of understanding instead of a tidal wave of devastation. I looked up, ready to brace myself for the fallout, but the disappointment that crossed her face felt like ice water poured over my head.

"He's my brother, you know?" Cassie's voice was barely above a whisper, tinged with something that could have been heartbreak or fury, or perhaps a complex mixture of both. "What if this ruins everything?"

The weight of her words crashed over me, and I could practically feel the chasm widening between us, ready to swallow both our hopes whole. Standing on the precipice of a decision that could fracture our lifelong bond felt as daunting as leaping from a cliff into unknown waters. I wanted to reassure her, to wave away her fears with a cavalier flick of my wrist, but the truth hovered, heavy and undeniable, in the charged air around us.

"Cassie, I never meant for it to happen. It's not like I planned this. It just... developed." I stammered, searching her face for any sign of understanding. The stars overhead continued their silent vigil, indifferent to our human frailties. "I love being with him. We have this connection that feels deeper than I ever expected."

"Connection? You mean chemistry," she scoffed, rolling her eyes, though the quiver in her voice betrayed her uncertainty. "You're talking about my brother, not some fling. This is serious, Lucy." The way she said my name felt sharp, as if she was etching it into the very air between us, reminding me of the gravity of the situation.

"I know it's serious!" I exclaimed, my frustration spilling over like a glass filled beyond the brim. "But I can't just pretend it's not happening. I care about him, Cassie. It's like there's this magnetic pull, and I'm not sure I can fight it."

Cassie crossed her arms, her expression softening slightly but still tinged with reluctance. "And what about me? What about our friendship? What happens if things go south? I can't lose you both." The fear etched in her brow made my heart ache. I'd known this moment would be fraught, yet the reality was more painful than I could have anticipated.

"I don't want to lose you either," I admitted, my voice barely above a whisper. The thought of her brother's face, full of laughter and warmth, twisted into something more complicated sent a jolt of fear through me. But the thought of losing Cassie, my lifelong confidante, sent a deeper pang through my heart. "I'm scared, Cassie. I really am."

A silence enveloped us, the kind that stretched thin, almost palpable. The stars seemed to twinkle in anticipation, as if they were spectators to our unfolding drama. Just then, a gust of wind rattled the trees, sending a cascade of leaves swirling around us, a swirl of chaos in an otherwise serene night.

Cassie sighed, her shoulders dropping in defeat. "Maybe you should just talk to Ethan," she suggested, her tone losing some of its earlier edge, replaced instead by a tinge of reluctant acceptance. "But be careful. If this goes wrong, I don't know what it could do to us. I need to protect him, Lucy. He's been through a lot already."

The sincerity in her voice wrapped around my heart, and I nodded, even though the idea of confronting Ethan filled me with dread. What if he didn't feel the same way? What if he did, and it turned everything upside down? Each scenario played out in my mind, a vivid tapestry woven with threads of hope and fear, love and loss.

"I'll talk to him," I promised, though the certainty in my voice felt as fragile as the stars overhead. "I just... need to find the right moment."

As the night deepened around us, the silence was both a comfort and a warning, a lullaby of uncertainty singing in the cool breeze. I knew this was just the beginning of a complicated journey, and the road ahead promised to be anything but straightforward. But perhaps, in the tangled mess of emotions, there was a chance for something beautiful, waiting patiently beneath the surface, like the soft glow of dawn creeping into the dark.

Morning crept in, splattering soft golden light across Cassie's porch, but my heart felt leaden, weighed down by the shadows of last night's conversation. I sat cross-legged on the worn wood, tracing patterns in the grain as I mentally rehearsed what I would say to Ethan. The world outside was alive, birds chirping a vibrant symphony, but inside me, a storm brewed. I could still hear Cassie's words echoing in my ears, her anxiety a tangible thread weaving through the fabric of my thoughts.

I glanced over at Cassie, who was absentmindedly sipping her coffee, a thoughtful frown creasing her forehead. The steam curled around her like a gentle fog, and for a moment, I envied how easily she seemed to navigate the murky waters of familial loyalty. Just then, Ethan's laughter drifted from the backyard, a sound so warm and genuine it could melt glaciers. I felt the familiar flutter in my chest, an unwelcome reminder of the conflicting emotions that had surfaced like a sudden spring thaw.

"Do you think I should tell him?" The question escaped my lips before I could swallow it back, the urgency in my voice startling even me. Cassie set her mug down with a deliberate clink, her eyes narrowing in concentration.

"I don't know, Lucy. It depends on what you want," she replied, a hint of mischief flickering in her gaze. "Are you prepared for the consequences? Because if you tell him and he doesn't feel the same, it might get awkward... and I mean 'awkward' in the sense of holiday dinners and family gatherings."

A nervous laugh bubbled up from my throat, momentarily lightening the tension. "So you're saying it could ruin Thanksgiving? That's just cruel."

Her laughter mingled with mine, filling the air with a semblance of ease, but underneath it all, the tension remained, coiling tighter.

"I just think you should tread carefully. If this is serious for you, it's worth considering."

The thought of serious wrapped around my mind, prickling with both excitement and dread. Did I want this? Did I want Ethan, with his easy charm and bright smile, or was it merely the thrill of the forbidden that captivated me? My thoughts were interrupted by a sudden rustling, and we both turned to see Ethan striding toward us, his tousled hair catching the light like a halo of mischief.

"Hey, ladies! What are you plotting? World domination?" he teased, his voice rich and inviting.

"Only if it involves free coffee and a couch," Cassie shot back, and I felt my cheeks warm. Her banter was a shield, a way to deflect the weight of our earlier conversation.

Ethan grinned, an easy expression that sent my heart racing. "Count me in. I've got just the couch for it." He plopped down on the porch steps, the sunlight gleaming off his skin, casting him in an almost ethereal glow. The casual way he leaned back, stretching his arms above his head, made me realize just how much I wanted to reach out and touch him, to break the invisible barrier that seemed to pulse between us.

"Lucy, how's the whole job hunt going?" Ethan asked, tilting his head slightly, his gaze keen and focused on me. There was something genuine in the way he asked, a kindness that made me want to spill my secrets, to let him in on the tumult swirling inside me.

"It's fine," I replied, trying to maintain a nonchalant tone. "I'm still sorting through options. You know how it is—keeping the options open." The words tasted bitter, a feeble attempt at distraction as I felt Cassie's eyes on me, scrutinizing my every move.

"Options, huh? I like it. More than one way to skin a cat, right?" Ethan grinned, mischief dancing in his eyes.

I caught Cassie's smirk in my peripheral vision, and her voice chimed in, playful yet pointed. "Just make sure you don't let the cat out of the bag, Lucy."

I shot her a warning glare, feeling the heat creep up my neck. "Very funny," I muttered, but a small smile betrayed my irritation.

Ethan, completely oblivious to our silent exchange, leaned closer. "I was thinking about hitting the trails later. You should join. It'll be fun—just the three of us, like old times. We can hike to the overlook and see if the view is as good as we remember."

There it was—the invitation, an open door that could either lead to a cherished day of friendship or a precarious moment of truth. I felt the pull of nostalgia tugging at me, wrapping around my heart with a comforting familiarity. But the looming question loomed larger than ever: Could I keep my feelings in check while hiking beside him?

Cassie nudged me with her shoulder, an unspoken encouragement that sent a ripple of nervous energy through me. "Sounds great!" I forced a smile, the words tumbling out in an attempt to disguise the turmoil swirling inside. "Right, Cassie? It's been ages since we did that."

"Absolutely! I'll even pack snacks. You know, just in case the hike turns into an expedition," she replied, her eyes sparkling with a mischief that made me grateful for her unwavering support.

As Ethan stood, the sunlight silhouetting his figure, I couldn't shake the sensation that I was being drawn into an adventure, one that could end in triumph or disaster. He was already moving toward the door, uncharacteristically animated, the excitement radiating from him. "I'll grab the water bottles. Don't take too long to get ready, okay?"

"Sure thing!" I called, the sound echoing as he disappeared inside. Cassie turned to me, her expression a mix of glee and concern.

"You've got this, Lucy," she said, her voice low but fervent. "Just breathe. And remember, whatever happens, I'm here for you."

The sincerity in her words warmed me, grounding me in the whirlwind of uncertainty. As I rose to head inside, my heart pounded against my ribcage, a staccato rhythm that echoed my swirling thoughts. What would I say to Ethan? How could I navigate this strange, new terrain between us without tripping over my own feelings?

Stepping through the door, I felt the air shift, a tension coiling in my chest, but perhaps this hike would lead to clarity. Maybe it was just a hike with friends, or perhaps it was the first step into uncharted territory—a place where the lines between friendship and something more blurred like watercolors on a canvas, vibrant yet unpredictable.

The air was crisp as we hit the trail, the world waking around us with the sounds of rustling leaves and distant birdsong. Sunlight filtered through the trees, dappling the path with soft patches of light that danced beneath our feet. Ethan led the way, his enthusiasm infectious as he recounted stories of our previous hikes—those carefree days of laughter and wild abandon, where the world felt smaller, and our lives were unburdened by adult complications.

I trailed behind with Cassie, who walked shoulder to shoulder with me, her eyes flickering between me and her brother. "You know, he's going to start asking questions if you keep looking like a deer caught in headlights," she whispered, a teasing smile playing on her lips. I shot her a glare, but the corners of my mouth betrayed me, curling upward in reluctant amusement.

"Thanks for the vote of confidence," I murmured, trying to suppress the whirlpool of anxiety churning in my stomach. As we ascended the trail, I could feel my heart racing in sync with our footsteps, each beat echoing the duality of my thoughts—half of me reveling in the beauty of the moment, and the other half bracing for the inevitable confrontation.

Ethan turned back, a playful glint in his eyes. "Are you two plotting my demise back there? Because if so, I'd like to know who's writing my obituary. 'Beloved brother, lost to the dark machinations of friendship.'"

Cassie laughed, her eyes sparkling. "Don't worry, we're just making plans for world domination. You're invited if you bring snacks."

I chuckled, grateful for the levity, but as we continued onward, the weight of my unspoken feelings pressed down on me like a heavy backpack. Every step felt laden with possibility, and I found myself glancing at Ethan, trying to decipher the unspoken tension swirling between us. His smile was disarming, his laughter a balm for my worries, but my resolve wavered with each passing moment.

As we reached a clearing, the view opened up before us, revealing the vast expanse of the valley below, a patchwork quilt of greens and golds stretching toward the horizon. Ethan paused, soaking in the beauty, his profile sharp against the brilliant backdrop of blue sky. "Can you believe how breathtaking this is?" he asked, his voice tinged with awe.

"It's gorgeous," I replied, my breath hitching as I drank in the sight, but my heart thrummed louder, demanding attention. This was it. The moment I'd been both longing for and dreading. I could feel the breeze caressing my skin, coaxing me to take the plunge. "Ethan, can we talk?"

His expression shifted, the casual joy fading as he nodded, the hint of concern shadowing his features. "Yeah, of course. What's on your mind?"

I glanced at Cassie, who shot me a look of encouragement. "Why don't you grab a seat on that rock?" I suggested, pointing to a flat boulder just off the path, its surface warmed by the sun.

As he settled on the rock, I felt the weight of the moment pressing down, heavy and consuming. "It's just... I've been thinking a lot about us," I began, my voice trembling slightly. "About what we have, and where it's going."

Ethan's brow furrowed slightly, and I could see the wheels turning in his mind. "Where it's going? Like, in terms of hiking destinations or—"

"No!" I interrupted, the urgency in my voice surprising even me. "I mean, what we are to each other." I took a deep breath, my heart pounding against my ribcage. "I like you, Ethan. More than I probably should, considering... well, everything."

Silence enveloped us, thick and suffocating. I could practically hear my heart thudding in the stillness, a chaotic drumbeat against the backdrop of the serene landscape. Ethan's expression shifted, surprise washing over his features, mingled with something I couldn't quite read. "You like me? Like how?"

"Like... like, I want to be with you," I blurted out, feeling the floodgates open. "I know this is complicated. I know it could ruin things between us and with Cassie, but I can't keep pretending it's just friendly anymore."

He was silent, the weight of my confession hanging in the air, an invisible barrier that seemed to stretch between us. "I... I didn't realize you felt that way," he finally said, his voice barely above a whisper.

My heart sank, the mixture of hope and dread creating a tumultuous whirlpool in my chest. "So you don't feel the same?"

"No, it's not that." He paused, running a hand through his hair, the motion familiar yet charged with an unfamiliar tension. "I just—this is a lot to process. You're Cassie's best friend. I always thought... I mean, I didn't want to complicate things."

"Complicate? Ethan, this is already complicated!" I felt a sharp edge to my voice, frustration bubbling beneath the surface. "I don't want to play it safe anymore. I care about you."

"I care about you too, but..." His voice trailed off, and I could see the struggle etched on his face, the way he wrestled with the truth.

Just then, Cassie ambled over, breaking the fragile tension that had crystallized between us. "Hey, you two! What's going on?" Her eyes darted between us, a flash of confusion passing over her features.

Ethan shifted, the moment suddenly fraught with a new layer of complexity. "We were just talking," he replied, his tone light, but the intensity of the moment lingered in the air like smoke.

Cassie's gaze sharpened, sensing the shift, the undercurrent of unspoken words hanging heavily. "Talking, huh? About world domination?"

"Something like that," I managed, forcing a smile that felt brittle against the rawness of what I had just confessed.

The three of us resumed walking, but the lightness had vanished, replaced by an invisible weight. I could feel the tension weaving around us, thick and unyielding, as we made our way to the overlook. Every word felt charged, as if the air crackled with electricity, and I couldn't help but feel that we were teetering on the brink of something monumental.

As we reached the overlook, I was struck by the view again, but it felt different now—darker, more mysterious. The sun hung low in the sky, casting a golden hue over the landscape, but shadows lurked in the corners of my vision, reflecting the chaos in my heart.

"Wow," Cassie breathed, taking in the vista, but her voice held a tremor, and I knew she felt it too. The air thickened with unspoken questions, the weight of what hung between us growing heavier.

Ethan turned to me, his expression unreadable. "Lucy, I..." His words were lost as a rustling in the underbrush startled us.

From the corner of my eye, I caught a flash of movement—a figure emerging from the trees. The hair on the back of my neck stood on end, and a jolt of adrenaline surged through me. My heart raced, my instincts screaming that something was very, very wrong.

As the figure stepped into the light, I froze, a chill washing over me. It was a face I hadn't seen in years, a ghost from my past, and suddenly, the fragile threads of my reality felt poised to unravel.

"Lucy? Is that really you?" The voice was hauntingly familiar, sending shockwaves through my heart and forcing me to confront not only my feelings for Ethan but the consequences of a past I thought I had left behind.

# Chapter 6: "Tension and Temptation"

The cabin loomed ahead, a rustic silhouette framed by towering pines that whispered secrets to the evening breeze. As I stepped out of the car, the cool air wrapped around me like an old sweater, a stark contrast to the suffocating heat that had built up in the car during the drive. Ethan leaned against the vehicle, arms crossed, his gaze fixed on the stars beginning to sprinkle the darkening sky. I couldn't help but admire the way the faint light illuminated his strong jaw and the mischievous curve of his lips, a reminder of the playful banter that had danced between us for weeks.

"Are you sure about this?" I asked, my voice unsteady, betraying the excitement and fear swirling inside me. The weight of unspoken words hung heavily in the air, as palpable as the scent of pine needles and damp earth.

Ethan turned, the corners of his mouth twitching upwards. "What, afraid of a little nature? Or is it just me?" His teasing tone was a balm, but it did little to soothe the undercurrent of tension coiling between us.

"I'm not afraid of the outdoors, Mr. Adventure. I'm afraid of what happens when the sun sets and we're alone in this cozy cabin," I shot back, my heart racing. He was too charming for his own good, and the last thing I wanted was to lose myself in that easy grin.

With a dramatic flourish, he gestured towards the cabin. "Then let's not waste time talking about it. Let's see if this cozy cabin lives up to the hype." He pushed open the door, and a burst of warm, inviting air greeted us, carrying the rich aroma of cedar wood and something sweet and smoky, like a distant campfire lingering in my memory.

Inside, the cabin felt like a warm embrace. A stone fireplace dominated one wall, its hearth waiting for a fire to crackle to life, while the open kitchen exuded a rustic charm, complete with mismatched mugs hanging from a wooden rack and a fridge adorned with a collection of magnets—each one a token from an adventure long past. My apprehension began to ease, replaced by a flicker of warmth that came from being here, with him.

"Help me unpack?" he asked, his eyes twinkling as he tossed his duffel bag onto the couch, where a plaid blanket lay draped like a welcome mat. I nodded, the suddenness of the moment pulling me deeper into his orbit. We moved about the small space, each action deliberate, each touch sparking electricity that buzzed beneath our skin.

"I brought some essentials," Ethan said, rummaging through his bag. He pulled out a bottle of wine, its deep red hue glowing in the soft light. "Thought we could toast to our daring getaway."

"Daring?" I laughed, setting down my own bag, which was more practical than exciting. "You mean to your questionable decision-making skills?"

"Exactly. But in my defense, I didn't know you'd be so good at banter. It was all part of my master plan." He grinned as he uncorked the wine, the pop resonating like a gunshot in the silence, and I could almost feel the tension leap between us.

We settled on the porch, the wooden planks creaking beneath us as we settled into the chairs that overlooked the vast expanse of woods, the moon spilling silver light over everything like a painter's gentle hand. The world felt hushed, the only sounds being the soft rustle of leaves and the occasional chirp of a cricket, as if the universe held its breath, waiting for us to make our move.

"Here's to... whatever this is," I said, raising my glass, and he clinked his against mine, the sound crisp and refreshing. "To whatever this is," he echoed, his eyes locking onto mine, a spark of something dangerous dancing in his gaze.

The wine slid smoothly down my throat, warming me from the inside out. I watched as he took a sip, the muscles in his arms flexing slightly as he lifted the glass. There was something intoxicating about this moment, something more than the wine swirling in my head. The air between us thickened, the way the world felt just before a storm.

"Tell me something real," he said, setting down his glass and leaning closer. The intimacy of the moment made my heart race, a thrilling mixture of exhilaration and fear washing over me. "What are you most afraid of?"

His question caught me off guard. I could have deflected, could have made a joke, but something about his serious expression urged me to be honest. "Being vulnerable, I guess. It's easy to hide behind sarcasm and wit, but letting someone in… that's terrifying."

"I get that." His voice softened, and he mirrored my body language, leaning forward, elbows resting on his knees, creating a bubble that felt cocoon-like and private. "But you know, vulnerability can be powerful. It opens doors."

"And sometimes it closes them," I countered, biting my lip. "What if the person I let in decides to walk away?"

"Then that's on them, not you," he replied, his gaze unwavering, a quiet intensity that felt like a challenge. "Life's too short to worry about things you can't control."

I chuckled, but it was a nervous laugh. "Easier said than done, Mr. Philosopher."

"Maybe, but I believe it. We can't let fear dictate our choices." He paused, his expression softening. "Besides, I'd never walk away from you."

My breath hitched at the weight of his words. There it was, that unspoken connection, palpable and simmering, igniting the space between us. I had always been good at building walls, but here, in this cabin surrounded by wilderness, the notion of vulnerability began to feel less like a curse and more like an invitation. And yet, beneath the surface of his promise, I sensed the very real danger of crossing that line, of letting the tension that pulsed in the air become something more.

But as the night deepened, our laughter floated away like smoke, mingling with the stars above, and the lines between friendship and something more began to blur. And so, caught in the delicate balance of tension and temptation, I wondered how long we could dance around the truth before one of us finally stepped forward, ready to claim what was waiting just beyond our grasp.

The fire crackled with a familiar warmth, but the tension lingering between us felt electric, sharper than the bite of the cold night air. We settled into a comfortable silence, the kind that spoke volumes, where every stolen glance was a question waiting to be asked. I wrapped my hands around the wine glass, its smooth surface cool against my skin, hoping to distract myself from the heat that radiated from Ethan's presence beside me.

"Are you always this charming, or is it just me?" I ventured, a playful edge in my voice to lighten the moment.

Ethan chuckled, a low, rumbling sound that sent a shiver down my spine. "Oh, I'm always this charming. It's a full-time job." He leaned back, propping his arms behind his head as if the night were his to claim. "But it's exhausting, you know? I might need to take a break. Like, say... after this weekend."

"Your ego is almost as big as the moon," I teased, but there was truth in his words. I could see the flicker of exhaustion in his eyes, the way he wore his charm like armor. "But let's not ruin it with reality just yet."

"Reality can wait," he said, turning serious for a moment, the weight of unspoken thoughts heavy in the air. "I want to enjoy tonight, whatever this is."

My heart raced, a wild creature clawing at the bars of its cage. It was the invitation I had been secretly hoping for, yet fear whispered insidiously in my ear. What did "whatever this is" mean? The words hung between us like a taut string, ready to snap. I wanted to pull away, to keep my distance, but the magnetic pull of his gaze held me captive.

"Then let's make a deal," I said, an idea sparking in my mind. "No talk of life, jobs, or where we see ourselves in five years. Just... this. Just us. For the next twenty-four hours, we can pretend."

He raised an eyebrow, a hint of mischief dancing in his expression. "Pretend? What exactly are we pretending about?"

"About not having a care in the world," I said, a smile tugging at my lips. "That we're just two people who stumbled into a cozy cabin and decided to indulge in a little escape."

"Deal," he said, raising his glass in a mock toast. "To pretending!"

We clinked our glasses again, laughter spilling into the night air, momentarily dissolving the invisible barriers between us. As the fire crackled, I leaned back, allowing the warmth to seep into my bones, the flickering flames painting the world around us in shades of orange and gold. I could feel Ethan's eyes on me, and the weight of that attention was both thrilling and terrifying.

As the wine flowed, the conversation became more relaxed, each topic shifting like the flames. We discussed everything from our favorite movies to the most embarrassing moments of our childhood. I found myself laughing freely, the tension slowly melting away, only to be replaced by something even more complicated. Ethan shared stories about his family that hinted at a depth I hadn't yet explored. He spoke of his younger sister, who was studying art, and the way their parents had always encouraged creativity, fostering a space where dreams could breathe.

"Sounds like a lovely upbringing," I remarked, a hint of envy in my voice.

"It was," he replied, his expression momentarily clouded. "But it had its challenges. I spent a lot of time feeling like I had to live up to everyone's expectations. It's easy to lose yourself in that."

"Tell me about it." I traced the rim of my glass, contemplating my own journey. "Sometimes I feel like I'm just a collection of others' hopes. I have my own dreams, but they often take a back seat."

"Don't let them." His voice was firm, his gaze steady. "You deserve to chase what makes you happy, even if it feels selfish sometimes."

"Easier said than done," I said, trying to inject some humor into the moment. "I'm still working on it. I'd need a manual."

"Manuals are overrated. Just jump in and figure it out as you go," he said, his tone lightening. "Think of it as an adventure."

"Adventuring is one thing, but the stakes get higher when you're aiming for happiness," I countered, feeling the weight of his gaze. There was something electric in the air, something unnameable that seemed to draw us closer, inch by inch.

With a sudden boldness, Ethan stood and stretched, his frame silhouetted against the glow of the fire. "Come on, let's explore the wilderness. There's a full moon, and I refuse to waste it cooped up in here."

"Exploring at night? That sounds like the plot of a horror movie," I joked, but my heart raced at the idea of being alone with him in the dark.

"Then I promise to protect you from any lurking monsters," he said with mock seriousness, his voice deepening in a way that sent a thrill racing through me.

"I don't think you can fight off my imagination," I replied, but I couldn't help the smile creeping onto my lips. The allure of the night, mixed with the intoxicating feeling of adventure, was hard to resist. I set my glass down and stood, following him into the cool embrace of the night.

The woods were alive with sounds, the rustle of leaves and distant hoots of owls echoing through the trees. Moonlight painted everything in silvery hues, the path ahead dimly lit but inviting. As we walked side by side, our shoulders brushed occasionally, sending sparks shooting through me like a live wire.

"So, tell me about your wildest adventure," Ethan prompted, his breath warm against the chilly air.

I paused, thinking. "There was this one time I hiked a mountain with friends. We got lost, but instead of panicking, we decided to make the best of it. We set up camp and ended up stargazing for hours, sharing stories and dreams."

"Sounds like a perfect escape," he said, glancing sideways at me. "And here we are, creating our own little adventure."

As the words left his lips, a moment of uncertainty crashed over me. Was this really an adventure, or was it something more? I couldn't help but wonder if this weekend was a turning point, a decision that could alter the course of our lives.

"Do you think we're making a mistake?" I asked, my voice softer than intended.

Ethan stopped, turning to face me fully. The moonlight illuminated his features, making his eyes shimmer with an intensity that left me breathless. "I think we're making memories. Whether they're mistakes or triumphs doesn't matter. What matters is that we're here, together."

His words hung in the air, rich and heavy with promise. I took a step closer, feeling the undeniable pull between us. Just then, a branch snapped in the distance, the sound jarring me back to reality. The moment felt too fragile, too perfect to last, and the shadows that lingered at the edges of my mind whispered their warnings. But as Ethan reached for my hand, threading our fingers together, the world fell away, leaving just the two of us, caught in the magic of the night.

The chill in the air was quickly forgotten as Ethan's fingers intertwined with mine, his warmth igniting a sense of safety and exhilaration that sent a thrill racing through me. We walked deeper into the woods, the moonlight spilling across the path, casting an ethereal glow on the forest around us. Each step felt like a heartbeat, steady and rhythmic, resonating with the quiet promise of the night.

"Tell me another story," he said, his voice low and inviting. The way he looked at me—like I was the only thing in his universe—made it hard to focus on anything other than the thrill of being so close to him.

"Okay, let's see," I pondered aloud, my mind racing for a tale that would encapsulate both adventure and vulnerability. "There was this time I went on a road trip with my best friend. We didn't have a map, just a vague idea of where we wanted to end up. We took a wrong turn somewhere and ended up at a tiny roadside diner, the kind you see in old movies." I paused, allowing the memory to wash over me. "The place was falling apart, but the pie? It was divine. Best I've ever had."

Ethan chuckled, squeezing my hand a little tighter. "I've heard the best adventures come from getting lost. What's the point of a plan if you can't veer off course once in a while?"

"Very philosophical," I shot back, a teasing lilt in my tone. "You're full of surprises tonight."

"Just trying to keep you on your toes," he replied, grinning. But the lightness of our banter didn't quite mask the tension that still crackled in the air. There was something undeniable brewing between us, a palpable chemistry that threatened to explode at any moment.

We reached a clearing, and I stopped, taking in the breathtaking view. The night sky stretched infinitely above us, stars twinkling like diamonds scattered across velvet. A shooting star streaked across the sky, and instinctively, I squeezed Ethan's hand. "Did you see that?"

"I did. Make a wish," he said, his eyes twinkling with a playful challenge.

I closed my eyes, my mind racing through a myriad of wishes. But as my heart swelled with hope, I couldn't help but think of the danger of wishing too hard. What if I wished for the wrong thing? What if I wished for him, and the universe had other plans?

"What did you wish for?" he asked, leaning closer, our breaths mingling in the cool air.

"It's a secret," I replied, trying to sound coy but feeling the heat rising in my cheeks. "You know that's how it works."

"Fair enough," he said, nodding with a smirk. "But I think I know what you wished for. Something thrilling, something reckless."

I arched an eyebrow. "Reckless? Me? Never."

"Come on. The way you tell stories? I can sense the wild spirit beneath that sensible exterior." He paused, his gaze steady and unwavering. "You just need a little push to unleash it."

"Is that so?" I challenged, emboldened by the moonlight and the wine coursing through my veins. "What makes you think I'm not already wild?"

"Because if you were," he said, his voice dropping to a conspiratorial whisper, "you wouldn't be here with me pretending to be someone else."

His words struck a chord deep within me, awakening a daring spark. "Alright then, Mr. Pushy," I said, an impish grin spreading across my face. "What do you suggest?"

Ethan studied me, a flicker of mischief dancing in his eyes. "How about we venture off the path? There's a legend about a hidden pond not far from here. They say it's enchanted."

"Enchanted?" I laughed, a mix of excitement and skepticism. "Are you trying to lure me into a fairy tale?"

"More like an adventure," he said, stepping closer, the distance between us narrowing as he leaned in slightly. "What do you say?"

For a moment, I hesitated, the voice of reason whispering warnings in my ear. But the thrill of spontaneity clawed at my mind, beckoning me to let go. "Lead the way," I finally said, determination lacing my words.

Ethan's grin widened, and he pulled me along, guiding us deeper into the woods. The underbrush rustled beneath our feet, the cool air filled with the scent of damp earth and pine. With every step, my heart raced not only with excitement but also with the understanding that this weekend had transformed into something I had never anticipated. The path wound tighter, shadows dancing around us, creating a tapestry of light and dark that reflected our tumultuous emotions.

"Do you ever get scared?" I asked suddenly, the question slipping out before I could stop myself. "I mean, really scared? Like, what if we get lost?"

"Scared? Of course," he admitted, the honesty in his voice disarming. "But fear isn't always a bad thing. It keeps you alert, makes every moment feel alive."

"True," I said thoughtfully. "But sometimes fear can be paralyzing. Like a deer in headlights."

"Or like someone standing at a crossroads, afraid to choose a direction." He stopped, turning to me, his gaze piercing through the darkness. "You don't have to be paralyzed, you know. You can choose."

As his words hung between us, I felt an undeniable connection, a bond forged in shared vulnerabilities and whispered dreams. It was intoxicating and terrifying all at once, and for a fleeting moment, I thought about stepping forward, closing the distance between us.

But then a loud crack echoed through the trees, a sharp noise that sliced through the tranquil atmosphere like a knife. We froze, eyes darting around, hearts pounding in unison.

"What was that?" I whispered, dread pooling in my stomach.

"I don't know," he replied, his voice low, his brow furrowing in concern. "Stay close."

We edged back towards each other, instinctively seeking comfort in our proximity. The woods that had felt alive just moments before now seemed foreboding, shadows creeping like uninvited guests.

Suddenly, from the darkness beyond the trees, a low growl echoed, sending chills racing down my spine.

"Did you hear that?" I breathed, my pulse quickening.

"Yeah, and it's not a friendly sound," Ethan replied, shifting slightly, the air thick with tension.

Before I could respond, a figure emerged from the shadows, its silhouette towering and menacing. My breath caught in my throat, a surge of fear gripping my chest. This wasn't a fairy tale anymore; this was real, and it was very, very dangerous.

Ethan stepped protectively in front of me, his stance firm, and for the first time, I could see the raw edge of fear in his eyes, mirroring my own. The night felt infinitely darker, the woods closing in, as the looming figure shifted closer, the growl intensifying, leaving us at the precipice of uncertainty and fear. The safety of our enchanted getaway faded into the night, replaced by the grim reality that we had wandered too far from safety, into the realm of the unknown.

# Chapter 7: "Falling Hard"

The weekend unfolded like a fairytale, vibrant and dizzying, each moment punctuated by stolen kisses and whispered secrets that pulled us deeper into each other's worlds. Ethan and I drifted through sun-drenched mornings, our laughter mingling with the sweet scent of fresh pastries from the café down the street. I could hardly remember a time when I felt this buoyant, as if I were a leaf caught in a soft breeze, twirling in the air, far from the weight of my reality.

One afternoon, we wandered hand in hand through a nearby park, where the trees stood like sentinels, their leaves shimmering like emeralds in the sunlight. Ethan's fingers intertwined with mine felt so natural, so right, that I could hardly believe I hadn't noticed him before. He spoke animatedly about his dreams of designing homes, each idea layered with passion. "I want to create spaces that inspire love and connection," he said, his voice laced with conviction. "Homes that don't just shelter people but embrace them. Where every room tells a story."

As he spoke, I felt a spark of understanding flicker between us, brightening the corners of my heart that had grown dim under the weight of responsibility and guilt. I hung onto every word, his dreams wrapping around me like the warmth of the sun on my skin, igniting something deep within. I could picture it vividly: a home filled with laughter, walls painted in hues that felt alive, spaces crafted for memories. But just as quickly as that vision bloomed, reality crashed over me like a sudden winter chill.

My phone buzzed violently in my pocket, shattering the moment. It was Cassie. I hesitated, glancing at Ethan, who was now distracted by a pair of children chasing bubbles. I stepped away, the laughter and warmth fading into a distant hum. Cassie's text hit me like a punch to the gut, her concern radiating through the screen.

"Hey, I'm worried about you. Have you talked to Ethan? You know what happened last time. I don't want you to get hurt."

The weight of my deception hung over me like a storm cloud, heavy and oppressive. I took a deep breath, trying to shake off the gnawing anxiety. I didn't want to hurt Cassie. She had always been my rock, the steadying force in my life, and the last thing I wanted was to betray her trust. But my heart, foolish and wild, urged me to embrace the love blossoming before me. Ethan was unlike anyone I'd ever met, a whirlwind of creativity and laughter that made me forget my worries—if only for a moment.

I typed a quick reply, forcing a smile to touch my lips as I returned to Ethan's side. "Everything okay?" he asked, his brow slightly furrowed, concern flickering in his eyes.

"Yeah, just a little something from Cassie," I said, attempting to downplay the turmoil swirling inside me. "She's just looking out for me."

Ethan nodded, his gaze penetrating, as if he could sense the turmoil churning beneath my calm exterior. "She cares about you. That's a good friend," he said, a hint of admiration in his voice. "I hope she knows how lucky she is to have you in her life."

"Trust me, I'm the lucky one," I said, forcing a lightness into my tone that felt strained. "But I know I can be a handful sometimes."

His laughter, bright and genuine, chased away the remnants of my tension. "I can handle a little chaos," he teased, nudging me playfully. "You'd be surprised what I can handle."

Our banter flowed effortlessly, like the river winding its way through the park, twisting and turning with each new joke, each lighthearted challenge. Yet, beneath the surface, my heart remained heavy, torn between two worlds that felt irreparably disconnected.

As the sun dipped lower in the sky, casting a golden hue over everything, I made a decision. I wouldn't let my fears steal this moment from me. I leaned into Ethan, reveling in the warmth of his body beside me. "Let's go on an adventure," I said, impulsively, my eyes shining with mischief.

"An adventure?" he echoed, feigning seriousness. "What do you have in mind? Climbing a mountain? Conquering a castle?"

"Or perhaps just exploring that ice cream shop I've heard whispers about?" I suggested, gesturing toward the street bustling with life.

Ethan grinned, his eyes sparkling with excitement. "Now that's a quest I can get behind."

We meandered through the lively streets, laughter spilling from our lips as we shared stories of our most embarrassing moments and our wildest dreams. With each tale, the bond between us deepened, weaving an intricate tapestry of connection and intimacy. I could feel the walls I had built around my heart beginning to crumble, each secret I revealed serving as a thread that pulled us closer together.

But then, just as we reached the charming little ice cream shop—its windows adorned with twinkling lights that seemed to dance with the evening breeze—my phone buzzed again, the screen illuminating with Cassie's name. I hesitated, an unease crawling up my spine. I could already feel the familiar pang of guilt tightening its grip around my heart.

"Everything okay?" Ethan asked, noticing my sudden stillness.

I glanced at the screen, then back at him, forcing a smile that felt like a mask. "Yeah, just... Cassie again."

"Want to take a minute?" he offered, his voice gentle, laced with understanding.

In that moment, I wanted to dive headfirst into the ice cream shop, to taste the sweetness of the moment with him, to forget the reality waiting just outside our bubble. But the words I'd left unspoken—the lies, the secrets—threatened to unravel everything. "Maybe just a moment," I finally said, my voice barely above a whisper, as I stepped aside to read the text.

And as I stood there, torn between two worlds, I felt the fragile joy we'd built together teetering on the brink, held together by nothing more than a promise of love and a hope that somehow, everything would work out.

The world around me faded as I stood in that moment, the tension between the screen of my phone and the warmth of Ethan's presence palpable. Cassie's message, filled with worry, seemed to echo in my mind, drowning out the joyful chaos of the bustling ice cream shop just a few feet away. My heart raced as I considered the choices before me—one path leading to the intoxicating thrill of a budding romance, the other tethering me to the unrelenting guilt I couldn't shake.

"Hey," Ethan's voice broke through my thoughts, gentle yet probing. "You okay? You seem miles away."

I managed a weak smile, hoping it would convey both my desire to be present and the storm brewing within. "Just a little... family drama," I replied, using a vague half-truth to mask the weight of my lie.

"Family drama, huh?" he mused, tilting his head. "Does that mean you need to leave? Because I could totally take you home, but I'd much rather find out what flavor of chaos you prefer in your ice cream."

His playful tone coaxed a genuine laugh from me, a sound that felt like sunlight breaking through a cloudy sky. "I think I'll survive without the chaos today. How about we tackle that ice cream?"

"Now you're speaking my language," he replied, his grin widening as he ushered me toward the door.

Inside, the shop was a wonderland of colors and scents, the air thick with the sweet aroma of waffle cones and rich chocolate. Rows of jars glimmered on the counter, each filled with sprinkles, nuts, and candies, beckoning like jewels in a treasure trove. I gazed at the flavors displayed, each one a promise of delight.

"What are you thinking?" Ethan asked, leaning closer, our shoulders brushing, the contact sending a thrill down my spine.

"I'm torn between the caramel sea salt and the raspberry sorbet. One's indulgent, and the other feels like summer on a spoon," I mused, pretending to weigh my options seriously.

"Go for the caramel sea salt. It has a little bit of everything," he suggested, raising an eyebrow with mock seriousness. "Sweet, salty, and utterly addictive. Just like life should be."

"Okay, Mr. Philosophical. I'll take your word for it," I teased, the corner of my mouth quirking up. I ordered my scoop, watching as the ice cream swirled and dipped, the creamy goodness glistening in the afternoon light.

As we settled at a small table outside, I tried to focus on the moment, on the way the sun painted Ethan's features in warm golds and deep shadows. The conversation flowed, light and easy, punctuated by laughter and the occasional playful jab. But my thoughts kept drifting back to Cassie, her unwavering loyalty a double-edged sword.

"What's that look for?" Ethan asked, his voice cutting through my reverie as he dipped his spoon into his own bowl of rocky road. "You're not secretly planning a heist, are you?"

I chuckled, grateful for the levity he brought. "No heists today. Just contemplating the mysteries of friendship," I replied, the weight of my words settling between us like an unwelcome guest.

"Mysterious, indeed. Care to elaborate?" he prodded, his eyes sparkling with curiosity.

I hesitated, caught between the desire to share and the instinct to protect. "It's just... sometimes friendships can feel like a balancing act, you know? You want to be honest, but you also don't want to hurt anyone."

Ethan's expression shifted, a flicker of understanding crossing his features. "Sounds like you're dealing with a lot. You don't have to carry that alone, you know."

The sincerity in his voice tugged at my heart, but I fought against the wave of guilt rising within me. I wanted to share my truth, to feel the weight lift off my shoulders, but the words seemed to stick in my throat like a stubborn piece of ice. "It's nothing I can't handle," I said finally, my voice a touch too bright, a weak attempt to deflect the impending confession.

"Liar," he teased, but there was no malice in his tone, just gentle encouragement. "Everyone needs someone to lean on now and then. Even superheroes."

I raised an eyebrow. "Superheroes? I'd like to think I'm more of a sidekick, really."

"Every sidekick needs their moment to shine," he said, leaning forward, his intensity drawing me in. "What's yours? What's the dream?"

The question caught me off guard, sending a rush of emotions cascading through me. My dream? It felt like a distant memory, something I hadn't dared to consider in ages. "I've always wanted to make a difference, you know? To inspire people, maybe even through my art," I admitted, the words tumbling out before I could stop them.

"Art? You paint?" he asked, genuine excitement coloring his tone.

"Sometimes," I said, feeling a flush creep up my cheeks. "More like a hobby, really. I've always loved capturing moments, though. A good sunset, a laugh shared with friends. I guess I see the beauty in the mundane."

"I'd love to see your work," he said, his enthusiasm infectious. "I can only imagine the kind of magic you create."

A warmth bloomed in my chest at his words, the kind that made me feel seen in a way I hadn't experienced in a long time. "Maybe one day," I replied, a teasing glint in my eye. "If you promise to keep your critiques gentle."

Ethan chuckled, shaking his head. "Oh, I can be very critical when it comes to ice cream flavors. But art? That's a sacred territory."

"Good to know," I shot back, my heart dancing as I took a spoonful of my caramel sea salt. The sweetness exploded on my tongue, a rich wave of flavor that sent my senses soaring. "Wow, this is amazing," I declared, savoring the blend of textures and tastes.

"See? I'm full of great ideas," he said, self-satisfied.

As we shared bites of ice cream and laughter, the shadows of my worries felt distant, almost manageable. But beneath the surface, the storm was still brewing. My phone buzzed again, the harsh jolt of reality crashing through our bubble.

I glanced down at the screen, a sinking feeling settling in the pit of my stomach. Cassie's name loomed larger than ever, a reminder that the bliss of this moment was precariously balanced on the edge of truth and deception.

The phone buzzed again, a persistent reminder of the tangled web I had woven. I hesitated, stealing a glance at Ethan, whose laughter echoed around us, bright and infectious. The carefree joy of the moment was a fragile bubble, and I couldn't help but feel the sharp edges of my lie threatening to burst it.

"What's the verdict?" Ethan asked, his curiosity piqued as he watched my expression shift from playful to serious.

"It's just Cassie again," I admitted, keeping my tone light but unable to mask the knot tightening in my stomach.

"Still worried about you?" he inquired, his eyes narrowing in concern.

"Just being a good friend," I replied, but the words felt inadequate, almost hollow.

Ethan reached across the table, placing his hand over mine, a gentle gesture that sent a ripple of warmth through me. "You know you can talk to me, right? I'm here for you."

The sincerity in his voice stirred something deep within. It would be so easy to lean on him, to unburden my heart, to tell him everything. But just as quickly, a wave of guilt crashed over me, suffocating that impulse. I couldn't drag him into my mess, especially when I was still untangling it myself. "I know, but... I'm just sorting things out. I promise it's nothing to worry about."

"Okay, if you say so," he said, his tone skeptical but accepting. "Just know I'm not going anywhere. And if you change your mind, I'll be waiting right here, spoon in hand."

I chuckled, the tension easing slightly. "You and your spoon—quite the image of loyalty."

We finished our ice cream, the flavors lingering like the echoes of our laughter. But the sweet aftertaste was dulled by the ever-present reminder of Cassie's worry. As we stepped back into the bustling streets, I felt the sun setting behind us, casting long shadows that seemed to whisper of secrets yet untold.

"I'm really glad we did this," Ethan said, his smile infectious as we walked side by side. "I've missed just hanging out. Life can get so serious sometimes."

"Tell me about it. I'm all for turning seriousness into ice cream," I replied, bumping my shoulder against his playfully.

"You're going to turn into ice cream if you keep this up," he shot back, his laughter lighting up the fading light.

As we strolled, the evening air grew cooler, wrapping around us like a soft embrace. I reveled in the ease of our conversation, the way our words flowed seamlessly, punctuated by the occasional playful nudge or teasing remark. But just as I started to forget my worries, my phone buzzed again, this time more insistent, as if it had a life of its own.

"Okay, seriously, what's going on?" Ethan asked, concern flooding his voice. "You're practically glued to that phone. Should I be worried?"

I sighed, glancing down at the screen. Cassie's name flashed, and beneath it, a new message that made my heart race: We need to talk. It's important. The weight of her words hung heavily in the air, an anchor dragging me back to reality. "It's just... Cassie," I said, forcing a casualness that felt forced.

"Just Cassie? That doesn't sound like just Cassie," he replied, raising an eyebrow, his intuition sharper than I'd like to admit.

"Trust me, it's fine," I insisted, trying to keep my tone upbeat. "She's just being her usual self."

Ethan studied me for a moment, the shadows of doubt lingering in his eyes. "You sure? Because you look like you just found out your dog ate your favorite pair of shoes."

"It's nothing that dramatic," I laughed, but the sound felt strained. "Really, it can wait."

"Alright, but I'm keeping my detective hat on," he replied, a smirk on his lips. "Just remember, I'll be asking questions later."

As we wandered through the streets, I tried to immerse myself in the vibrant atmosphere around us—street performers, couples strolling hand in hand, the rich aroma of coffee wafting from a nearby café. Yet the vibrant hues of the evening dimmed against the growing storm within me, the shadows of my truth creeping closer, wrapping around my heart like a vice.

We found ourselves in a small courtyard, a hidden gem lined with twinkling fairy lights, their glow casting a warm ambiance over the stone benches. Ethan's laughter drew my attention back, a reminder of the joy I was so desperate to cling to. "Look at this place! It's like something out of a movie," he said, spinning in delight.

"It's beautiful," I agreed, taking a moment to appreciate the setting. But as I turned back to him, the warmth of the scene felt tainted.

"Let's make a pact," Ethan said suddenly, his expression serious. "No more secrets between us. It's too easy to hide behind the laughter and not share what really matters."

The weight of his words struck me like a bell tolling at midnight, resonating deep within. "You know what? That sounds fair. No secrets," I echoed, the sincerity of his plea wrapping around my heart. But how could I promise that when my very existence felt like a web of lies?

"Good. So, what do you say we keep this momentum going?" he suggested, his excitement infectious. "Maybe grab dinner? I know a place that serves the best burgers."

"I'm in," I replied, allowing myself to sink into the moment, if only for a little while longer.

But as we began to walk again, a sudden flash of movement caught my eye. A figure darted through the courtyard, their silhouette flickering in and out of the shadows. My heart skipped a beat as I recognized the familiar face—Cassie, her expression a mixture of anger and urgency.

"Wait," I said, my voice barely a whisper, as she approached us, breathless.

"Cassie?" Ethan said, his tone shifting to confusion. "What's wrong?"

"Can we talk?" she demanded, ignoring Ethan's presence entirely, her eyes locked onto mine, burning with intensity. "Now. It's important."

My heart sank, a thousand unspoken words hanging in the air, heavy and fraught with tension. I glanced at Ethan, whose expression was a mix of surprise and concern, and then back to Cassie, who was waiting expectantly, urgency radiating from her like a force field.

The moment felt suspended in time, a precarious balance between the joy I had found and the reality that threatened to unravel everything.

# Chapter 8: "The Breaking Point"

The woodsy aroma of pine and damp earth enveloped me as I stood on the porch of the cabin, the air thick with an unsettling tension. A gentle breeze rustled the leaves overhead, but the whispering trees felt more like spectators to a looming storm. My heart raced, not from the exhilaration of the romantic tension that had been building between Ethan and me, but from a sense of impending dread that hovered just beyond the threshold of my happiness.

Ethan's words lingered in the air like smoke, his confession hanging between us, vibrant and alive. I had never seen him so raw, his eyes reflecting a depth of emotion that made my heart leap and falter all at once. Just as I was about to gather my thoughts, to find the right words to respond, the sound of crunching gravel pulled me back to reality. Cassie was approaching, and every instinct screamed at me that this moment would change everything.

The door swung open with a creak, and there she stood, her figure framed by the soft golden light spilling out from within. The brightness contrasted sharply with the pallor of her face, her usually radiant complexion dulled by a shadow of distress. I felt a pang of guilt stab through me, as if I had been caught in the act of something illicit, even though the truth was less straightforward than that.

"What's going on here?" Cassie's voice was steady but laced with an undercurrent of vulnerability that tore at my heart. I exchanged a glance with Ethan, a silent plea passing between us. The weight of his gaze made me feel both grounded and painfully aware of the precarious situation we were in.

"Cassie, wait," I began, stepping down from the porch, my heart pounding in rhythm with the anxiety pooling in my stomach. "It's not what you think."

But the protest felt flimsy in my mouth, an echo of words I had rehearsed a thousand times but never quite believed. Cassie's eyes were like storm clouds, swirling with confusion and hurt. She crossed her arms defensively, and I could see the way her knuckles whitened as she gripped her elbows.

"Then what is it? Because it looks like something to me," she shot back, her voice sharp as the snapping of twigs beneath our feet. "You and Ethan, alone in a cabin... It doesn't take a genius to figure this out."

I could almost hear the clock ticking, each second stretching between us like an insurmountable chasm. The camaraderie we had once shared felt fragile, like glass on the brink of shattering. The thought of losing Cassie, of being the reason for this rift, filled me with an unbearable ache.

"It's complicated," Ethan interjected, stepping closer to Cassie, his hand raised as if to placate her. "We were just talking—"

"Talking?" she interrupted, her voice rising with indignation. "That's rich coming from you, Ethan. You think you can just—what? Confess your feelings and everything is supposed to be fine? What about our friendship? What about—"

She faltered, the fury giving way to a wave of pain that washed over her features, softening the hard lines of her anger into something deeply heart-wrenching. I wanted to reach out to her, to bridge the gap that was rapidly widening between us, but I was frozen in place, caught in a whirlpool of emotion.

"It doesn't have to be like this," I said, my voice trembling slightly. "We can figure this out. We care about each other, Cassie. You know that."

"Care about each other?" she repeated, a bitter laugh escaping her lips. "You mean you care about each other while I'm just left out in the cold?" Her gaze swept between us, and I could see the storm brewing behind her eyes. "I've been your friend through everything. You're both so caught up in whatever this is that you can't even see how it's tearing me apart!"

Each accusation struck me like arrows, piercing through the flimsy defenses I had built around my heart. I felt tears prick at the corners of my eyes, but I refused to let them fall. I had to be strong, not just for myself, but for Cassie too.

"This isn't just about you and me, Cassie," I said, my voice steadier now, as I tried to find the right words to heal rather than hurt. "It's about all of us. I never wanted to hurt you. You have to believe me."

"But it's too late for that, isn't it?" she spat, the edge of her hurt morphing into something sharper, more dangerous. "You've both crossed a line, and I'm just supposed to sit here and take it?"

The air grew thick with silence, a heavy blanket that pressed down on all of us. I could feel the emotional divide expanding, swallowing all the moments we had shared, the laughter, the camaraderie. Ethan shifted beside me, his brow furrowed in concern, and I sensed his own inner turmoil as he grappled with the fallout of his confession.

"I never meant for this to happen," he said, his voice quiet yet filled with urgency. "I care about you both. We're all friends here. I just—"

"Just what?" Cassie shot back, her eyes blazing. "You just thought you could waltz in and declare your feelings and everything would magically resolve? Newsflash, Ethan: life doesn't work that way!"

In that moment, I felt the weight of the world pressing down on my shoulders. All my hopes, dreams, and the delicate threads that wove our friendship together felt like they were about to unravel. Would we manage to repair this rift, or was this the end of everything we had cherished?

I looked at Ethan, who was equally trapped in this whirlwind of emotion, and I knew that the confrontation was inevitable. But as the air crackled with unresolved feelings, I couldn't shake the feeling that the true battle was just beginning, one that would test our bonds in ways we had never anticipated.

The silence that followed Cassie's accusation hung heavy, a tangible entity that filled the space between us like thick fog. The quiet was a sharp contrast to the tempest brewing within me, emotions swirling chaotically. I stole a glance at Ethan, who stood beside me, his expression torn between regret and defiance. He opened his mouth as if to speak, but the words never came. Instead, he seemed to shrink, his confidence wavering under the weight of Cassie's hurt.

"Look, Cassie," I ventured, desperate to soothe the storm, "I know this is all shocking. I wish things had played out differently. But we're not enemies here. We're friends. This was never meant to hurt you."

Her laugh was bitter, a quick exhale of disbelief that made my heart clench. "Friends? Is that what we're calling it now? Because it feels more like betrayal to me." She turned her gaze to Ethan, her eyes narrowing. "You were supposed to be my best friend, and now you're just... well, whatever this is."

"Don't you think I realize that?" Ethan shot back, his voice rising slightly. "I never wanted to hurt you, Cassie! This wasn't a decision made lightly. I didn't just wake up one day and decide to confess my feelings for Margo. It's complicated. You know that."

"Complicated," she scoffed, the word dripping with disdain. "You think that makes it any better? You think saying it's complicated somehow absolves you from the mess you've created?"

"I'm not trying to absolve myself!" he replied, frustration creeping into his tone. "I'm trying to explain that this isn't just about you or me or her. We're all tangled up in this."

"Nice try, but it sure sounds like you made your choice," Cassie shot back, her voice rising to a near shout. "So, what? I'm just supposed to sit here and watch this unfold? Pretend that I'm not hurt? That I'm okay with all of this?"

She gestured wildly, her fingers trembling as she struggled to contain the whirlwind of emotions that threatened to spill over. I felt the suffocating heat of guilt settle in my chest, knotting like a tight coil.

"Cassie, please," I interjected, stepping closer, wanting to bridge the divide that felt like a chasm between us. "You know how much you mean to me. I never wanted to hurt you. It's just... I can't deny how I feel about Ethan anymore."

"That's the problem!" she exclaimed, her voice rising with every word. "You think your feelings matter more than our friendship? More than the history we share?"

I opened my mouth to respond, but nothing came out. The truth was too complicated, too raw, and I felt as if I were standing on a tightrope, precariously balancing over the abyss of shattered trust.

Ethan stepped forward, his gaze fixed on Cassie with an intensity that made me hold my breath. "What do you want me to say? That I regret it? I can't do that, Cassie. I can't pretend I don't feel this way about Margo. It's real. It's been building for so long, and I can't just ignore it because it makes things uncomfortable."

Cassie's breath caught, and for a fleeting moment, vulnerability flashed across her features. "You think this is easy for me? Watching you two? I feel like I'm losing both of you at once." Her voice trembled, revealing the cracks beneath her bravado.

The realization hit me like a gust of wind, sharp and biting. I stepped closer to Cassie, closing the distance between us. "You're not losing us. We're all here. We can figure this out together. We've been through so much, and I refuse to believe it ends like this."

"Together?" she echoed, skepticism lacing her words. "How do you expect us to move forward when everything feels broken?"

"Because that's what we do," Ethan said softly, his voice suddenly calm, an anchor amidst the turmoil. "We don't run away from problems; we face them. This hurts like hell, but we owe it to ourselves to try. I don't want to lose you, Cassie. You mean too much to me."

Cassie's gaze flickered between us, her defenses wavering. I could see the battle within her, the heartache wrestling with a glimmer of hope. "You want to fix this?" she asked, her voice almost a whisper. "You really think we can just... go back to how it was?"

"Not back," I clarified gently. "Forward. We can't erase what's happened, but we can build something new. A new understanding, if you'll let us."

She shook her head slowly, the tears pooling in her eyes catching the light as she took a step back, creating space that felt palpable, heavy. "I don't know if I can do that. I don't know if I can be okay with this."

"None of us know what this looks like," Ethan admitted, his tone sincere. "But I know I want to try. I can't imagine my life without either of you in it."

Cassie's breath hitched, the anguish twisting her expression into a mask of uncertainty. "It just feels so messy."

"Life is messy," I replied, hoping to inject a bit of lightness into the dark tension hanging over us. "Like my attempts at baking—always a disaster but somehow deliciously unpredictable. We can make it work, even if it's a little burnt around the edges."

Her lips twitched, a flicker of amusement cutting through her despair. "Only you would compare our emotional turmoil to cookies."

"Well, I'm nothing if not creative," I said, offering a small smile, willing her to join me. "Plus, it's a testament to our resilience. We can rise from the ashes of this mess, just like a failed soufflé."

Cassie's laughter broke through the thick air like a ray of sunshine, warming the chill that had settled in my bones. "I can't believe I'm even considering this," she said, shaking her head, but there was a softness in her voice now.

"It's not going to be easy," Ethan warned, a seriousness creeping back into his expression. "We have a lot of work to do, and it won't always be pretty. But if we're committed to being honest, I think we can find our way through."

"I just hope it's worth it," Cassie murmured, glancing between us with a vulnerability that tugged at my heartstrings.

"It will be," I assured her, feeling a surge of determination. "Together, we can navigate this, even if it means redefining what friendship looks like. We owe it to ourselves to at least try."

As the sun dipped lower, casting a golden glow across the cabin, I felt a sense of hope unfurling within me, tentative but present. In the face of this emotional upheaval, perhaps we could emerge stronger, even if the path ahead was fraught with challenges. The flicker of connection was still there, simmering beneath the surface, waiting for us to ignite it anew.

As Cassie's laughter faded, I could feel the tension shift ever so slightly, as if the air had released its stranglehold on us. A flicker of something akin to hope ignited in my chest, though it was still wrapped in layers of uncertainty. Cassie took a deep breath, her shoulders relaxing just a fraction, but her eyes were still clouded with doubt. I knew we were treading on fragile ground, and the path forward would be riddled with obstacles.

"I just don't want to feel like I'm the third wheel in my own life," she said, the vulnerability in her voice like a soft melody against the backdrop of our earlier confrontation. "You two seem to have this connection I didn't even know about. It's like I've been living in a bubble, and it's just... popped."

Ethan shifted uncomfortably beside me, his gaze drifting to the horizon where the sun dipped low, painting the sky in shades of orange and lavender. "That's the last thing I want for you," he said softly. "You're my best friend, Cassie. Always have been. Always will be."

"Will you two stop with the declarations? I'm not ready for a group hug or anything," she retorted, but the corners of her mouth twitched upward, a glimmer of humor breaking through the clouds of tension.

"Just testing the waters," I teased, relieved to see her smile, even if it was tentative. "Maybe we can have a group hug later. After the cookies are baked. You know, in case they burn again."

Ethan chuckled, his tension easing. "Only if you promise not to burn them this time."

"Fine! But if they do burn, I'm blaming the emotional chaos." I gestured grandly to the surrounding woods, which had witnessed our emotional upheaval, making the trees unwitting witnesses to our melodrama.

Cassie rolled her eyes, but I caught the glimmer of warmth returning to her expression. "Okay, then. Let's figure this out. I refuse to lose both of you over a bunch of feelings."

"Deal," Ethan said, relief washing over him. "But we need to lay everything on the table. No more secrets. No more half-truths."

With a nod, I felt the gravity of the moment settle over us. It was a pact of sorts, one that would require honesty and bravery in equal measure. "Agreed. I've been keeping so much bottled up; it's time to spill."

As the sun dipped lower, the golden light began to wane, casting long shadows across the cabin. We settled onto the porch steps, the chill of the evening creeping in, but it felt almost comforting, a reminder that we were still here together.

"So, what do you want to know?" I asked, glancing at Cassie, who seemed to take a moment to gather her thoughts.

"Everything. For starters, how long have you two been... whatever this is?" she asked, her tone light yet probing. "Did you have a secret rendezvous while I was at work?"

Ethan shot me a look, a mixture of surprise and amusement. "I'm not sure I'd call it a rendezvous," he said, raising an eyebrow. "More like accidental confessions over board games and bad coffee."

I couldn't help but laugh at that. "Oh yes, the moment I knew I was in trouble. Ethan almost beat me at Monopoly. I mean, who does that?"

Cassie leaned in, intrigued. "And you both just sat around pretending everything was fine while you were battling over property rights and fake money?"

"Pretty much," Ethan admitted, a grin spreading across his face. "It was a master class in denial."

"Hey, it wasn't just denial!" I countered, a mock indignation rising in my throat. "We did have some great conversations about life and our aspirations. And then—"

"Then you made it weird," Cassie interrupted, an exaggerated pout on her lips. "Why do all my friends suddenly feel the need to get romantic? Is this a conspiracy?"

Ethan chuckled, his laughter infectious, easing the tension even more. "Maybe it's just the magical atmosphere of the cabin. You know, the pine trees and the rustic charm?"

"Or the fact that you both kept glancing at each other like lovesick puppies," Cassie shot back, crossing her arms with mock seriousness.

As the banter continued, the heaviness of earlier seemed to lift, but I couldn't shake the gnawing anxiety that this fragile peace could unravel at any moment. Cassie was opening up, but the wounds of betrayal were still fresh. I watched her closely, trying to gauge whether she truly believed we could navigate this new territory together.

"Okay, how about you tell me your side of the story?" Cassie said, her tone suddenly more serious, drawing the laughter to a halt. "How did you both get here, to this point?"

I hesitated, the weight of the moment pressing down again. "I didn't mean for this to happen," I began slowly, searching for the right words. "At first, it was just friendship. Ethan and I had a connection, sure, but it wasn't until things shifted after... after that night."

"What night?" Cassie asked, her brow furrowing in confusion.

"The night I told you about my fears of being stuck in my career," I explained, my heart racing. "Ethan was the one who listened, who really listened, and somewhere in all those conversations, something changed. But I never intended for it to go this far. I just... didn't know how to stop it."

Cassie's expression softened, and I could see her grappling with her emotions, a mix of hurt and understanding playing across her features. "And you?" she turned to Ethan, her voice steady yet laced with an uncharacteristic fragility. "What happened on your end?"

Ethan ran a hand through his hair, the gesture both familiar and endearing. "It crept up on me," he admitted. "I didn't want to feel this way. I kept telling myself it was just friendship. But the more time we spent together, the more I realized I couldn't ignore it anymore. I had to say something. I thought it would clear the air. Instead, I'm the cause of all this mess."

"That's the thing about feelings," Cassie said, her voice softening further. "They're messy and unpredictable, and they have a way of making you act without thinking."

Silence enveloped us again, but this time it was different—less charged, more contemplative.

"I just want to be clear," Cassie said suddenly, her tone shifting. "I don't want to lose you both. But you need to understand that this changes everything. We can't just sweep it under the rug and pretend it's all fine. We have to be honest about what's happening."

"I get that," I said, the words spilling out with urgency. "But I also don't want to make any rash decisions. We need time to process. We can take baby steps, right?"

"Baby steps," Ethan echoed, a faint smile on his lips, but I could see the flicker of uncertainty in his eyes.

Just then, the rustle of leaves caught my attention, an unexpected sound breaking the fragile moment. I glanced toward the tree line, the sudden shift in atmosphere igniting an instinctual tension within me. "Did you hear that?"

Cassie followed my gaze, her expression shifting from contemplation to alarm. "What was that?"

"Probably just a deer," Ethan suggested, but his voice held an edge of uncertainty.

Yet, as the rustling grew louder, a chill settled in the air, and it felt far too deliberate to be a simple animal. The branches trembled, and I could sense something looming just beyond the treeline, a presence that sent a shiver racing down my spine.

"Maybe we should head inside," I suggested, but the words fell flat as the rustling crescendoed into a cacophony of chaos. A figure burst from the trees, cloaked in shadows, and I felt my heart drop.

"Get inside!" I screamed, but before I could react, the figure lunged forward, shattering the fragile peace we had just begun to build, leaving us teetering on the edge of chaos once again.

# Chapter 9: "Heartstrings and Complications"

The air crackled with tension, a palpable reminder of the words that had passed between Cassie and me like venomous darts, each one striking deep. The vibrant chatter of the school hallways seemed to swirl around me, a cacophony I could no longer tune into. I moved through the throngs of students, a ghost haunting the halls of my own life. My backpack felt heavier than usual, burdened not just with textbooks and notebooks, but with the weight of my choices and the gnawing anxiety that refused to let me go.

As I rounded the corner near the science lab, the fluorescent lights flickered overhead, casting erratic shadows that danced along the walls. I could almost hear the whispers of our shared secrets echoing in my mind, memories of laughter and late-night talks that now felt like fragments of a different universe. Cassie and I had been inseparable since the first day of kindergarten, our friendship woven together with threads of trust and countless shared moments. Yet, now, our connection felt like a delicate web, fraying at the edges with every unspoken word.

Each day I sat in our usual spot in the cafeteria, my eyes scanning the room for any sign of Cassie. She had taken to sitting with a new group of friends, laughter bubbling from their table, but it only reminded me of the void her absence created. The vibrant smells of pizza and fries wafted through the air, and I poked at my untouched food, my appetite lost in the tumult of my emotions. I could hear the clinking of forks and the murmur of gossip, but the laughter seemed to taunt me. I was the outsider now, watching the world I once belonged to slip away like sand through my fingers.

In the far corner, Ethan sat with his friends, a familiar yet distant figure. The way he tossed his head back in laughter sent a ripple of longing through me. Memories of his gentle smile and the warmth of his hand on mine crashed over me like a tidal wave. The look in his eyes during our last encounter still haunted my dreams. A mixture of longing and regret tied my stomach in knots, every glance at him a reminder of the chasm that had opened between us. It felt like watching a beautiful painting fade under the harsh light of day; once vibrant, now dulled and frayed.

After school, I found myself wandering toward the park, the air tinged with the earthy scent of autumn leaves and the sweet note of impending rain. The clouds gathered overhead, heavy and gray, promising a storm that mirrored the tempest in my heart. I settled onto a weathered bench, its wood splintered and rough beneath me, yet oddly comforting. I could almost pretend the world was normal, that my heart wasn't a cacophony of confusion and despair.

The sound of rustling leaves drew my attention, and I glanced up to find Ethan approaching, his hands shoved deep into the pockets of his jacket. The sight of him sent a jolt through me, electrifying and terrifying all at once. There was a moment, a suspended breath where everything around us faded into a blur, and all that existed was the two of us. He stopped a few feet away, uncertainty etched across his features, as if he was battling a tempest of his own.

"Hey," he said, his voice soft but laced with the weight of unspoken words.

"Hey," I replied, my heart racing, a wild, uncooperative beast. The air thickened with the gravity of our shared history, the moments we had stolen away from the world and now had to navigate in the aftermath of our choices.

"I—I've been thinking about what happened," he began, his gaze searching mine for something, perhaps forgiveness or understanding. "I didn't mean for it to get so... messy."

"Neither did I," I whispered, the confession tasting bittersweet on my tongue. "But it did, and now I don't know how to fix it."

A small sigh escaped his lips, a sound that seemed to echo the heavy burden we both carried. "I miss you, you know? The way things were."

I felt a pang of guilt stab at me, the memory of Cassie's hurt flashing through my mind like a warning sign. "It's not that simple," I replied, a sharpness creeping into my voice. "We can't just pretend this didn't happen."

Ethan ran a hand through his hair, frustration evident in his movements. "I'm not asking you to pretend, but can't we at least talk about it? Find a way to navigate through the mess?"

I looked away, my heart twisting at the idea of diving deeper into this complicated web we'd woven. My thoughts drifted to Cassie again, the image of her hurt face pulling at my conscience. "What about Cassie?" I asked, my voice barely a whisper. "She's my best friend. This has hurt her too."

Ethan's expression darkened, and for a moment, I could see the shadows of regret lurking in his eyes. "I know, but we can't ignore what we feel just because it complicates things. I care about you, and I thought you cared about me too."

His words hung in the air, heavy with implications, and I felt the ground shift beneath my feet. A part of me wanted to lean into this connection, to embrace the warmth that his presence brought, but another part screamed in protest, echoing Cassie's name like a lifeline.

Before I could respond, a rumble of thunder rolled through the sky, the storm finally breaking loose as droplets began to fall. We both stood there, caught in the middle of our conversation and the downpour, the rain blurring the lines between longing and despair. My heart raced as the world around us blurred, and I couldn't help but wonder if this storm was a sign, a prelude to a confrontation far more significant than either of us had anticipated.

As the rain soaked through our clothes, I took a step back, putting distance between us, a desperate attempt to shield myself from the conflicting emotions that raged within. "I can't do this right now," I said, my voice trembling. "I need time."

With that, I turned and fled, leaving Ethan standing there, a haunting silhouette against the storm. Each step felt like a betrayal, but I couldn't shake the feeling that I was being pulled into a vortex, where every decision had the power to change everything. The world felt darker, the rain a stark reminder of the complications that lay ahead. As I ran, I hoped to outrun the chaos, but deep down, I knew the storm was just beginning.

The rain hammered down relentlessly, each drop a tiny reminder of the chaos I was trying to escape. I dashed home, drenched but numb to the cold, my heart racing not from exertion but from the weight of my spiraling thoughts. I had thought I could outrun the storm, but with each step, I felt the repercussions of my choices looming closer.

Once inside, I kicked off my soaked shoes, the sound echoing through the silent hallway. The scent of freshly baked cookies wafted through the air, a warm contrast to the turmoil swirling within me. My mother, ever the domestic goddess, was in the kitchen, her hands dusted with flour as she hummed an old tune, blissfully unaware of the storm brewing in her daughter's heart.

"Hey, sweet pea," she said, her voice brightening the dimness that seemed to cling to me like the dampness of my clothes. "I made your favorite! Chocolate chip with a hint of sea salt."

I forced a smile, hoping it would hold my worries at bay. "Thanks, Mom. They smell amazing."

But the sweet aroma was no match for the bitterness coiling in my stomach. I plopped onto a barstool, resting my head on the cool granite countertop, feeling the exhaustion seep into my bones. The cookies were nothing more than a pleasant distraction; my mind still reeled from the confrontation with Ethan, the taste of his words lingering like an unwelcome aftertaste.

"Everything okay?" she asked, her brow furrowed as she wiped her hands on a towel. "You look a little pale. Did something happen at school?"

I opened my mouth to respond, but the words tangled in my throat. How could I explain the mess of emotions that felt like a live wire, sparking and sizzling, demanding to be acknowledged? Instead, I shrugged, hoping it would suffice. "Just school stuff."

"Ah, teenage drama," she said with a knowing smile, pouring herself a cup of coffee. "You know, I once had a friend who—"

"Mom," I interrupted, not wanting to hear another story about how she survived the trials of youth. I appreciated her intention, but my own drama felt monumental, too significant to be bundled into the cute anecdotes of her past.

She sighed, placing her cup down with a soft thud. "Alright, I get it. Just know I'm here if you need to talk. Or if you want to eat your feelings with a batch of these cookies."

I couldn't help but chuckle softly at that. "Cookies do help, I suppose."

After a moment, I took one, the warm chocolate melting on my tongue, a fleeting moment of comfort amidst the chaos. But with each bite, I felt my thoughts drift back to Ethan, the way his eyes sparkled with unspoken promises, and the memory of Cassie's hurt gaze. The guilt churned in my stomach, making the sweet treat sit heavy in my chest.

Later that evening, I curled up on my bed, the sheets cool against my damp skin, the weight of the world resting on my shoulders. My phone buzzed, a jolt of electricity against the quiet of my room. I picked it up to see Cassie's name flashing across the screen. My heart thudded as I hesitated, my fingers hovering over the screen. What would I say? Would it open old wounds or offer a chance for healing?

Taking a deep breath, I opened the message: Can we talk? I need to clear the air.

The words felt like a lifeline thrown into a turbulent sea, but I didn't know if I had the strength to grab hold. I typed a quick response: Sure, when?

A few seconds later, her reply came through: Meet me at our spot?

The spot—our secret place by the old oak tree in the park, a sanctuary from the chaos of our lives. It was where we'd shared secrets and dreams, where laughter had once flowed as freely as the breeze. I could feel my heart rate quicken as I realized I couldn't postpone this any longer. I needed to face the music, no matter how out of tune it might sound.

I slipped on my jacket, the cool evening air wrapping around me like a shroud as I headed out. The walk to the park felt longer than usual, each step a reminder of the weight of unspoken words. The rustling leaves seemed to whisper doubts, and the shadows danced menacingly in the dim light. When I arrived, I found Cassie sitting under the sprawling branches of the oak, her silhouette framed against the twilight sky.

"Hey," she said, her voice soft yet steady.

"Hey," I replied, my throat dry as I took a seat beside her. The silence stretched between us, thick and uncomfortable, punctuated only by the distant sounds of crickets and the gentle rustle of leaves overhead.

"I've missed this," she finally said, her gaze fixed on the horizon. "You know, just us. I feel like everything's changed."

"Everything has changed," I admitted, the words tumbling out before I could censor them. "I messed up, Cassie. I never meant for you to get hurt."

She turned to me, her expression a mix of pain and understanding. "You weren't the only one who messed up. I just... I thought we were in this together. I thought I could trust you."

"I know," I said, my voice trembling. "And I wish I could take it all back. It's just... Ethan and I, there was something there, something I couldn't ignore. But I never wanted it to come between us."

Her eyes softened, the anger melting away to reveal a deeper hurt. "You should have talked to me. I would have understood, or at least tried to."

I nodded, shame washing over me. "You're right. I let my feelings cloud my judgment, and I didn't want to hurt you. But in trying to protect you, I hurt us both."

Cassie took a deep breath, her shoulders rising and falling as she collected her thoughts. "I'm not angry anymore. Just... confused. It feels like we're walking on eggshells, and it shouldn't be like this."

The admission hung in the air, heavy with implications. "I want to fix this," I said earnestly. "I want us to go back to being how we were, but I also don't want to hide things from you anymore."

She studied me for a long moment, and I could see the wheels turning in her mind. "So, where do we go from here?"

"I don't know," I admitted, feeling the weight of uncertainty settle in my chest. "But I want to try. I don't want this to be the end of our friendship. We can work through this, together."

Her gaze softened further, and for the first time since the fallout, I felt a flicker of hope. "Okay," she said, her voice steady. "Let's take it one step at a time. No more secrets, promise?"

"Promise," I replied, relief washing over me. The tension that had coiled tightly between us began to loosen, the air feeling lighter, as if the storm clouds of our past had finally begun to part.

As we sat there, side by side under the sprawling branches of the oak, I felt the weight of the world shifting ever so slightly. The evening breeze carried away the remnants of our worries, leaving behind the comforting sense of possibility. We may have been entangled in complications, but for the first time in what felt like ages, I could see a path forward—uncertain and winding, but there nonetheless.

As the days rolled on, the delicate threads of my life began to weave a new, complex tapestry, frayed at the edges but vibrant in its contradictions. Cassie and I had reached a tentative truce, our conversations peppered with the sharp humor we once shared, yet the unspoken tension lingered like a stubborn fog. At school, we navigated the hallways with a practiced ease, but beneath the surface, the undertow of our complicated emotions constantly threatened to pull us under.

Ethan lingered in the corners of my mind like a ghost, haunting and alluring. Despite our fragile truce, I found myself wandering into the realm of what-ifs. What if I had chosen differently? What if I hadn't crossed that line? I replayed our last conversation over and over, dissecting each word as if they held the secrets to a puzzle I desperately wanted to solve. I caught glimpses of him in the cafeteria, laughter ringing out like music, but I felt as though I was listening to a song played just out of tune—beautiful yet tragically misaligned.

One particularly crisp autumn afternoon, Cassie suggested we attend a school football game together. I hesitated, my mind flickering to the possibility of running into Ethan among the raucous crowd. Yet, as I looked at her hopeful face, I couldn't bear the thought of disappointing her again. "Sure," I said, my voice betraying none of the anxiety churning inside me.

The stadium was alive with energy, the scent of popcorn and hot dogs wafting through the air as we joined the throng of students, excitement buzzing like static electricity. The stands were a kaleidoscope of colors, each cheer and shout resonating with the exhilaration of competition. Cassie and I settled into our seats, her enthusiasm palpable as she painted the scene with animated descriptions of our team's chances.

"Just watch," she said, her eyes sparkling with mischief. "They're going to crush it tonight. You'll see."

I forced a smile, hoping to share in her excitement while my gaze drifted across the field, scanning for a familiar figure. A few rows down, I spotted Ethan, his laughter ringing out like a melody that only I could hear. He was surrounded by friends, his easy charm captivating those around him, and for a moment, my heart fluttered, caught in the conflict of longing and regret.

"Are you even listening?" Cassie nudged me, pulling me from my reverie.

"Of course!" I replied, too quickly, and she raised an eyebrow, unimpressed.

"Right. Just staring off into the distance like you're about to be whisked away by a fairytale prince."

"Oh, please, it's just a football game." I chuckled, trying to play it off, but she wasn't buying it.

"Sure, sure. Keep telling yourself that," she teased, rolling her eyes.

The game began, and with each whistle and cheer, I tried to immerse myself in the experience. Yet my attention inevitably wandered back to Ethan. As the scoreboard ticked down, he caught my eye, and in that split second, everything else faded away. The noise of the crowd dulled to a whisper, and it felt like the world had narrowed down to just the two of us. There was a glimmer of something in his gaze—curiosity, perhaps even longing—that sent my heart racing.

Cassie's voice broke through my thoughts as she cheered, "Touchdown!" The crowd erupted, and I clapped along, trying to match her energy. But my mind was elsewhere, caught in the tumult of emotions swirling between Ethan and me. I could feel the magnetic pull of his presence even from afar, the gravity of our connection undeniable despite the chaos.

As the halftime show began, Cassie suggested we grab snacks. We navigated through the crowd, the energy around us intoxicating. I kept glancing back at Ethan, who was now surrounded by a different group, his laughter ringing out in a way that tugged at something deep within me. The realization hit me like a brick—he was moving on, and I was still stuck in the past.

"Hey, you're daydreaming again!" Cassie teased, elbowing me playfully as we stood in line for nachos.

"I'm not daydreaming," I protested, but the words sounded hollow, even to me. The tension that had simmered beneath the surface now threatened to boil over, and I could feel the weight of my choices pressing down, heavy and unyielding.

Just then, my phone buzzed in my pocket, a reminder of the outside world crashing into my moment. I pulled it out to see a message from Ethan: Can we talk?

A jolt of surprise raced through me. My fingers trembled slightly as I typed back, Now?

His response came quickly: Yeah, meet me at the bleachers in five minutes?

I glanced at Cassie, who was absorbed in her nachos, blissfully unaware of the turmoil unfolding within me. "Hey, I'll be right back," I said, my heart racing as I slipped away, leaving her with her snack.

As I approached the bleachers, my breath hitched in my throat. What did he want? Did he want to clear the air, or was it to say goodbye? I could feel the energy in the air shift, the anticipation thickening like fog.

Ethan was leaning against the railing, the glow of the stadium lights casting a halo around him, making him look impossibly handsome. He turned as I approached, his expression a mix of determination and uncertainty.

"Thanks for coming," he said, his voice steady but soft.

"What's up?" I asked, trying to keep my tone casual even as my heart pounded like a drum.

He took a deep breath, his gaze unwavering. "I can't stop thinking about you, about us. I know things have been complicated, but I can't pretend like I don't feel something for you."

I felt my heart leap, the warmth of his words wrapping around me like a comforting blanket. But that comfort was quickly overshadowed by the thought of Cassie, her laughter echoing in my mind like a warning. "Ethan, I—"

"Wait, let me finish." He stepped closer, his eyes intense, searching mine for understanding. "I don't want to lose you. I know it's messy, and we're walking a tightrope, but I can't walk away from this. I won't."

The sincerity in his voice made my heart race, but doubt crept in, twisting the joy into something darker. "But what about Cassie?" I breathed, the words tasting like ash on my tongue.

He hesitated, the air crackling with the weight of the moment. "I don't want to hurt her, but I can't ignore what we have either. You need to know how I feel."

Before I could respond, a loud cheer erupted from the stadium, the sound drowning out the tumult of our emotions. It was a brief distraction, a momentary reprieve, but it left us hanging in uncertainty.

"Ethan, I..." I began, but a sudden commotion from the crowd interrupted me. A figure stumbled from the stands, crashing onto the field, drawing the attention of everyone around. The buzz of excitement turned to alarm, and in that split second, the world spiraled into chaos.

Ethan's gaze shot toward the disturbance, and I followed suit, my heart racing. In the fray, a familiar face emerged, but before I could process it, everything shifted. The moment hung heavy, poised on a precipice, as reality collided with an unexpected turn. The air thickened with tension, and in that moment, I realized our conversation was far from over, our tangled hearts hanging in the balance of uncertainty, with the storm still brewing on the horizon.

# Chapter 10: "A Stolen Moment"

The night air was thick with the sweet scent of honeysuckle and damp earth, a fragrant reminder of the summer that lingered too long, stubborn and intoxicating. My heart thumped in my chest, a wild drumbeat urging me onward as I made my way to the old bridge, that cherished remnant of our childhood escapades. Each step was punctuated by the soft rustling of leaves overhead, as if the trees themselves were whispering secrets only the night could understand. The moon hung low in the sky, a silver coin that had fallen from the heavens, casting an ethereal glow on the world below. The water beneath the bridge danced and shimmered, a mirror to the stars, inviting yet foreboding.

Ethan stood there, leaning against the weathered wooden railing, the shadows playing tricks on his features, turning him into a specter of my past and a promise of my future. There was an urgency in his stance, an unspoken gravity that pulled me toward him as if the very fabric of our lives had woven a thread too strong to sever. I could see the conflict in his eyes, the way they flickered like candle flames caught in a draft. They were deep pools of vulnerability and strength, a dangerous combination that sent a jolt of electricity through me.

"Sorry for dragging you out here," he said, his voice low and smooth, like honey drizzling over warm bread. He took a step closer, and I could feel the heat radiating off him, mingling with the cool night air. "I just... I had to see you."

I tucked a stray hair behind my ear, suddenly aware of how my pulse quickened at his proximity. "You know I'm supposed to be studying for that big exam next week," I replied, attempting to sound playful but failing miserably. The truth was, I would have ditched studying for a lifetime of exams just to be here, under the moonlight, with him.

He chuckled softly, a sound that wrapped around me like a comforting blanket. "Studying can wait. This..." He gestured to the world around us, the night, the bridge, the star-speckled sky, "...this is what you should be focusing on. Besides, you've already aced every test they've thrown at you."

His faith in me felt like a warm embrace, but as I looked deeper into his gaze, I saw the flicker of something darker, an undercurrent of worry that tugged at my own heart. I had been grappling with my feelings, caught in a tangled web of loyalty to my best friend, Cassie, and this undeniable chemistry with Ethan. They were like two magnets, each pulling me in opposite directions, and I was stuck in the middle, feeling the strain of the pull.

"I know, but..." I hesitated, my breath catching. "Cassie... she's been distant lately, and I can't help but feel like it's because of us."

His expression hardened for a moment, a shadow passing over his features, before he softened again. "I don't want to come between you two, but I can't pretend I don't feel this," he said, his voice thick with emotion. "It's like a spark, igniting everything inside me. I've never felt this way about anyone before, and I know you feel it too."

The world around us seemed to blur, the night filled with the tension of unspoken words and unshed tears. I wanted to confess my feelings, to share the tumult of emotions swirling inside me, but the thought of losing Cassie made my stomach churn. She had always been my anchor, the one constant in a life filled with uncertainties. Yet here I was, standing on the precipice of something beautiful and terrifying, and Ethan was the only one who could pull me from the edge.

"Maybe we could just take a moment, you know?" I suggested, my voice a whisper as I stepped closer, closing the gap between us. "Just be here, right now, without thinking about everything else."

His lips curved into a smile that lit up his entire face, and I felt my resolve waver. I had never seen him look so alive, so free, and it ignited a flame within me that had long been dormant. "Just this moment, then," he replied, his tone playful but laced with a seriousness that made my heart race.

He reached out, brushing his fingers along my arm, sending a shiver cascading down my spine. The contact was electric, a charge that sparked between us, igniting all the thoughts I had tried to suppress. I looked into his eyes, those dark orbs filled with intensity, and felt the world around us fade away.

"I've been thinking about us," he said, his voice barely above a murmur. "About what it would be like if we just—"

The sound of laughter in the distance interrupted him, sharp and jarring. My heart sank. Cassie. She was nearby, probably with her group of friends, oblivious to the storm brewing in my chest. I pulled back, the warmth of Ethan's presence dissipating as reality crashed back in. "Ethan, we can't—"

"Can't what?" he pressed, frustration and longing mingling in his expression. "Can't acknowledge what's right in front of us? You feel it too. Don't pretend you don't."

I opened my mouth to respond, but the words tangled in my throat. I could hear the distant sounds of Cassie's laughter, a reminder of everything I stood to lose. A whirlwind of emotions surged through me—fear, desire, guilt—each vying for dominance in my mind. "I don't want to hurt her," I finally managed, my voice barely a whisper.

"But are you willing to hurt yourself?" he challenged, his gaze unwavering. "Every moment we deny this connection, we're stealing from ourselves."

His words hung in the air, heavy and poignant, cutting through the noise of my thoughts. There was a truth in them that resonated deep within me, but the weight of loyalty pressed heavily on my heart. I could almost hear the ticking of time, reminding me that choices had consequences. As the laughter grew closer, I took a step back, my heart racing with the gravity of the situation.

"Maybe we should just... go back," I suggested, the words tasting bitter on my tongue. My mind raced, caught between the magnetic pull of my feelings for Ethan and the loyalty that bound me to Cassie.

Ethan's expression fell, the flicker of hope dimming in his eyes. "If that's what you want..." he started, but his voice trailed off, filled with a disappointment that pierced my heart like an arrow.

"No, it's not what I want," I said quickly, the truth rushing out before I could second-guess myself. "I want to be here with you, but I can't ignore what this could do to Cassie."

"Life isn't about playing it safe, Ella," he replied, frustration bubbling just beneath the surface. "What about what you want? Don't I get a say in this?"

The air crackled with tension, each word we exchanged pulling at the threads of my resolve. I wanted to fight for us, to embrace the passion sparking between us, but the weight of my friendship with Cassie loomed large, an invisible chain shackling my heart. "You deserve someone who can be all in, not someone who's half-heartedly hiding in the shadows," I said, my voice trembling.

Ethan stepped closer, his eyes dark and stormy. "And you deserve more than just a friendship based on guilt. You deserve to feel alive, to be happy. What do you think I want? To steal you away? No! I want you to choose me because you want to, not because you feel obligated."

His words lingered in the air, heavy with the gravity of his sincerity. And in that moment, with Cassie's laughter echoing in the background, I realized I was standing at a crossroads, torn between the familiar comfort of loyalty and the thrilling unknown that beckoned with Ethan. The choice loomed before me, tantalizing yet terrifying, promising both joy and heartbreak. The stakes were higher than I had ever anticipated, and the night around us grew colder, the moon casting long shadows on the ground as if urging me to take a step into the darkness, to embrace the stolen moment that might just change everything.

Ethan's breath warmed my skin, the tension between us thick enough to cut with a knife. Each heartbeat echoed the uncertainty swirling in my chest, a constant reminder of the delicate balance I was trying to maintain. I had always been the good friend, the reliable one, and yet here I stood, dangerously close to crossing a line that could unravel everything.

"What are you thinking?" he asked, searching my face as if he could decipher the secrets etched in my expression. There was a flicker of hope in his eyes, and I felt a pang of guilt. How could I pull him into my storm while I wrestled with my own demons?

"I'm thinking this feels... right," I admitted, the words spilling out before I could cage them. "But also terribly wrong."

He squeezed my hands tighter, grounding me in that moment, and the world around us faded even further into the background. "What if it doesn't have to be wrong?" he countered, his voice a soft challenge that curled around my resolve. "What if we're just two people who happen to have this connection, and it's okay to explore it?"

The breeze rustled the leaves above us, as if nature itself conspired to affirm his words. The night was thick with possibility, yet the thought of Cassie's disappointed face haunted me. Would I betray her by following my heart?

"I wish I could be that person," I replied, the frustration seeping into my voice. "But I can't shake the feeling that I'm standing on the edge of a cliff, and one wrong move could send everything spiraling."

Ethan's expression softened, and he stepped closer, his warmth enveloping me like a blanket against the chill of the night. "Then let's not think about the cliff. Let's just take one step back from the edge."

His eyes were captivating, holding me in a trance that made it easy to forget the world outside our bubble. I wanted to believe him, to let go of the weight pressing on my heart, but the reminder of my friendship with Cassie pulled me back like a tether.

"Okay, one step," I echoed, a shaky smile creeping onto my face. "But just one. And then we're back to reality."

"Deal," he said, grinning, the tension between us shifting into something lighter. "Let's talk about something that isn't existential."

"Like?" I asked, the playfulness creeping back into my voice, sparking a flicker of joy in my heart.

"Your ridiculously stubborn study habits," he suggested, his tone teasing. "Seriously, do you ever give yourself a break?"

I rolled my eyes, the laughter bubbling up like a fizzy drink. "And miss out on my chance to become the town's youngest overachiever? Never!"

"Overachiever or not, you need a little chaos in your life. It'll make for better stories," he replied, winking. "Remember that time you tried to build a treehouse and it ended up looking like a sad excuse for a fort?"

"Oh please, that was a masterpiece!" I protested, laughter spilling from my lips. "A structurally unsound masterpiece, but a masterpiece nonetheless."

He laughed, the sound deep and rich, wrapping around me in the cool night air. "A bit of an architect, you are," he teased. "If we'd left it up, I'm pretty sure it would've become a local landmark."

"More like a local hazard," I quipped back, our banter weaving a thread of lightness through the heavy air. In that moment, we slipped away from the weight of the world, if only temporarily.

But the laughter faded as reality seeped back in, a creeping shadow threatening to overshadow our stolen moment. I turned serious, my heart beating a little faster. "Ethan, do you really think we could be... something more?"

He didn't hesitate. "Absolutely. I can't imagine feeling this way about anyone else. It's not just the thrill of sneaking out; it's everything else that comes with it."

"Everything else?" I repeated, my heart fluttering as I searched his face for clarity. "What does that mean?"

"It means that I can see a future with you, Ella. The late-night talks, the laughter, the chaos. You make everything feel... alive." His honesty wrapped around me, filling the cracks of my heart with warmth.

The pull was magnetic, the energy between us sparking like fireflies dancing in the twilight. Yet a dark cloud loomed overhead, reminding me of the impending storm. Cassie. What would she think if she knew? Would our friendship survive?

Before I could voice my concerns, the distant sounds of laughter drew nearer, bringing with it a sharp reminder of reality. The brightness of their voices sliced through the intimacy of our moment, and I felt a sudden rush of panic. "Ethan, we should—"

"I know," he cut in, his tone shifting as he glanced over his shoulder toward the approaching sound. "Let's make this quick."

In a heartbeat, he leaned in, closing the distance between us. My heart raced, caught in the whirlwind of emotions, as his lips brushed against mine. It was a soft caress, tentative yet electric, and in that fleeting moment, the world fell away, leaving just the two of us suspended in time.

The kiss sent shockwaves through me, igniting a fire that radiated warmth through my veins. I melted into him, forgetting everything else—the laughter, the uncertainty, even the looming consequences. For a heartbeat, I let myself be swept away, losing myself in the heady blend of our shared breath and lingering warmth.

But just as quickly as it began, the moment shattered. A voice called out, pulling me back from the edge, from the euphoria of our shared kiss. "Ella! Are you out here?" It was Cassie, her voice bright and cheerful, cutting through the atmosphere like a knife.

I pulled away, my heart plummeting as reality crashed back in. Ethan's expression mirrored my own confusion, a blend of exhilaration and dread, our secret punctured by the arrival of the outside world. "I think we need to—" I started, but the urgency in my voice was drowned out by Cassie's approach.

"Ella, come on! We're heading to the party at Sam's!" she called again, her tone carefree. I could hear the laughter of her friends trailing behind her, a cheerful cacophony that felt like an impending storm.

Ethan stepped back, his expression hardening as he glanced in the direction of the noise. "Right. Party time." The spark that had danced between us dimmed, replaced by a weight of unspoken words hanging in the air.

"Yeah, party time," I echoed, feeling the warmth drain from my cheeks as I struggled to compose myself. "Just... just give me a second."

"Ella, we don't have all night!" Cassie shouted, her voice growing closer.

"Coming!" I called back, my heart racing. Turning back to Ethan, I took a deep breath, my mind racing with the implications of what had just happened. "We'll talk later?"

"Yeah, later," he replied, but there was a tension in his voice, a flicker of doubt that sent a chill down my spine.

I felt as though I was standing on the precipice of a cliff, staring down at the swirling waters below. "I'll text you," I promised, and as I stepped back, I could see the unyielding weight of my decision hanging between us, thick and palpable.

With one last look, I turned toward the laughter that had become my tether to reality. The moonlight shimmered on the water behind me, a fleeting reminder of what I had just tasted. I walked away, my heart heavy with uncertainty, knowing that the stolen moment we had shared had changed everything. As I crossed the threshold of the bridge, I felt the ground shift beneath me, and I knew I was entering a world that could never go back to the way it was before.

As I stepped away from the bridge and the warmth of Ethan's lingering touch, the air turned heavy, thickening with the weight of unspoken words and uncharted feelings. The laughter from Cassie and her friends grew louder, a chorus of joy that rang out like a bell, summoning me back into the fold. I quickened my pace, my heart a wild drum in my chest, each beat echoing the conflict within me.

"Ella! Finally!" Cassie exclaimed, her face lighting up with the kind of enthusiasm that always warmed my heart. She swept me into a hug, the scent of her floral shampoo enveloping me like a comforting embrace. "We thought you'd gone AWOL! You know how Sam gets when he thinks he's the life of the party."

"I'm here, aren't I?" I replied, forcing a smile that felt slightly stretched. The pang of guilt settled deep, a weight that settled in the pit of my stomach as I glanced back at the bridge, knowing Ethan was still there, feeling the echo of his kiss tingling on my lips.

Cassie, oblivious to my internal struggle, looped her arm through mine as we headed toward the thrumming music that emanated from Sam's backyard. The path was lined with fireflies, flickering like tiny stars fallen to earth. I tried to focus on the warmth of the evening and the friendship that had always felt like a safety net, but the nagging doubt kept creeping in, whispering questions I didn't want to confront.

As we approached the party, the atmosphere shifted, becoming a whirlwind of excitement and noise. A cluster of our friends had gathered, laughter punctuating the night air, and the smell of barbecued food wafted over us, mingling with the scent of fresh-cut grass.

"Let's grab some drinks!" Cassie suggested, pulling me toward the makeshift bar where Sam had set up an impressive array of beverages, both alcoholic and non. I could see Ethan in the distance, standing by the cooler, his eyes scanning the crowd. The moment our gazes locked, a jolt of awareness shot through me. He smiled, but it didn't quite reach his eyes, and I felt the tightening in my chest return.

"Want something fruity or strong?" Cassie asked, oblivious to the tension dancing between Ethan and me.

"Fruity sounds great," I said, trying to keep my voice light.

As we grabbed our drinks, I caught Ethan's gaze again, this time more intense, filled with a question I could barely decipher. My heart raced, a mix of excitement and dread swirling within me. I knew that no matter how hard I tried to blend into the vibrant atmosphere, my mind was still tethered to that moment by the bridge, that electrifying kiss that changed everything.

"Hey, Ella!" A voice cut through my thoughts, pulling my focus. It was Ben, one of our mutual friends, his grin wide as he approached. "You finally made it! We were just debating who would win in a fight: a bear or a shark."

Cassie laughed, her eyes sparkling. "I'm on Team Shark. Bears can't swim!"

I couldn't help but chuckle, though my laughter felt hollow. "I'm not sure that's how it works, but I'm in!" I replied, trying to immerse myself in the friendly banter.

As the night unfolded, I moved through the crowd, my mind racing. Conversations ebbed and flowed, music pulsed in the background, and yet, all I could think about was Ethan's expression—part hope, part despair. Every laugh from Cassie tugged at my conscience, a reminder of the delicate balance I was trying to maintain.

A game of charades began, the group forming a circle, and Cassie dragged me to the front. "You have to go first! Show us what you've got!" Her enthusiasm was infectious, and despite the turmoil swirling inside me, I found myself smiling.

I stood in the center, channeling my inner performer, mimicking various animals and celebrities, the crowd erupting in laughter. Just as I was about to reveal my pièce de résistance—a dramatic rendition of a lion—I caught Ethan's eye again. He was standing at the edge of the circle, his arms crossed, a faint smile on his lips that didn't quite reach the depths of his gaze.

"Seriously, what's the deal with you and Ethan?" Cassie whispered as I resumed my place beside her, her tone playful but her eyes narrowed with curiosity.

I opened my mouth to reply, but the words tangled in my throat, the truth eluding me. "He's just... I don't know. He's complicated," I finally managed, the honesty catching in my chest like a bird trapped behind bars.

Cassie raised an eyebrow. "Complicated, huh? Sounds like someone has a crush!"

I shot her a glare, but the smile tugging at my lips betrayed me. "Not a crush. Just... an interest in his existential thoughts about life and bears versus sharks."

"Uh-huh," she smirked, clearly unconvinced. "You've always been terrible at lying."

Before I could respond, Sam called out, "Hey, who's next for charades?" The group turned their attention back to the game, and I breathed a sigh of relief, grateful for the distraction.

As the game continued, my laughter mixed with the warm night air, but I couldn't shake the feeling of Ethan's gaze on me. Each glance ignited a fire in my belly, a reminder of the connection we shared, of the possibility that lingered just beyond the horizon of friendship. Yet, the reality of Cassie's presence loomed over me, casting shadows over my thoughts.

As the game wound down, I slipped away from the group, needing a moment to breathe. The night sky was a canvas of stars, twinkling like the secrets I held close. I wandered toward the edge of the yard, the sound of laughter fading into the background.

"Ella?"

I turned, and there was Ethan, stepping out from the shadows, the moonlight catching the edges of his features. "I thought you might need a break."

"Or an escape route?" I shot back, my tone teasing but my heart racing.

"Maybe a bit of both," he replied, the corner of his mouth lifting in a grin. "This is the most chaotic party I've been to in ages. It's exhausting keeping up with all the bear and shark debates."

I laughed, the tension in my chest easing ever so slightly. "You're the one who signed up for this chaos. I'm just trying to keep my sanity intact."

"Maybe you should join me in chaos once in a while," he suggested, stepping closer, the warmth radiating from him pulling me in. "What are you really afraid of, Ella?"

The question hung in the air, heavy with meaning. "I don't know," I admitted, my voice barely above a whisper. "I guess I'm just scared of what happens if I choose you and it all goes wrong."

"Or what happens if you don't?" he countered, his gaze unwavering. "You've been given this moment, and it's slipping away."

His words struck a chord, resonating deep within me, and for a heartbeat, I felt the pull of possibility. "You're right," I breathed, uncertainty swirling in my chest. "But I can't just abandon everything I've built."

Ethan sighed, his expression shifting to something more serious. "Ella, this is about you. You deserve to chase after what makes you happy. You can't let fear dictate your choices forever."

"I wish it were that simple," I replied, my voice trembling.

"Maybe it could be," he urged, stepping even closer. "Maybe if you let go, you'd find something incredible waiting on the other side."

The intensity in his gaze held me captive, and I felt my resolve waver. The chemistry between us crackled in the night air, a storm building with each passing second. Just as I was about to voice my feelings, the loud laughter from the party erupted again, pulling me back to reality.

"Ella!" Cassie's voice cut through the moment like a blade. "We need you for a photo! Come on!"

I glanced toward the gathering, my heart sinking at the thought of returning to the chaos. "I—" I started, torn between my desires and the loyalty that anchored me.

"Go. I'll be here," Ethan said softly, his voice a soothing balm against the chaos.

The moment felt like a fragile thread, stretched taut between us, and I turned reluctantly toward the party, my heart heavy. As I walked back to the group, laughter and music swirling around me, I couldn't shake the feeling that I was leaving something vital behind.

"Get in close, Ella!" Cassie called, waving me over. I plastered on a smile, yet the nagging ache of what could have been lingered as I stood in the circle, the warmth of Ethan's gaze still echoing in my mind.

"Say cheese!" Sam shouted, and as the flash of the camera captured the moment, my heart raced with uncertainty. The reality of the night weighed on me, heavy and unyielding, and I could feel the fracture lines forming, threatening to pull me in two directions.

As the group erupted into laughter, I couldn't shake the feeling that the storm I had been avoiding was finally here, looming just on the horizon. The cliff was no longer a distant threat but a precipice I was about to confront. And with every laugh, every moment shared, I felt the pull of that decision growing ever stronger.

And then it happened. A sharp shout rang out from the crowd, an

# Chapter 11: "Choosing Sides"

Cassie stood with arms crossed, a storm brewing in her hazel eyes. The soft hum of the staff room faded into silence, the kind that comes just before thunder rumbles in the distance. I could hear the rustle of papers and the clinking of coffee mugs, but it all felt distant, muted by the weight of her ultimatum. The afternoon sun streamed through the tall windows, casting warm rays across the room, illuminating the tension that sparkled in the air like electricity.

"Choose, Emma. It's either him or me." Her voice was low, edged with a steel that pierced through my hesitation. The bright glow of the sun did nothing to soften the chill creeping into my bones. I opened my mouth to respond, but the words tangled in my throat, caught between loyalty and desire.

I had always admired Cassie's fierce loyalty, the way she defended her friends with the ferocity of a lioness. Yet, here I was, feeling like a deer caught in the headlights of an oncoming train, paralyzed by the weight of her demand. On one hand, there was Cassie, my confidante and the sister I never had, a person who had been by my side through thick and thin. On the other hand, there was Noah, with his easy smile and the way he seemed to see right into my soul, igniting a fire within me that I didn't even know existed.

"Why are you doing this?" I finally managed to whisper, my heart pounding in my chest. "Can't we find a way to make this work?"

Cassie shook her head, her curls bouncing defiantly as if they shared in her refusal. "It's not that simple. He's... different. You know he is. He's not who you think he is, Emma."

My heart twisted at the edge of her words. There it was, the shadow of doubt she cast over Noah, the boy who had brought laughter back into my life after a season of gray. "What do you mean different?" I pressed, the heat of anger surging through me. "He's kind, he's funny, and he makes me feel... alive."

Cassie's expression softened, just for a moment, the protective shield wavering like the flicker of a candle in a gust of wind. "I don't want to see you get hurt. You deserve better than someone whose past is shrouded in mystery. I just... I need you to understand."

A shroud of confusion enveloped me. Cassie had always been my rock, yet this felt like a betrayal—a rift forming between us that could split me in two. I wanted to trust her, to believe that her heart was in the right place, but something deep inside whispered that she was letting fear dictate her actions.

I took a step closer, the space between us thick with tension. "You think I can't make my own choices? That I don't know what I'm doing?"

Her gaze held mine, fierce yet pleading. "I'm not saying that. I just think you're blinded by infatuation. Love doesn't come without risk, and sometimes the person you want the most can be the one who hurts you the deepest."

"Noah wouldn't hurt me," I insisted, feeling my voice rise slightly, my emotions a tempest threatening to spill over. "He's been nothing but good to me. You're judging him based on rumors, Cassie. I need to find out for myself."

The silence hung heavy, and I could feel the divide widening between us, a chasm deepening with each word. Cassie's hands dropped to her sides, the fight draining from her, leaving behind a vulnerability I had rarely seen. "I can't watch you walk into something that could destroy you. I just can't."

The rawness of her emotion broke through my resolve. I wanted to reach out, to soothe her worries, to bridge the gap that was threatening to swallow us both whole. "What if it doesn't destroy me? What if it makes me stronger?"

Her eyes glistened with unshed tears, and my heart twisted with regret. "It's not just about you, Emma. It's about us—what happens to our friendship if things go wrong. You'll have to choose sides, and I fear that if you choose him, you'll lose me."

The weight of her words pressed down on me, and I felt the walls of the staff room closing in. My mind raced, flipping through memories like a photo album, each image a snapshot of laughter shared and secrets whispered. Our bond had been forged in the fire of shared experiences, and I could feel that flame flickering, teetering on the edge of extinction.

"I can't lose you," I finally admitted, my voice barely above a whisper. "But I can't deny what I feel for him either."

Cassie's shoulders sagged, the fight in her dimming like a candle struggling against the wind. "Then you have to understand that choosing him means choosing a path I can't follow. You'll have to navigate this alone."

The finality of her words sent a chill through me. I stood there, rooted to the spot, as a maelstrom of emotions swirled inside. The staff room felt increasingly like a cage, its familiar warmth now stifling. Outside, the world continued to spin, oblivious to the turmoil raging within me. I could feel the weight of choices pressing down, each one laden with consequence, each path branching out into an unknown future.

The door swung open, and the laughter of students filtered in, a stark contrast to the heaviness that hung between us. I blinked, trying to clear my head, desperate for clarity in the haze of uncertainty. The vibrant chatter felt like a reminder of everything I stood to lose—the friendships, the connections, the laughter that colored my life.

"Just think about it," Cassie said softly, her eyes glistening as she turned away. "Please."

And with that, she stepped back, leaving me to grapple with the weight of my decisions, my heart fractured between two worlds, each one pulling me in different directions.

The air felt charged as Cassie walked away, the door clicking shut behind her, leaving me alone in the dimly lit staff room. My heart raced, and I could still feel the imprint of her fierce gaze as if it were seared into my skin. The walls around me seemed to close in, the laughter of students outside drifting through the glass like a distant melody I no longer felt connected to.

I sank into a chair, running my fingers through my hair as I attempted to unravel the knot of emotions swirling inside me. I could still hear Cassie's words echoing in my mind, a persistent reminder of the impossible choice laid before me. Love or loyalty? A question as old as time itself, yet here I was, utterly unprepared to answer it.

Noah's smile danced before my eyes, warm and inviting, a lighthouse guiding me through the fog of uncertainty. Every moment spent with him was like stepping into a sunbeam on a chilly day. He had a way of making everything feel lighter, as if the world held just a little less weight when he was near. But the shadows of Cassie's warnings crept into my thoughts, dark and unwelcome, whispering doubts about his intentions and the shadows lurking in his past.

I couldn't shake the feeling that I was balancing on a tightrope stretched between two cliffs, each side promising both ecstasy and agony. My phone buzzed on the table, a welcome distraction. I grabbed it, hoping for a text from Noah, a lifeline that could pull me from my spiraling thoughts. Instead, it was a message from Cassie.

Let's meet after school. I need to talk to you. No more secrets.

My heart sank. Secrets? Did she have something else to reveal? I knew she'd been keeping something from me, a hidden truth about Noah that she was too afraid to voice outright. The anxiety bubbling in my stomach felt like a stone sinking deeper and deeper as the minutes passed.

The afternoon dragged on, the clock ticking with cruel deliberation. Each chime of the bell sent ripples of apprehension through me. When the final bell rang, signaling the end of the day, I hurried out, weaving through the bustling hallways filled with students' laughter and chatter. My heart raced with every step toward the café where Cassie had suggested we meet, a small corner of our town that had become our sanctuary—a place filled with the comforting scent of freshly brewed coffee and sweet pastries.

As I pushed open the door, the familiar sound of the bell chiming overhead brought a rush of nostalgia. The café was warm, inviting, with its rustic wooden tables and eclectic decor. Cassie was already seated in our usual booth, her fingers tapping nervously on the table. She looked up as I approached, and for a moment, I saw the cracks in her brave facade.

"Hey," I said, sliding into the seat across from her. "What's going on?"

Cassie took a deep breath, her eyes searching mine for understanding. "I didn't want to put you in that position, Em. You know I'd never want to hurt you."

"Then why did you?" I felt a sharpness in my voice, a mixture of anger and hurt. "You didn't need to give me an ultimatum. It felt... cruel."

Her gaze fell to the table, and I could see the internal battle raging within her. "I know, but you're my best friend, and I just wanted to protect you. I thought if I could make you see the danger—"

"Danger?" I interrupted, my frustration bubbling over. "Are we talking about Noah, or are you projecting your own fears onto me? He's not a villain in some fairytale. He's just a guy, and I like him. A lot."

Cassie's eyes flashed, a spark igniting in the depths of her frustration. "You don't know what you're getting into. People like him don't change. They can't. They carry their past with them like a shadow."

My breath caught at the weight of her words. "What do you mean by people like him?" I asked, my voice lowering. "What do you know about him that I don't?"

Her silence spoke volumes, and I felt the temperature drop in the small booth. "Cassie, please," I urged, desperate for clarity. "Tell me. If there's something I should know..."

Finally, she leaned in, her voice dropping to a whisper, as if she were afraid someone might overhear. "He's been in trouble, Emma. Real trouble. I heard things from people who know him. You deserve someone who doesn't come with baggage that could crush you."

The confession hung in the air like a fog, suffocating and thick. My heart raced as I processed her words. Trouble? What kind? I had sensed an air of mystery about Noah, an untold story lingering in the space between us. But this?

"Who told you this?" I pressed, needing more than vague accusations.

"A friend of mine who knows him from school—someone who's seen what he's been involved in." She paused, her gaze steady on mine. "He's not what you think, Em. And if you think you can save him, you're only setting yourself up for heartbreak."

I took a moment to absorb her words, feeling as if the ground beneath me was shifting. "But you don't really know him. Not the way I do," I argued, the defiance in my voice rising. "What if he's changed? What if he's trying to be better?"

Cassie looked away, her expression pained. "And what if he hasn't? What if you end up caught in the crossfire of his past? I can't stand by and watch you walk into a disaster."

The tension crackled between us, thick and suffocating. I could see the love and concern etched into Cassie's features, but it felt overshadowed by the walls she was trying to build between us. "So what am I supposed to do? Just turn my back on him because of what someone said?"

"Maybe it's not just about him. Maybe it's about us," she said quietly. "I can't risk losing you, Em. Not like this."

"Then don't ask me to choose!" I shot back, my voice rising in the cozy café, drawing a few glances from nearby tables. "I won't. I refuse to live my life dictated by fear. I need to figure this out on my own."

Cassie's shoulders slumped as if I had struck a physical blow. "Then just promise me you'll be careful. I want you to be happy, but I can't just stand by and let you hurt yourself."

"Maybe you should trust me a little more." I leaned back, crossing my arms defiantly. The conversation had reached an impasse, leaving an unsettling void where our laughter and camaraderie usually flourished. I didn't want to lose this—her, us—but how could I hold onto a friendship that felt conditional?

The café buzzed around us, life continuing on as I wrestled with the weight of the decisions that lay before me. I could feel the foundation of my reality crumbling, the landscape of my life shifting beneath my feet, and I wasn't sure which way to turn. Cassie's fierce love had always been a shield, but now it felt like a shackle, binding me to fears that didn't belong to me.

As the conversation dwindled into silence, I glanced out the window, the world outside moving in a blur of color and sound. Somewhere out there was Noah, waiting for me to take that leap into the unknown. And I couldn't shake the feeling that every moment spent hesitating was a moment stolen from the possibility of something beautiful.

The café's cozy atmosphere felt stifling, as if the air itself had thickened with unspoken truths. I took a sip of my lukewarm coffee, the bitterness matching the tension that clung to the edges of our conversation. Cassie's eyes searched mine, a mixture of hope and fear dancing in her hazel depths. I could almost hear her internal dialogue, wrestling with the weight of what she had shared and the potential fallout.

"Emma," she said, her voice softer now, as if trying to breach the wall that had formed between us, "I don't want to be the villain here. I just care about you. I need you to know that."

"I know you do," I replied, letting the words hang in the air like an olive branch. "But it feels like you're trying to control my life, Cassie. I'm not a child anymore."

"Neither am I," she shot back, her tone sharper, but I could see the frustration bubbling under the surface. "But that doesn't mean we don't look out for each other. If you were in my shoes, you'd be worried, too."

"Worried about what, exactly? That I might fall in love with someone who isn't perfect? Who has a past? Newsflash: We all have baggage, Cassie. Just because Noah's is a little heavier doesn't mean he doesn't deserve a chance."

Her brow furrowed, and I could tell my words had struck a nerve. "What if he drags you down with him? What if—"

"Stop!" I interrupted, unable to hold back my mounting frustration. "I need to make my own mistakes. You've always told me that's how I learn."

Cassie opened her mouth, perhaps to argue, but then she closed it again, taking a breath as if steeling herself for whatever came next. The clatter of dishes and laughter from other tables faded into the background, leaving just the two of us in our small bubble of discord.

"Fine. You want to figure this out on your own? Then do it," she said, her voice laced with resignation. "But if you get hurt, I won't be here to pick up the pieces."

"I'd rather have you in my life, even if it's complicated, than lose you altogether," I said, my heart aching at the thought of severing this bond. "Just promise me you'll support me, no matter what."

"I can't promise that," she said, her voice a whisper, filled with sorrow. "But I can promise I'll be here if you need me."

With that, we both fell into a heavy silence, each lost in our own thoughts. I knew I had to speak to Noah soon, to face whatever shadows he carried with him. My heart ached for clarity, yet fear whispered reminders of Cassie's warnings, creating a tangled web of hesitation in my mind.

As I stepped out of the café into the late afternoon light, the sun dipped lower in the sky, casting a warm golden hue across the town square. I paused for a moment, letting the breeze flutter through my hair, grounding me in the present. It was a beautiful day, one of those rare afternoons where everything seemed to sparkle with possibility, yet I felt the weight of impending choices suffocating my every breath.

My phone buzzed again, and I pulled it from my pocket, heart racing with anticipation. It was a text from Noah, and a smile crept across my face despite the heaviness in my chest.

Hey, can we meet up? There's something I want to tell you.

I felt a shiver of excitement mixed with anxiety, and I texted back, agreeing to meet him at the park, where we had spent countless afternoons wrapped in laughter and dreams. The park was a pocket of serenity, an oasis where the world seemed to fade away. I could already envision the soft rustle of leaves overhead, the vibrant flowers bursting with color, and the sound of the fountain splashing in the background, a reminder of happier times.

As I walked toward the park, my heart raced, each step a mixture of anticipation and dread. I thought about how Noah had opened up to me, sharing pieces of himself in fragments like a jigsaw puzzle waiting to be completed. Yet Cassie's words loomed over me like a dark cloud. What if he had secrets that could unravel everything we had built?

When I arrived, the sun hung low in the sky, casting long shadows that danced along the pathways. Noah was already there, leaning casually against the wooden railing of the bridge that arched over the small pond. The golden light framed him perfectly, highlighting the contours of his face and the easy smile that never failed to make my heart skip a beat.

"Hey," I said, a smile breaking through my apprehension.

"Hey." His eyes sparkled with mischief, but there was an undercurrent of seriousness that made my stomach flutter. "I'm glad you came."

"I wouldn't miss it," I replied, attempting to keep my voice steady, though my heart was racing like a runaway train. "What's going on?"

He stepped closer, the distance between us shrinking, and I could feel the warmth radiating from him like a beacon in the cool evening air. "I've been doing some thinking... about us, about everything."

The weight of his words settled around us like an impending storm, and I braced myself. "Okay," I said, trying to keep my voice light despite the sudden tension curling in my stomach. "What about us?"

Noah looked down at his hands, his fingers fidgeting as if he were trying to collect his thoughts. "I didn't want to burden you with this. I really didn't, but I feel like you deserve to know."

My heart sank as the worry I had pushed aside rushed back in full force. "What is it?" I asked, my voice barely above a whisper.

He hesitated, his eyes darting away from mine as if he were searching for the right words in the fading sunlight. "I've had some trouble in the past, Emma. I was involved in things I'm not proud of. It's why I moved here. I needed a fresh start."

The confession hung in the air like a thundercloud, heavy and charged. "What kind of trouble?" I managed to ask, my voice shaky.

"Things I can't change," he said, looking up, his gaze earnest but shadowed by something deeper. "I got involved with the wrong crowd. It spiraled out of control, and I ended up—"

Before he could finish, a commotion erupted from the far side of the park. A group of teenagers burst into view, their laughter punctuated by shouts, but one voice rose above the chaos, sharp and panicked. "Noah! We need to go, now!"

Noah's expression shifted in an instant, the light in his eyes dimming as a flash of recognition crossed his face. "What are they doing here?" he murmured, his voice tight.

"Who? Who are they?" I demanded, my pulse quickening with confusion.

The group was moving closer, their laughter now tinged with urgency. As they neared, I recognized one of them—a familiar face from school, a boy who had always hung around with the wrong crowd. A chill crept down my spine as Noah's tension radiated off him like heat from a fire.

"Emma, I think we need to—" he started, but the boy interrupted him, stepping forward, eyes wild.

"Dude, we don't have time! You promised you'd help us. We're in deep, and we can't get out without you."

The atmosphere shifted dramatically, the idyllic park suddenly feeling like a stage for a drama I wasn't prepared to witness. I could see the panic in Noah's eyes as he looked back at me, torn between two worlds. I opened my mouth to speak, to ask what was happening, but no words came.

In that moment, I realized I was standing at a precipice, one foot in the realm of love and trust, the other in a world I had never wanted to touch. I felt the ground shift beneath me, the weight of my decisions crashing down like a wave, and I knew whatever choice I made next would change everything.

Then, before I could voice my thoughts, the air crackled with tension, and I heard Noah whisper, "I have to go."

And just like that, everything I had hoped for, everything we had built, teetered on the edge of a cliff, threatening to tumble into the abyss below.

# Chapter 12: "The Echoes of the Past"

The air was heavy with the scent of blooming jasmine as I stepped into the familiar embrace of our old park, a tapestry of vibrant greens and sun-dappled paths. The oak tree stood sentinel, its branches sprawling like a protective canopy, and beneath it lay a patch of earth worn smooth by the countless afternoons Cassie and I had spent laughing, plotting, and sharing secrets. I could almost hear the echoes of our past—her laughter twinkling like chimes on a summer breeze, the way her eyes sparkled with mischief whenever we embarked on one of our adventures. Today, though, I wasn't sure if those memories would carry the same magic.

I laid out the picnic blanket, its cheerful checkered pattern a stark contrast to the weight in my chest. I had filled the basket with all her favorites: artisanal sandwiches with creamy avocado and tangy feta, fresh strawberries, and homemade cookies that crumbled at the slightest touch. Each item was a labor of love, a silent plea for forgiveness wrapped in foil and wax paper. I poured us each a glass of lemonade, the condensation dripping down the sides, pooling on the blanket like unspoken words.

The park buzzed with life, children chasing one another, their squeals of delight punctuating the air like joyful punctuation marks. I glanced toward Cassie, who was still standing a few feet away, her arms crossed tightly over her chest, her gaze fixed on a distant group of children rather than the feast I had laid out. The sunlight flickered through the leaves, dancing on her auburn hair, but the warmth that usually radiated from her seemed eclipsed by an impenetrable cloud.

"Hey," I ventured, forcing a smile that felt more like a grimace. "Remember the last time we had a picnic here? You dared me to eat a whole jar of pickles."

She turned her head slightly, a fleeting spark of recognition lighting her eyes before it faded, leaving behind a shadow of something harder to decipher. "Yeah, and you lost your lunch over it," she replied, her tone light but with an edge that suggested she was still clinging to our earlier fallout like a lifeline.

"Good times," I said, trying to infuse a sense of nostalgia into the moment. "I thought maybe we could create new memories today."

Silence fell like a curtain between us, thick and suffocating. I busied myself with the food, my fingers fumbling with the lids and wrappings, wishing desperately for the right words to tumble out. "I made your favorite cookies," I added, as though that could bridge the chasm that had opened between us.

Her eyes flickered toward the basket, then back to the horizon, where the sun dipped lower, casting long shadows across the park. "You always knew how to bribe me with food," she remarked, her voice teasing but devoid of the warmth that usually accompanied such jests.

"Bribery is my love language," I shot back, attempting to keep the mood light. The corners of her lips quirked upward for a moment, but it vanished too quickly.

I sighed, the weight of my heart settling heavily in my stomach. "Cassie, I—"

"I know," she interrupted, her voice suddenly sharp, cutting through the air like the snap of a twig underfoot. "You're sorry. You want to fix everything. But it's not that simple."

I took a breath, the warm air filling my lungs, reminding me of all the times I had found comfort in her presence. "I miss you. I miss us. I thought we could just—"

"Rewind?" she finished for me, her tone biting. "You can't just erase what happened, not with a picnic or a basket of cookies. It's not that easy."

Each word felt like a dagger, each syllable infused with the history of our friendship, the moments that had built us and the shadows that now loomed over. I swallowed hard, the lump in my throat rising as memories flashed before my eyes: the late-night talks that stretched until dawn, the spontaneous road trips fueled by nothing but our shared dreams, the way we used to finish each other's sentences without thinking.

"I never meant to hurt you," I said quietly, my voice barely above a whisper. "You have to know that."

Cassie finally met my gaze, her eyes a tumult of emotions. "You've changed, and I don't know how to navigate that. It feels like we're standing on opposite sides of a chasm, and every time I reach out, it only gets wider."

The breeze rustled through the trees, a soft whisper of nature that contrasted starkly with the storm brewing between us. I felt the familiar ache of nostalgia tugging at my heart, the longing for the uncomplicated bond we once had. "What if we tried to find a way back?" I asked, my voice trembling slightly. "What if we started small?"

Her expression softened, but the resolve in her stance remained. "Like how? You can't just force a friendship back to life. It doesn't work like that."

"I don't want to force anything," I replied, my voice steadying. "I just want to try. Even if it means starting over, I'm willing to do that. You're worth it."

She paused, her gaze drifting toward the children laughing nearby, a bittersweet smile breaking through. "Starting over feels like a nice idea, but it's more complicated than that. The past isn't just going to fade away, and I can't pretend it didn't happen."

"I know," I said, a mix of frustration and understanding swirling inside me. "But I'm here. I'm willing to work through it. You don't have to shoulder this alone."

Cassie took a step closer, her walls still standing tall but the distance between us lessening. "And what if I can't let you in? What if this is as good as it gets?"

The question hung in the air, heavy and laden with doubt, a reminder of the risk that lay ahead. The laughter of children faded into a soft echo as I searched for the right words, feeling as though I stood at the edge of a precipice, the ground shifting beneath my feet. "Then we'll figure it out together," I said finally, the determination in my heart flaring brightly against the shadows. "Because I refuse to give up on us, Cassie. Not now, not ever."

The moment hung between us, taut with unsaid words and unresolved feelings, like the stillness before a summer storm. Cassie's gaze, once so familiar, now felt like a closed door, and the laughter of the children seemed to mock the silence stretching between us. I could feel the tension tightening like a noose around my heart. The sweet aroma of strawberries and lemonade wafted in the air, mingling with the faint scent of grass and earth, but even the most fragrant picnic could not disguise the bittersweet taste of our estrangement.

"Can we just... talk about it?" I ventured, my voice barely above a whisper, afraid that raising it would shatter the fragile moment we were teetering on. "What happened? How did we get here?"

She hesitated, her fingers absently tracing the edge of the blanket, a delicate gesture that spoke volumes. "It's complicated," she replied, her voice soft but laced with a tension that betrayed her calm exterior. "Things changed, and I don't know if we can just pick up where we left off."

"But what if we don't have to?" I countered, leaning forward, eager to breach the divide. "What if we can create something new? Different but still... us?"

Cassie looked up, her blue eyes swirling with a mixture of hope and uncertainty, like the sea on a windy day. "You really think it's that easy? You say you want to rebuild, but it's not like we have a blueprint for this."

"I don't need a blueprint," I replied, my heart pounding in my chest. "I just need you. If we're going to fix this, we have to be honest. With each other. No more pretending."

Her gaze flickered, revealing a hint of vulnerability before the walls crept back up. "I wish it were that simple. I wish I could just forget how things unraveled. I wish I could erase the hurt."

A silence fell again, heavier this time, suffocating the laughter around us. I felt a familiar spark of frustration igniting in my chest, a fire I couldn't extinguish. "You know I'd never hurt you intentionally," I said, my voice rising with emotion. "It was never about that. It was about what I thought was best for you."

Her laugh was bitter, a stark contrast to the laughter of children nearby. "Best for me? Or best for you? You can't deny that you've changed. You're not the same person I used to know."

"Maybe I've grown," I shot back, not bothering to hide the hurt in my voice. "But that doesn't mean I care about you any less. It just means I'm trying to find my way, and it seems like you're lost too."

The sunlight flickered through the leaves, casting shadows that danced around us as if the universe itself was holding its breath, waiting for us to find a way back. Cassie's expression softened slightly, the corner of her mouth twitching as if trying to recall the warmth of our shared laughter. "I don't know if we can just go back to the way things were," she said, her voice barely a murmur.

"Who says we have to go back?" I countered, my mind racing. "What if we redefine what we are? We've both changed; why not embrace it? We could be something even better."

For a fleeting moment, I caught a glimpse of the girl who had shared dreams with me under this very tree, a reflection of the past shimmering in her eyes. But just as quickly, that light dimmed. "I'm not sure if that's possible," she replied, her voice heavy with resignation. "You have your new life, your new friends. I'm just... still here, stuck in the past."

The ache in my chest intensified, a bittersweet reminder of how far apart we had drifted. "Stuck?" I echoed, incredulity creeping into my tone. "Cassie, you're not stuck. You're standing still while the world spins around you. I know it's hard, but you don't have to face it alone."

Her gaze fell to her hands, fingers entwined like the vines that climbed the oak tree, struggling to find their way. "Maybe I don't want to move forward. Maybe I'm afraid of what lies ahead without you."

The admission hung in the air, raw and unguarded. I reached out, resting my hand gently over hers, a gesture of solidarity. "I'm not going anywhere. I'm still here, and I want to help you. We'll figure this out together."

She met my gaze, uncertainty and longing swirling in her expression. "You really mean that?"

"Of course," I replied, my heart racing with a mix of hope and fear. "We can start small. Maybe just by being honest about how we feel. No more dancing around the issue."

Cassie smiled weakly, a flicker of the warmth I had missed igniting in her eyes. "Honesty, huh? You might regret that."

I chuckled softly, the tension easing just a little. "Trust me, I'm ready for the truth. No more sugarcoating."

"Alright, then." She took a deep breath, her shoulders relaxing as if a weight had been lifted. "I guess I'm tired of pretending everything is fine when it's not. I've missed you, but I've also felt abandoned. It's like watching you move on while I'm stuck in a loop, reliving our best moments without being able to join you."

Her words pierced through me like a shard of glass, each syllable resonating with the pain we both felt. "You were never abandoned," I said, my voice steadying. "I didn't mean to push you away. I was just trying to find my way, and in the chaos, I forgot to reach back for you. I was too wrapped up in my new life to notice how far apart we were drifting."

Cassie sighed, the sound heavy with unspoken burdens. "It's hard for me to understand how you can just... shift so easily. I'm still figuring out where I fit without you."

"Then let's figure it out together," I urged, squeezing her hand gently. "We're both in uncharted territory, but it doesn't mean we can't create a new map. We just need to be willing to take that first step."

As she processed my words, the sun dipped lower, casting a warm golden hue over the park. A moment of silence lingered between us, filled with the soft rustle of leaves and the distant laughter of children. Then, slowly, Cassie nodded, a tentative agreement sparking in her eyes. "Alright, let's try. But I warn you, my honesty comes with a side of sarcasm."

"Perfect," I said, relief washing over me. "I've always preferred my truths with a sprinkle of humor. After all, what's life without a little laughter?"

As Cassie and I sat beneath the sprawling oak, the shadows shifted like our conversations, flickering between light and darkness. The tension, once a quiet hum, had transformed into an electric current, coursing through the air and making my skin tingle with apprehension. I could sense her hesitation, the way her laughter felt like a fragile glass ornament, beautiful yet ready to shatter at the slightest touch.

"So," I said, breaking the silence with a lightness I didn't quite feel. "What's your honest opinion on my sandwich-making skills? I mean, aside from the fact that I'm obviously a culinary genius."

Her smile was tentative, as if she were testing the waters, and the moment felt precarious. "You do have a knack for turning even the simplest things into a five-star meal," she quipped, taking a cautious bite of her sandwich. "Though I think the secret ingredient is always a dash of desperation to win me back."

I chuckled, but beneath the laughter lay a thread of anxiety. "Desperation? More like determination. I've got my eye on the prize, and that prize is a friendship that doesn't involve passive-aggressive texts and awkward silences."

She raised an eyebrow, an expression that reminded me of our playful banter from days gone by. "Oh, so we're back to the grand prize now? What's next, a trophy for Best Attempt at Reconciliation?"

"Absolutely," I shot back, my smile widening. "It'll be a stunning gold-plated award, presented at a ceremony filled with all our favorite people. I'm thinking it'll even have fireworks."

The corner of her mouth twitched, a ghost of her old self flickering to life. "Fireworks? Are you sure you can handle that? You have a tendency to blow things out of proportion."

"I'm more of a 'let's-light-some-sparklers-and-hope-for-the-best' kind of girl," I retorted. "But that's just part of my charm."

With a soft laugh, Cassie relaxed slightly, her shoulders lowering from their tense perch. "Well, at least you haven't lost your flair for the dramatic. That's comforting."

As the conversation flowed, I felt the distance between us shrink, like a fabric pulled tight finally loosening its grip. Yet, the shadows lingered in the background, a constant reminder of the unresolved tension that loomed large. "Seriously, though," I said, leaning closer, my tone shifting to something more earnest. "What do you think we need to do to get back on solid ground?"

Cassie's expression grew thoughtful, her gaze drifting to the distant horizon where the sun began to dip low, painting the sky with hues of orange and pink. "I think... I think we need to be willing to be vulnerable. Like, really vulnerable. Not just the fun stuff, but the messy, ugly bits too."

"Messy, huh?" I echoed, the weight of her words sinking in. "Are we talking about emotional spaghetti and sauce all over the place, or more like a full-blown kitchen disaster?"

"More like the kind of disaster that makes you question your life choices," she replied, a faint smile creeping onto her lips. "But honestly, I've missed that level of openness between us. The way we could talk about anything and everything, no holds barred."

"I miss that too," I admitted, feeling a lump form in my throat. "But how do we get back to that? It's like trying to navigate a maze blindfolded."

"Maybe we start by taking off the blindfold," she suggested, her eyes meeting mine with newfound determination. "Let's strip away the pretense and just be real. No more pretending we're fine when we're not."

"Agreed," I said, heart racing. "So, here goes nothing. I'll start: I've been feeling lost since everything went down. I thought I could handle it alone, but it's been harder than I expected."

Cassie nodded slowly, her expression shifting from light-heartedness to sincerity. "I get that. I felt the same way, like I was adrift in a sea of memories, unable to find solid ground. There were moments when I wondered if we'd ever find our way back to each other."

"Every time I reached for you, it felt like I was touching a ghost," I confessed, the words spilling out like a long-held secret. "I wanted to scream, to demand answers, but the fear of losing you kept me quiet."

"I thought about reaching out too," she admitted, her voice barely above a whisper. "But I was scared you'd moved on for good. I didn't want to burden you with my feelings when I thought you were living your best life."

"I was trying to build something new," I replied, the frustration bubbling up again. "But I didn't realize that the foundation was crumbling without you there to hold it up. You were always my rock, and I took that for granted."

Cassie's eyes glistened, a reflection of shared pain and understanding. "We can't go back to what we were, can we?"

"No," I said firmly, shaking my head. "But we can create something new, something stronger. We just have to be willing to embrace the changes, even when it's uncomfortable."

She took a deep breath, the atmosphere charged with an electric anticipation, like the moments before a storm. "Okay, then," she said, her voice steadying. "Let's be honest. What's the one thing that scares you most about our friendship right now?"

A silence fell, thick with unspoken fears. I hesitated, feeling the weight of my own truth. "That we'll never fully recover from this. That we'll always be haunted by what happened, like ghosts lurking in the corners of our hearts."

Cassie nodded, the understanding etched across her features. "Same here. But maybe if we confront those ghosts together, we can turn them into something else. Something that doesn't feel like a weight around our necks."

"I'd like to think that's possible," I said, my heart pounding in my chest as I took a chance. "But it means being open to the scary stuff. You know, like when we were kids and we dared each other to explore the haunted house in the neighborhood."

A flicker of mischief returned to her eyes, and for a moment, I saw the old Cassie peeking through. "You mean that dilapidated mess with the creaky floors and the ominous shadows?"

"Exactly!" I exclaimed, feeling a rush of nostalgia. "And if I recall correctly, we came out unscathed, albeit with slightly more fear than when we went in."

"Right," she laughed, the sound brightening the atmosphere. "But it felt good to face that fear together, didn't it? We were invincible."

"Invincible," I echoed, a smile spreading across my face. "Let's reclaim that feeling. Together."

Just then, a loud commotion erupted nearby, pulling us from our introspection. A group of children had gathered around something on the ground, their excited shrieks echoing through the park. Curiosity piqued, we both turned our heads, straining to catch a glimpse of what had captured their attention.

As the crowd parted, a shimmering object caught the light—a locket, glinting like a lost treasure. I felt a tug of recognition, a familiar weight pressing against my heart. "Isn't that...?" I started, my voice trailing off as I stood to get a better look.

Cassie followed my gaze, her face paling as she took in the scene. "That's... that's mine," she breathed, a mix of shock and confusion washing over her. "But how? I lost it years ago!"

Before I could respond, a little girl picked up the locket, holding it aloft like a trophy. "Look what I found!" she called out, her voice full of triumph.

A chill ran down my spine, and I exchanged a glance with Cassie, the weight of that moment settling heavily between us. "It can't be a coincidence," I murmured, the air thickening with unspoken tension. "This could mean something."

Cassie's expression shifted, a flicker of unease crossing her features. "What if it's a sign? What if we're meant to find this now, at this moment?"

My heart raced as the implications hung in the air, unanswered questions swirling in my mind. "Or maybe it's a warning. Something we need to pay attention to."

As the little girl approached us, the locket swinging from her hand, I felt the walls closing in, the past and present colliding with a force that was both exhilarating and terrifying. The laughter of children faded into a distant murmur as a new chapter loomed ahead, one fraught with uncertainty and the ghosts we were just beginning to confront.

# Chapter 13: "Building Bridges"

The sun dipped below the horizon, casting a warm golden hue over the backyard as the tantalizing scent of grilled burgers wafted through the air. Laughter echoed off the fence, mingling with the clinking of glasses, creating a symphony of camaraderie that should have made me feel at ease. Instead, I felt like a marionette with tangled strings, pulled in too many directions, caught between my desires and the unyielding tension brewing beneath the surface. Cassie stood near the grill, her smile bright but her eyes—oh, her eyes told a different story. They flickered with uncertainty, the corners of her mouth betraying a heart that was not entirely present.

"Burgers ready!" Ethan called out, his voice buoyant and confident, effortlessly drawing the attention of our friends. I watched him from across the yard, his infectious energy bringing people together like moths to a flame. In that moment, he was a lighthouse amidst a storm, but I couldn't help but feel that we were both lost at sea.

"Do you think she'll like them?" I asked, sidling up next to him as he flipped the patties, the sizzle providing a rhythmic backdrop to our conversation.

Ethan glanced at me, his eyes sparkling with mischief. "Unless she's suddenly become a vegetarian, I think we're safe."

I chuckled, but the laughter felt hollow, a thin veneer over the turmoil swirling within. Cassie had always been my anchor, a constant in my chaotic world, yet tonight, she felt more like an enigma—beautiful and frustratingly elusive.

As the evening progressed, I tried to weave through the laughter, engaging in conversations that felt increasingly superficial. I forced smiles and nods, my heart heavy with the unspoken truths that hovered like clouds threatening rain. Ethan caught my gaze from across the table, his brow furrowing slightly. He understood the weight of my thoughts, our shared history acting as an invisible tether binding us in mutual concern.

"You've got to talk to her," he murmured when we found a moment alone by the drinks table, the laughter of our friends fading into a comforting hum around us. "This isn't the time for half-measures."

I sighed, feeling the tension in my shoulders. "I know, but how do I say it? 'Hey, Cassie, I know we've been best friends forever, but I think I might be in love with you.' That's a conversation starter, right?"

"Subtlety has never been your strong suit," he teased, nudging my shoulder with his, and the warmth of his touch sent a shiver down my spine, momentarily distracting me from my dilemma.

I shot him a look, half-heartedly annoyed but mostly grateful for the levity. "Thanks for the vote of confidence. But maybe we need to ease her into it. She's not exactly the queen of feelings."

Ethan nodded, his expression growing serious. "Then we build the bridge. This is a small gathering for a reason—let the atmosphere work for you." He leaned in, his voice dropping to a conspiratorial whisper. "Make her feel safe enough to let down her walls. And then you can drop the truth bomb."

Just then, Cassie walked past us, her laughter bubbling like champagne, drawing everyone's attention like a magnet. I couldn't help but admire her; she always had this effortless way of lighting up a room, her presence like sunlight breaking through the clouds. But there was a flicker of apprehension behind her smile that gnawed at me.

"Hey, Cass!" I called out, summoning all the courage I could muster. "Come help us with the burgers!"

She hesitated, glancing between us, and for a moment, I could see the gears turning in her mind. Finally, she joined us, her smile faltering for just a fraction of a second as she approached. The tension was palpable, but I pushed it aside, determined to draw her in.

"Ethan has a secret ingredient that makes these burgers extraordinary," I said, trying to inject some lightness into the moment. "You have to check it out!"

"Is it love?" she quipped, rolling her eyes playfully. "Because I'm allergic."

"Ah, but it's the secret sauce of friendship!" Ethan shot back, a playful grin plastered on his face. "And that's the most potent ingredient of all."

As we continued to banter, I felt the atmosphere shift, the weight of unspoken words lifting slightly. We were in our element, sharing memories and inside jokes, the familiarity of it all wrapping around us like a warm blanket. I caught Cassie's eye again, and this time, there was a spark of something deeper—a flicker of understanding.

"Okay, but seriously," she said, wiping her hands on a kitchen towel, "what's your secret?"

I could feel Ethan's eyes on me, a silent reminder that this was my moment. "You really want to know?" I asked, leaning in closer, a playful challenge in my tone.

Cassie nodded, curiosity dancing in her gaze.

"Fine," I said, taking a deep breath. "It's about honesty. The kind that isn't easy but is essential. I think we've all been tiptoeing around some things. Especially you."

Her smile faltered, and the laughter around us faded into a whispering silence. The air thickened with anticipation, and for a heartbeat, everything stood still. I had opened the door, and now it was up to her to step through.

"What do you mean?" she asked, her voice barely above a whisper, but I could see the flicker of fear in her eyes.

I steadied myself, ready to build that bridge we had talked about. "Cassie, I think we need to talk about how we feel—about everything."

The moment hung between us, a fragile connection teetering on the edge, as I awaited her response, hoping that whatever happened next would guide us both toward a truth that had been hiding in plain sight for far too long.

The air felt electric, charged with the unspoken words hanging between us. Cassie's eyes narrowed slightly as she took a step closer, her brow furrowing in that way I had always found endearing. "What do you mean by how we feel?" she pressed, her voice a mixture of curiosity and wariness, like a cat inching toward a particularly tempting piece of yarn while keeping one eye on the nearest exit.

I swallowed hard, suddenly aware of how much hinged on my next words. "You know, the usual—friendship, feelings, that pesky little thing called love," I said, attempting a nonchalant tone that faltered in the face of my growing anxiety.

"Love?" she echoed, disbelief mingling with a hint of amusement, her smile wavering between flirtation and frustration. "Are you sure you didn't accidentally throw a bottle of red wine into your own grill?"

"Maybe I did," I shot back, the warmth of my own teasing pushing back against the chill of uncertainty. "But this isn't just a drunken confession, Cassie. I mean it."

For a moment, her eyes softened, and I dared to hope I'd pierced the veil of her reluctance. "And what makes you think that I—"

"Because you've been different lately," I interrupted, heart racing. "More distant, almost like you're standing on the edge of something and can't decide whether to jump or walk away."

She looked away, the shadow of vulnerability crossing her face, and for a second, I feared I had lost her. But then she turned back, the flicker of anger igniting something fierce within her. "Maybe I'm just trying to figure things out, okay? It's not like I can just waltz in here and spill my guts without thinking it through first."

The truth hung heavy in the air. "And what exactly are you thinking?" I dared to ask, my voice steady despite the turmoil churning in my gut.

"Maybe that it's easier to pretend everything is fine than to deal with... whatever this is." She gestured vaguely between us, her frustration spilling over. "You think I want to put everything at risk?"

"Risk?" Ethan chimed in, having deftly maneuvered back to our side, a beer in hand and an eyebrow raised as if he had just stepped into a particularly entertaining drama. "What kind of risk are we talking about? The risk of turning friends into something more? Because I can assure you, that's the least risky thing I've ever seen."

Cassie shot him a glare, but the tension cracked like dry twigs beneath a sudden weight. I could feel the smile creeping up on my lips, a mix of relief and something sharper. Ethan always had a way of cutting through the chaos with his blunt humor. "See?" I said, grabbing onto the moment. "Even he agrees! Maybe we should just lay it all on the table."

Cassie huffed, crossing her arms in a way that made her seem both fierce and adorably defensive. "It's not that simple," she insisted, though her resolve appeared to be wilting like a wilting flower in late summer.

"No, it really isn't," Ethan said, setting his beer down on the table with a purposeful thud. "But pretending that this awkward dance we're doing is okay? That's far more complicated."

"Awkward dance?" Cassie raised an eyebrow, an incredulous smirk teasing the corners of her mouth. "I thought we were doing the tango."

"Let's be honest, it's more like an off-beat shuffle at this point," I quipped, my heart pounding with an exhilarating mix of trepidation and exhilaration.

Cassie laughed then, a genuine sound that seemed to break through the wall of tension. "So we're terrible dancers, is that it?"

"Terrible but determined," Ethan added with a wink. "And if we're going to trip over our own feet, let's at least do it together."

I watched as Cassie took a deep breath, her shoulders relaxing slightly as the laughter wove a fragile thread between us. "Maybe it's not that I don't want to talk about it," she admitted, her voice softer now, almost tentative. "It's just... I don't want to ruin what we have."

"But what if it's already changed?" I asked, my heart pounding, the truth trembling on my tongue. "What if pretending it's all fine is the thing that's going to ruin everything?"

She hesitated, searching my eyes as if trying to glean the depth of my sincerity. "You really think that?"

"I do," I replied, my voice steadying. "And I think there's something beautiful waiting for us if we're brave enough to face it."

Cassie's expression shifted, something flickering behind her gaze. "And if it's terrible? What if it changes everything and not for the better?"

"Then we'll deal with it," I said, feeling an unexpected surge of confidence. "But at least we'll have been honest with each other. Isn't that worth it?"

Silence enveloped us, punctuated only by the sounds of our friends enjoying the evening around us, blissfully unaware of the seismic shift taking place in our corner of the yard. I felt the weight of our shared history behind every word, the countless moments we had navigated together, supporting each other through highs and lows, and I knew we could face whatever lay ahead.

Finally, she reached for my hand, her fingers brushing against mine, igniting a spark that sent shivers racing down my spine. "Okay," she said, a tentative smile playing at the corners of her lips. "Let's see where this goes."

And just like that, the world around us seemed to fall away, the laughter fading into a soft murmur as our connection solidified into something real and exhilarating. The warmth of her touch grounded me, a reminder that we were not alone in this venture. In that moment, I could almost hear the metaphorical music playing—our hearts entwined in an unsteady dance, unsure yet undeniably eager to take the next step.

The evening stretched before us like a vast, open sky, and for the first time, I felt ready to explore its limitless possibilities. Cassie's gaze held mine, the uncertainty slowly dissipating, leaving behind a thrill that promised new beginnings. The bridge had been built; now all we needed was the courage to cross it together.

The gentle tension in the air felt almost palpable as Cassie held my gaze, her fingers intertwined with mine, a silent promise flickering between us like the stars that had just begun to twinkle above. The evening breeze rustled through the trees, carrying the distant sound of laughter from our friends, but in this moment, it was as if we existed in our own private universe, suspended between the thrill of possibility and the weight of uncertainty.

"What now?" she asked, her voice barely a whisper, as if raising it too high might shatter the fragile connection we had forged.

"Now?" I echoed, a teasing glint in my eye. "Now we navigate the murky waters of our emotions like seasoned sailors." I forced a grin, hoping to lighten the air, but underneath it, my heart raced with the gravity of our situation. "We might need a map, though."

Cassie laughed softly, the sound warming my chest. "I was thinking more along the lines of a life raft." Her playful tone was a welcome relief, yet I could see the apprehension still dancing in her eyes, a shadow lurking beneath her bravado.

"Okay, fair point," I admitted, squeezing her hand gently. "But I think we can weather this storm together. Besides, what's the worst that could happen? We sail off into the sunset, hand in hand, living happily ever after?"

Her laughter faded, replaced by a contemplative frown. "Or we capsize and drown in our feelings."

I shook my head, determined to keep things light. "I didn't take you for a pessimist, Cassie. Besides, if we do capsize, we'll just swim back to shore and try again."

She paused, her expression softening, and I could sense the walls she had built beginning to crack. "You really think it could work? Us, I mean?"

The sincerity in her voice sent a rush of warmth through me. "I do. But it's going to take honesty, bravery, and maybe a little more grilling. I can't promise it will be easy, but I can promise it'll be worth it."

The moment hung between us, and I held my breath, wondering if I had miscalculated. But then her features relaxed, the tension in her shoulders easing. "Alright," she said, her voice steadier now. "Let's do it. Let's face whatever this is together."

The clarity of her words felt like a beacon in the night, illuminating the path we were about to embark on. Just as I opened my mouth to respond, a burst of laughter erupted from the group, snapping me back to the reality of our surroundings. Ethan, clearly the instigator, was regaling a particularly outrageous story about one of our past adventures, the warmth of his charisma drawing everyone in like moths to a flame.

"Come on, let's join them," I said, feeling a surge of excitement. "We can't leave them hanging on our every word."

As we approached the gathering, I felt Cassie's hand slip from mine, the physical contact lost but the connection lingering like a sweet aftertaste. Ethan turned to us, a broad grin on his face. "Look who finally decided to join the party! We were starting to think you two were plotting world domination or something."

Cassie shot him a playful glare, her cheeks flushed, and I couldn't help but smile at the ease with which she fell back into the rhythm of our group. "More like relationship domination," I retorted, winking at her, and the playful banter returned, lifting the atmosphere higher.

"Ah, so it's true!" Ethan exclaimed, feigning shock. "You've finally admitted it. I knew it! I knew you couldn't resist my matchmaking skills."

"Sure, let's give you all the credit," Cassie quipped, rolling her eyes, but her smile betrayed her delight.

As we settled back into the familiar rhythm of the evening, I marveled at how easily we shifted from tension to laughter. But beneath the surface, I felt the current of unspoken words surging like an underground river, ready to break free at any moment.

"Hey, who wants a drink?" Ethan announced, grabbing the attention of everyone around. "I'm mixing up something special!"

"I'll help!" I volunteered, eager for a moment away from the crowd, and Cassie joined me, her presence a comforting anchor. We made our way to the makeshift bar, and as Ethan rifled through the coolers, I stole a glance at Cassie.

"What do you want?" I asked, leaning in closer. "We can make it anything—a classic cocktail, a sweet lemonade, or maybe something wild like tequila shots?"

Cassie smirked, her eyes glimmering with mischief. "Tequila shots? Now that's a tempting offer."

"Ah, but remember the last time we tried that?" I reminded her, chuckling as I recalled the raucous laughter that had ensued, the aftermath a blend of regrettable decisions and shared memories.

"True, but that was also the night you confessed your lifelong dream of becoming a cat whisperer," she shot back, laughter spilling from her lips.

"Touché," I conceded, laughter mingling with the fading sunlight. "But I'm still waiting for that chance. Cats have an uncanny way of understanding emotions, you know."

"Or maybe they just enjoy watching us suffer," she replied with a mock-seriousness that sent us both into fits of laughter.

Just as the air turned light with our banter, a sudden crash broke through the night, the sound reverberating ominously as a nearby tree branch gave way, snapping and falling to the ground.

"What was that?" Cassie asked, her smile fading, and I felt the tension in the air shift like a cloud passing over the moon.

Ethan rushed over, concern etched on his features. "It's probably just a branch. Don't worry!" But I could see the flicker of unease in his eyes.

"Let's check it out," I suggested, feeling a strange pull of curiosity mingling with caution. Cassie nodded, her expression serious as we made our way toward the source of the noise, the laughter of our friends fading into the background.

As we approached the fallen branch, something glinted beneath it—metal, sharp and foreboding. I crouched down, the hairs on the back of my neck prickling, and as I brushed away the debris, my breath hitched in my throat.

"Guys, come look at this!" I called out, my heart racing. The atmosphere shifted once more, and as the others gathered around, I felt a wave of apprehension wash over me, a realization dawning that this was far from an ordinary night.

Cassie leaned closer, and I could see the shock reflected in her eyes. "What is it?" she whispered, her voice trembling slightly.

And as I lifted the object into the fading light, the truth settled like a heavy weight in the pit of my stomach—a discovery that would change everything.

# Chapter 14: "The Big Reveal"

The sun dipped low on the horizon, casting a warm golden hue over the riverbank, where the water shimmered like liquid glass, reflecting the sky's transformation into a canvas of oranges and purples. I could feel the cool breeze teasing my hair, its gentle caress a stark contrast to the tempest brewing in my chest. With every step I took, the weight of what I was about to reveal grew heavier, pressing against my ribs. I had invited Cassie for a walk, knowing that this moment, charged with vulnerability, could redefine everything.

As we strolled, her laughter filled the air like music, a sweet melody that I had grown to cherish. The way she tossed her hair back and tilted her head made my heart swell, even amidst my trepidation. I could almost forget the truth I needed to share, the truth that hovered between us like an uninvited guest at a wedding, but the reality was inescapable. The evening felt alive, as if the trees whispered secrets and the river murmured encouragement. My fingers fidgeted with the delicate chain around my neck, a nervous habit that had become all too familiar.

"Isn't it beautiful here?" Cassie said, her voice laced with delight as she paused to gaze at the water. I nodded, unable to find the words. It was indeed beautiful, but my heart ached with an ugliness that contradicted the serene surroundings. I wanted to bottle this moment of carefree joy, yet I knew it was time to release the bottled-up storm brewing inside me.

"Cassie, there's something I need to talk to you about," I finally managed, the words tumbling out in a rush, as if the dam had burst. Her expression shifted instantly, the glimmer in her eyes dimming to a flicker of concern. "It's about Ethan."

At the mention of his name, she stiffened slightly, the air suddenly thick with tension. "Ethan? What about him?" The way her voice rose at the end, like a fragile bird taking flight, sent a shiver down my spine. The current of the river behind us echoed my turmoil, rushing past with a relentless force.

I took a deep breath, the cool air filling my lungs, steadied by the resolve surging within me. "I... I have feelings for him. More than just friendship." The words landed between us like a stone, sinking deep into the soil of our relationship. Cassie's eyes widened, disbelief mingling with hurt, and I felt the world tilt ever so slightly beneath my feet.

"I don't understand," she said, shaking her head slowly, as if trying to dislodge the truth from her mind. "You're just friends, right? You've always been just friends."

A lump formed in my throat as I watched her process my confession. "I thought so too, but it's more than that for me. It's deeper, and I can't pretend anymore." My heart raced, pounding in my ears as I prepared for the fallout. Cassie's face, usually so expressive, seemed to lose its vibrancy, the hurt creeping in like shadows at dusk.

"But what about me?" she asked, her voice barely above a whisper, a tremor revealing the cracks in her composure. "You can't just change the rules like that."

"I never meant to hurt you," I said, my voice thick with emotion. "You're my best friend, and I cherish that, but I can't ignore what I feel. I have to be honest."

For a moment, silence enveloped us, the kind of heavy silence that feels like the world is holding its breath. The river continued its relentless journey, indifferent to the turmoil swirling in my heart. I saw Cassie blink back tears, her vulnerability laid bare, and it twisted something inside me. I wanted to reach out, to comfort her, but I had to let her process this in her own way.

Finally, she spoke, her voice breaking the stillness like a pebble thrown into the water. "I just want you both to be happy." Her admission hung in the air, a fragile peace amidst the chaos. Tears pooled in her eyes, and I felt the sharp stab of guilt. I wanted to take her pain and bear it myself, but the truth was already out, the words echoing like a haunting refrain.

"I don't want to hurt you, Cassie," I said, my own voice trembling. "You mean too much to me."

"I need time," she replied, turning her gaze back to the river, where the water rushed past, carrying away the remnants of sunlight. "This is a lot to take in."

I nodded, understanding that this moment of raw honesty had cracked open the facade of our friendship. It was a pivotal moment, one that could either bind us closer together or tear us apart. I had laid everything bare, but now I had to navigate the aftermath of my choices.

As we continued our walk, the air thick with unspoken words, I found myself grappling with the uncertainty of what lay ahead. Cassie's silence was deafening, and each step felt heavier than the last. I hoped that this would lead to healing, that the truth would somehow create a bridge instead of a chasm between us.

The shadows deepened as the sun dipped further below the horizon, and the river, once a source of comfort, now mirrored the turbulence in my heart. I wanted to reach for her, to comfort her, but the words escaped me, swirling in a tempest of fear and hope. Would we emerge from this moment stronger, or would it signal the beginning of a painful unraveling? In that moment, the future seemed as murky as the waters flowing beside us, and I could only hold onto the fragile hope that we would find our way back to each other.

The silence stretched like a taut wire, vibrating with the unsaid. As we walked, the rhythmic lapping of the river against the bank felt almost mocking, a steady reminder of the calm that contrasted sharply with the storm brewing in Cassie's heart. I could feel her processing my confession, each footfall heavy with the weight of our shared history. We had weathered storms before—breakups, betrayals, life's unexpected turns—but this felt different, the kind of change that reshapes the very landscape of our friendship.

"I don't know what to say," Cassie finally uttered, her voice a fragile whisper. I caught the flicker of her gaze as she glanced at the water, as if seeking answers from its depths. "I didn't see this coming. Not at all."

"I didn't want to hide it from you any longer," I replied, my tone earnest yet tinged with the trepidation that bubbled beneath my skin. "You deserve to know the truth."

Her laughter came then, sharp and sudden, slicing through the tension like a knife. "Truth? Or your version of it? Because this sounds more like a plot twist in a bad rom-com." There was a playful spark in her eyes, a sign that she was clinging to humor to fend off the hurt. I couldn't help but smile, relieved that a glimmer of our old banter was still intact.

"Okay, you got me," I said, attempting a lighthearted tone. "This is definitely more 'chick flick' than 'epic love story.' But you know how I feel about Ethan. I didn't want to keep pretending."

"Pretending? You mean like when you tried to convince me that you actually liked kale smoothies?" she shot back, and the corner of her mouth quirked up. "Now that was an epic failure."

"Don't remind me! I thought I could embrace the whole 'health kick' thing," I admitted, laughing despite the weight of the conversation. "Turns out I'm more of a pizza and Netflix kind of gal."

Cassie rolled her eyes, but the tension in her shoulders eased, if only slightly. "So, what happens now? Are you and Ethan going to start a podcast on dating disasters? Because I can already hear the cringe."

I appreciated her humor, even as it masked the genuine concern lurking just beneath the surface. "That's not the plan, I swear. It's just... I don't want to lose you, Cassie. You're the sister I never had."

She stopped walking, turning to face me fully, the sunset casting her features in soft relief. "And you think dating Ethan won't complicate things? You're both such good friends with me. It could get messy."

"Messy is the last thing I want," I said, a knot tightening in my stomach. "But I can't ignore how I feel. I would never put you in a position where you have to choose."

"I appreciate that," she murmured, her expression softening. "But it's going to take me time to process this. Feelings get tangled, you know? And I'm not sure how I fit into this new dynamic."

"I promise to give you space," I said, meaning every word. "Just know that whatever happens, I want you to be happy. If that means stepping back from Ethan, I'll do it."

Cassie's eyes sparkled with unshed tears, reflecting the twilight as it deepened into night. "You really are a good friend, aren't you? Just when I thought I had you all figured out."

We resumed our walk, the conversation drifting into the easy familiarity of shared memories—the ridiculous antics of our college days, the late-night heart-to-hearts over pizza, and the endless laughter that had filled our lives. Each story was a balm, soothing the raw edges of our earlier exchange. I relished in those moments, grateful for the laughter, even as my heart ached for the uncertainty ahead.

Yet, the specter of Ethan lingered at the edges of our conversation, a shadow we couldn't quite escape. I had left him back at the apartment, blissfully unaware of the emotional whirlwind that was now shaping our lives. I imagined his face lighting up when I mentioned Cassie's name, his bright smile—warm and inviting. And I felt the pang of guilt all over again. How could I want him and still protect the person who meant so much to me?

As we approached a bench overlooking the water, the stars began to pierce the darkening sky, tiny diamonds twinkling overhead.

Cassie sank onto the bench, resting her elbows on her knees, and I joined her, the cool metal a grounding force. The river flowed on, indifferent to our struggles, and I envied its clarity.

"I think," she began, breaking the comfortable silence, "that you need to talk to Ethan. This isn't just about us anymore."

"I know," I said, the thought weighing heavily on my chest. "It's just... What if he doesn't feel the same way?"

Cassie raised an eyebrow, a familiar challenge flickering in her gaze. "What if he does? What if this is the start of something amazing for all of us?"

Her optimism caught me off guard, an unexpected twist that sent a ripple of hope through my worry. "You really think that could happen?"

"Why not? You've always been the one to look for the silver lining, even when things seem grim," she replied, nudging my shoulder. "You can't back down now. You owe it to yourself to see where this goes."

"Okay, fine," I conceded, feeling a mix of excitement and fear. "But I'm not ready to throw our friendship away over a guy, even if he is adorable and charming."

Cassie laughed, the sound like a breath of fresh air, lifting some of the heaviness. "Trust me, I don't think you'll lose me that easily. Just promise to keep it real, okay? No more pretending, whether it's about Ethan or kale."

"I promise," I said, feeling the warmth of our friendship wrap around me like a comforting blanket. "Just... don't throw a pizza at me if I mess up."

"Only if it's extra cheese," she grinned, and the easy banter felt like a much-needed balm on the wounds that had just been exposed. We sat in companionable silence, the stars now fully illuminating the night, while the river sang its eternal song. Whatever lay ahead, I felt fortified by the bond we shared, the unyielding friendship that had weathered storms and would continue to do so. The road might be rocky, but at least we were walking it together.

The evening air carried a hint of coolness as we settled into a comfortable rhythm, our laughter rippling through the atmosphere like the soft current of the river. I leaned back against the bench, gazing up at the stars, their twinkling glow reminding me that even in darkness, there was beauty to be found. Cassie, still processing our earlier conversation, seemed to find solace in the constellations too, her brow furrowing as she attempted to navigate the emotional labyrinth I had thrust her into.

"I guess I always thought you and Ethan were like, I don't know, a sitcom couple. You know, the ones where there's an unspoken chemistry, and the audience is just waiting for the inevitable 'will they, won't they' moment?" she mused, tapping her chin thoughtfully.

"Maybe I was hoping for that too," I admitted, feeling a warmth spread through me at the thought. "But it wasn't just about the chemistry. It's like—" I paused, searching for the right words, "—when we're together, everything feels effortless, like I can finally breathe."

"Wow, you just got all poetic on me," Cassie said with a playful smirk. "Next, you'll be reciting Shakespeare under the stars."

"Only if you promise to be my enthusiastic audience," I shot back, laughter bubbling between us again, lightening the tension.

Cassie's smile faded slightly as she leaned back, her fingers tracing the cool metal of the bench. "Okay, but what if he doesn't feel the same way? What if you dive in and end up face-first in the shallow end?"

I considered her words, the shadows of doubt creeping in. "That's the risk, isn't it? But what's the alternative? Staying silent while I watch him with someone else? I can't bear the thought."

She nodded slowly, her gaze drifting back to the river. "Just promise me you won't lose yourself in him. You're more than a supporting character in his story."

"Right back at you," I said, giving her a nudge. "You're not a sidekick in my life. We're the co-stars, remember?"

She chuckled, the sound a balm against the uncertainty swirling around us. Just then, my phone buzzed in my pocket, pulling my attention away from our heartfelt moment. It was a text from Ethan: Hey, can we talk?

A knot tightened in my stomach. "Uh-oh, speaking of co-stars..." I murmured, glancing at Cassie, who raised an eyebrow.

"What's the verdict? Did he get caught in the Netflix void?"

"Or he's had an epiphany about his feelings for me," I replied, half-joking, though a flicker of hope ignited within me. "Either way, it's now or never."

Cassie's expression shifted to one of encouragement. "Go! I'll be right here, practicing my stand-up comedy routine for when you return."

"Noted," I said, shooting her a grateful smile as I stood up. The night felt charged with possibility, each step toward my apartment echoing with the weight of my choices. I could practically hear my heart racing, each beat resonating with the urgency of the moment.

As I approached the door, I could see the glow of the lamp inside, a comforting sight in the uncertain twilight. I paused for a moment, steeling myself for whatever conversation awaited me. What if Ethan felt the same way? What if he didn't?

With a deep breath, I pushed the door open. He stood by the window, silhouetted against the light, his profile sharp and striking. My heart raced, and I felt a rush of emotions collide within me. "Hey," I said softly, and he turned, his expression unreadable.

"Hey," he replied, his voice low and tinged with something I couldn't quite place—was it anxiety? Excitement?

I stepped closer, my heart hammering in my chest. "You wanted to talk?"

"Yeah, I did." He ran a hand through his hair, a nervous habit I had come to recognize. "I've been thinking a lot about us."

"Us?" The word hung in the air, weighted with the significance of our shared moments—the laughter, the inside jokes, the unspoken tension.

"Yeah. I don't know how to say this without sounding ridiculous, but..." he trailed off, his eyes searching mine as if he were deciphering a complex code. "I think I might have feelings for you too."

The world shifted on its axis, the words washing over me like a warm wave. "You—what?" I barely managed to breathe out the question, disbelief mingling with hope.

He stepped closer, the space between us shrinking as the tension thickened. "I didn't realize it at first. I thought it was just the friendship, but every time you're around, it feels like... I don't know, like there's something more. Something I can't ignore."

"I can't believe this," I said, my heart soaring and plummeting all at once. "I thought I was imagining things!"

A slow smile spread across his face, lighting up the room like the dawn breaking through the night. "You weren't imagining anything. I've been trying to wrap my head around it, and it's been driving me crazy."

"Crazy might be the understatement of the year," I joked, my nerves still dancing like fireflies. "So... what do we do now?"

"I guess we take a leap of faith," he suggested, his voice steady despite the uncertainty swirling between us. "What do you think?"

Just as I opened my mouth to respond, a loud crash echoed from outside, jolting us both. The sound of shattering glass shattered the moment, and I turned to the window, dread pooling in my stomach. The street below was in chaos, a flurry of flashing lights and frantic voices.

"What the hell?" I whispered, fear threading through my words as I rushed to the window. My heart sank as I caught sight of Cassie, standing amidst the crowd, her face pale and stricken with shock.

"Cassie!" I shouted, adrenaline coursing through me as I rushed to the door, Ethan close behind. "What happened?"

As we burst outside, the reality of the situation crashed over me like a wave. Sirens wailed, and a group of onlookers had gathered, their faces illuminated by the harsh glow of police lights. I squeezed through the crowd, my pulse racing, panic clawing at my throat.

Then I saw it—a broken storefront window, glass glittering like shattered stars on the pavement. Cassie stood frozen, her eyes wide as she stared at something on the ground. I rushed to her side, my breath catching in my throat as I followed her gaze.

There, in the shadow of the shattered glass, lay a familiar object—Ethan's leather wallet, unzipped, its contents spilling out like confetti of secrets.

"Cassie, what did you see?" I asked urgently, trying to steady my voice against the chaos surrounding us. But as I turned to face her, I caught the glimmer of something darker in her eyes, an understanding that sent chills down my spine.

"I saw someone," she whispered, her voice shaking. "And they were wearing a mask."

My heart dropped, and the night, once filled with possibilities, suddenly felt ominous, laden with unanswered questions. The ground beneath us shifted, and I knew, in that instant, that everything was about to change.

# Chapter 15: "A New Beginning"

The sun hung low in the sky, casting a golden glow across the verdant landscape of Evergreen Creek. Each evening, as the world transitioned from day to night, the air thickened with the scent of blooming jasmine and the crispness of approaching autumn. I often found myself losing track of time while wandering through the winding trails, the delicate crunch of leaves beneath my boots accompanying the soft symphony of crickets and distant laughter. This was our sanctuary, a hidden world where Ethan and I could escape the prying eyes of our neighbors.

One particular evening, we stumbled upon a secluded glen, the kind that felt like a secret only nature had the right to hold. A canopy of trees swayed gently overhead, their leaves whispering secrets of ages past. Ethan, ever the charming troublemaker, suggested we have an impromptu picnic. He spread an old plaid blanket on the grass, its fibers rough against my fingertips. The contents of his backpack—sandwiches with slightly squished bread, a bag of homemade cookies, and two thermoses filled with iced tea—felt so right against the backdrop of this hidden haven.

"Okay, you have to tell me your most embarrassing childhood story while we eat," he said, a mischievous glint in his eyes. It was a challenge, and I could see that he was already concocting ways to one-up me.

I laughed, the sound echoing softly in the tranquil space. "You first," I shot back, taking a generous bite of my sandwich. He hesitated, pretending to mull over his options.

"Fine," he relented, leaning back on his elbows. "When I was eight, I thought it would be a brilliant idea to impress Emily Callahan by climbing to the top of the old oak tree behind the school. Only, I got stuck. For hours. And when the fire department finally came to get me down, they made me wear a helmet and a harness like I was some kind of squirrel superhero."

"That's not embarrassing," I giggled, shaking my head. "That's legendary!"

"Legendary, huh? Well, I did have a pretty great view of her running away when they cut me down," he smirked, and my heart swelled. He was so effortlessly charming, effortlessly human.

As I took a sip from my thermos, the sweet tang of the tea enveloped me, almost as comforting as Ethan's presence. "Alright, you've convinced me," I began, drawing a breath for dramatic effect. "When I was ten, I thought it would be a good idea to dye my hair blue. My mom was furious, and the neighbors still talk about the 'blue-haired girl' from that summer. Turns out, I'm not cut out for the dye job."

Ethan laughed, his voice warm and inviting. "You must have looked like a work of art, a masterpiece in the making."

I tossed a cookie at him, which he caught with ease, raising an eyebrow in mock surprise. "This is the part where you reveal that you were actually a blue-haired punk rock star in your youth?"

"I can neither confirm nor deny that," I replied, my laughter mingling with the chirping crickets. The world around us blurred, and for a moment, it was just us—the picnic, the laughter, the gentle rustling of leaves.

But as twilight descended, a shadow flickered at the edge of my joy. I had always loved the thrill of small-town life, the comfort of familiarity. Yet, lately, the whispers I sensed around town were sharpening like daggers. It started with the passing glances from my neighbors at the grocery store, the murmured conversations that quieted when I approached. I could practically feel the weight of their judgment on my shoulders, especially as Ethan and I became more visible together.

"What are you thinking about?" Ethan asked, his voice softening, breaking through my spiraling thoughts.

"Just... you know how small towns are. I feel like we're under a microscope," I admitted, my gaze flickering to the ground.

He nodded, a crease forming between his brows. "Let them talk. We're making our own story here."

His confidence was a balm, soothing the edges of my uncertainty. "You're right," I said, though the knot in my stomach remained. There was a quiet strength in his words, an assurance that together we could weather whatever storms lay ahead. I reached for his hand, intertwining our fingers. The warmth of his skin against mine felt like an unspoken promise—a commitment to face this together.

As we sat in the gathering dark, sharing silly stories and savoring the sweetness of each cookie, I felt the world around us come alive with possibility. Just as the first stars began to twinkle overhead, our laughter rang through the glen like a melody, bright and unwavering. In that moment, the worries of the town seemed far away, eclipsed by the light we found in each other.

"Hey," Ethan said suddenly, breaking the gentle silence. "What do you say we make this a regular thing? The picnics, the stories, all of it."

"Absolutely," I replied, my heart racing at the thought of more stolen moments like this. "Just us against the world."

The moon peeked through the branches above, casting a silvery glow across the ground, and I felt a sense of hope unfurling within me. Perhaps, against the whispers and the scrutiny, we could carve out a little piece of paradise together—one adventure at a time.

As we finished our picnic and packed up our belongings, I noticed Ethan's gaze lingering on me, a soft intensity in his eyes. "You know, I've never felt this way about anyone before," he confessed, his voice barely above a whisper.

My breath caught, the gravity of his words settling between us like a delicate balance. "Me neither," I said, and in that moment, it was as if the world had shifted. Whatever storm awaited us, I knew we would face it together, stronger and braver than before.

Ethan and I drifted deeper into the rhythm of our newfound connection, each moment a vibrant brushstroke in a painting that was quickly taking form. Days unfolded like petals in the sun, and our laughter became the soundtrack to my life. With each hike, each late-night ice cream escapade, I discovered layers of him I hadn't expected—his fascination with constellations, the way his eyes sparkled when he talked about his childhood adventures, and his uncanny ability to find the humor in everything. We were like two rivers merging, carving out a path that felt uniquely ours.

One particularly memorable Saturday, as the sun dipped low on the horizon, we found ourselves at Willow Creek Falls. The water tumbled down the rocky precipice, sparkling under the waning light like a cascade of diamonds. I leaned against a weathered wooden railing, mesmerized by the beauty of it all, when Ethan sidled up beside me, his presence as comforting as the soft breeze that rustled through the trees.

"Do you think the water's cold?" he asked, peering over the edge as if contemplating a leap of faith.

"Definitely," I replied, my eyes twinkling with mischief. "But you'd never know until you tried, right?"

"Is that a challenge?" he grinned, his smile broadening into that crooked version that made my heart do a little flip.

"Maybe," I teased, biting my lip to stifle a laugh. Before I knew it, he was shedding his shirt and sneakers, leaving a trail of clothing behind like breadcrumbs.

"Let's find out!" With a sudden leap, he launched himself into the water, creating a splash that sent droplets dancing into the air like sparkling confetti. The shrieks of laughter that followed were unmistakably joyful, echoing against the stone walls of the falls.

"Ethan! You're insane!" I called, half-laughing, half-worried he'd lose his footing. He surfaced, hair slicked back and grinning from ear to ear, like a child who had just discovered the best secret in the world.

"Come on in! The water's fantastic!"

With a laugh and a shake of my head, I followed suit, casting aside my own shoes and top, letting the cool water envelop me. A shiver raced down my spine, but the thrill of being immersed in the moment banished any reluctance. "Okay, you were right! This is amazing!"

Ethan swam closer, and the playful splashes turned into a lighthearted water fight, both of us dissolving into fits of laughter as we tried to outmaneuver each other. "You'll never win!" he declared, lunging forward. I dodged just in time, laughing so hard I nearly forgot how to float.

"Don't be so sure!" I shot back, and in a bold move, I splashed him right in the face. The surprised look on his face was priceless, and we both burst into uncontrollable giggles.

As the sun began to set, painting the sky in hues of orange and pink, we finally climbed out of the water, breathless and exhilarated. We lay side by side on the warm rocks, letting the sun dry our skin while the cool evening air settled around us like a soft blanket.

"Best day ever," I murmured, turning my head to look at him. His gaze was fixed on the sky, a small smile playing on his lips.

"Agreed. But I think it's only going to get better," he replied, a teasing lilt in his voice.

Just then, a rustle in the bushes drew our attention. We both sat up, curiosity piqued, and out of the foliage emerged a small, scruffy dog, its fur matted and muddy. It paused, looked at us with wide, hopeful eyes, and then bounded forward, tail wagging furiously.

"Oh my gosh, look at this little guy!" I exclaimed, reaching out to pet him.

"Hey there, buddy! You lost?" Ethan said, his voice warm and inviting. The dog barked happily, licking my hand enthusiastically as if we were long-lost friends.

"Looks like he decided we were his new best friends," I laughed, scratching behind the dog's ears. "What should we call him?"

Ethan contemplated, a smirk playing on his lips. "How about Splash? Seems fitting."

"Or maybe Mischief," I countered, laughing at the dog's rambunctious energy.

"Definitely Mischief. I'm sure he's gotten into plenty of trouble," Ethan agreed, and as if on cue, the dog leapt up, playfully nipping at Ethan's shoelaces.

We spent the next hour bonding over our newfound furry companion, tossing sticks and laughing as Mischief chased them with uncontainable enthusiasm. It felt like a slice of pure bliss, a fleeting moment that I wished would stretch into eternity. But as dusk approached and the sky deepened into indigo, a sudden pang of reality struck me.

"We should probably take him to a shelter or find his owner," I said reluctantly, glancing at the dog's muddy paws and eager face.

"Yeah, but do you think we can just... keep him for a little while? I mean, just until we figure things out?" Ethan's eyes twinkled with mischief again, his charm spilling over.

I laughed. "You're trying to adopt a dog on our second date?"

"Maybe! He clearly loves us. And how could we turn away such a cutie?"

A rush of warmth filled me as I watched Ethan interact with Mischief, the tender way he knelt down to rub the dog's belly, his laughter mingling with the night sounds around us. "Fine, we can keep him for a bit. But we need to make a plan."

"Deal! We can be the coolest dog parents ever," he declared, a boyish excitement radiating from him.

Just as we began to formulate our "cool dog parent" strategies, the distant sound of voices approached, breaking the serene atmosphere. I recognized the tones, the sharp inflections that belonged to a few local residents. My heart sank. The whispers I had sensed from the townsfolk had materialized into the looming reality I had dreaded.

"Great," I murmured under my breath, suddenly acutely aware of the tension in the air.

"What's wrong?" Ethan asked, his brow furrowing with concern.

"The locals. They're coming," I said, a hint of apprehension creeping into my voice.

"Let them come. We're just enjoying the evening," he insisted, standing tall as if to shield me from whatever gossip might follow.

And there it was—the familiar clamor of voices grew closer, more pronounced, and suddenly I felt the walls of our little sanctuary beginning to close in. I watched as they neared, faces shifting from curiosity to judgment, and I could practically hear the unspoken questions dancing around us like fireflies.

"Just act normal," I whispered, plastering on a smile that didn't quite reach my eyes.

"Normal? With a muddy dog and a half-drenched picnic?" Ethan chuckled, his confidence unwavering. "I think we're past normal at this point."

He was right, of course. But as the group drew nearer, their glances flickering between us and the dog, I braced myself for the inevitable.

The laughter and warmth of the day clashed with the growing unease in my chest as the voices approached. I could make out a few familiar faces from the neighborhood, their expressions a mix of curiosity and judgment, their silhouettes cast in the fading light like ominous shadows. Ethan's confident stance beside me did little to quell my apprehension; he looked at me with an encouraging smile, but I could sense the palpable tension hanging in the air.

"Look who we have here, the adventurous duo!" one of the women called out, her tone light but laced with an undercurrent that made my skin prickle. It was Linda, the self-appointed town gossip, and her presence often felt like a dark cloud looming over otherwise sunny days.

"Just enjoying the falls and a little mud therapy," Ethan replied with a casual wave, earning him a chuckle from another voice, but my heart raced. The playful tone felt out of place amidst the rising scrutiny.

"Oh, and I see you've adopted a new friend," Linda continued, her eyes narrowing as they landed on Mischief, who was busily sniffing at a nearby rock. "How very... noble of you both."

Ethan's smile remained, but I could feel the cool air shift. "We found him by the falls. Thought he could use some love." His casual demeanor masked the defensive edge in his voice, but I knew better than to believe it could last.

"Love, huh?" Linda's brow arched, her expression turning condescending. "You know how these things go. Strays can be a bit of a handful. What if he's got... issues?" Her words hung in the air, and the unspoken "what if" loomed larger than the actual question.

I bristled, my instinct to defend our newfound friend bubbling to the surface. "He's just a dog, Linda. And he's got a great personality," I shot back, unable to temper my irritation. Mischief had wormed his way into my heart with his boundless energy and charm; I wouldn't let anyone tarnish that.

"Personality or not, dogs can bring trouble," she countered, a glimmer of satisfaction dancing in her eyes.

As the group settled in closer, I could feel the heat of their scrutiny, dissecting our every move. I cast a quick glance at Ethan, who remained unwavering, but I could sense his tension beneath the surface, the subtle way his hands flexed at his sides.

"Speaking of trouble, what's your plan for tonight?" one of the men piped up, his voice dripping with insinuation. "A little moonlit rendezvous by the river?"

"Just enjoying a picnic, actually," Ethan replied smoothly, his tone light and unaffected. "You know, the usual romantic getaway."

"Right," Linda interjected, her smirk widening. "Because nothing says romance quite like mud-stained shorts and a rescue dog."

I could feel the laughter bubbling within me, fighting against the need to shield our little adventure from the biting comments. "Well, at least we're doing something interesting. What have you all been up to? More gossiping?"

The group shifted uncomfortably, a moment of silence stretching between us like an unyielding rope. "Just checking in, you know," Linda said with a saccharine smile, but the disdain lingered beneath her words.

"Glad to see you're so dedicated to your community service," I replied, a hint of sarcasm threading through my voice. "Let us know if you ever need help picking up the pieces of your gossip column."

A murmur of surprise rippled through the group, and I immediately regretted my sharp retort. Ethan looked at me, a mix of amusement and concern in his eyes, but there was no backing down now. I had crossed an invisible line, and the air crackled with tension.

"Wow, feisty," Linda said, her surprise quickly morphing into mock admiration. "Guess we're not the only ones having a little fun today."

"Fun? That's one way to put it," I shot back, crossing my arms as Mischief settled at my feet, blissfully oblivious to the rising drama.

As the awkward silence lingered, the sun dipped lower, leaving only traces of light behind. I felt a surge of defiance, a protective instinct for both Ethan and Mischief igniting my resolve. "If you'll excuse us, we were just about to leave," I announced, turning my back on them, ready to escape the suffocating atmosphere.

"Wait, wait!" Ethan said, his voice urgent but light, pulling me back gently. "Let's not be hasty. I think we're just getting to know each other, right?" He addressed the group, trying to smooth the edges of the situation, but I could feel his discomfort.

"We're just enjoying our evening," I echoed, trying to channel a more neutral tone. "Nothing wrong with that."

"True," Linda said, her voice dripping with faux sweetness. "But you know how people talk in small towns. You two are quite the topic of conversation lately."

"Glad to know we're keeping you entertained," I retorted, unable to resist.

"Oh, it's more than entertainment. It's about community," she countered, a calculating gleam in her eye. "And I'd hate for you to get swept up in something you can't control. Love can be messy, you know."

"I appreciate the concern," Ethan interjected, "but we're more than capable of handling our lives."

"Really?" Another woman chimed in, her voice dripping with skepticism. "Because it seems to me like you're both a little too... naïve for this town."

A knot tightened in my stomach as I felt the weight of their words. Naïve. The word hung in the air like a challenge, and I could almost hear the unspoken thoughts that followed. What did they know of our connection, of the moments we shared? The bond we were building was a fragile thing, and I was painfully aware of how quickly it could be shattered by judgment.

"Thanks for the advice, but we're doing just fine," Ethan replied, his voice steady. But the spark of unease lingered in his eyes, and I knew we were teetering on the edge of a cliff, every word a potential misstep.

Before I could respond, a voice rang out from behind the crowd, cutting through the tension like a knife. "What's all this then?"

I turned to see Ben, my childhood friend, striding toward us, his presence a sudden reprieve in the thickening atmosphere. "Hey, guys!" he called out, a jovial tone masking the tension. "Didn't expect to see a party out here. You didn't invite me?"

Relief washed over me, and I exchanged a quick glance with Ethan. "No party, just a dog and some uninvited guests," I said, trying to inject some humor back into the situation.

"Well, I love a good dog story," Ben said, kneeling to scratch Mischief behind the ears. "And I could always use a break from the usual drama."

"Yeah, well, you've found it," Ethan replied, a touch of gratefulness threading through his words.

As Ben engaged the group, I felt a surge of hope. Maybe, just maybe, we could defuse the tension together. But as I caught a glimpse of Linda's disapproving frown, I couldn't shake the feeling that this wasn't over. Her eyes flickered with a knowing glint, and the whispers would only intensify.

"Mischief is just what this town needs," Ben declared, glancing around at the group with a mischievous glint. "A little chaos to spice things up!"

"Careful, Ben," Linda warned, her voice low and pointed. "You don't want to get mixed up in their little drama."

"Drama? This is just fun," Ben shot back, his laughter infectious. "And if anyone's going to stir things up, it's going to be us."

The moment felt precarious, balancing on a tightrope strung between camaraderie and the ever-present threat of judgment. I could feel the eyes of the group drilling into us, their scrutiny as sharp as the twilight air.

Just as I opened my mouth to respond, a sudden rustle in the bushes startled everyone. Mischief perked up, his ears twitching, and for a heartbeat, we all froze. Then, from the shadows, a figure emerged—tall, imposing, and utterly familiar. My breath caught as recognition washed over me, a surge of emotions colliding.

"Ethan?" I whispered, my voice barely above a gasp as the figure stepped into the fading light.

The laughter died in my throat, and all eyes turned to the newcomer. I felt the weight of the moment shift, the atmosphere thickening with anticipation. I knew then that this encounter would change everything.

# Chapter 16: "Whispers and Shadows"

The sun hung low in the sky, casting a golden hue over the school grounds as I stepped outside, my heart racing like the children on the playground. It felt surreal to walk these familiar halls, now infused with a heady mix of excitement and trepidation. Ethan and I had crossed a threshold, leaving the realm of friendship behind, and I was giddy with the possibilities that lay ahead. But that afternoon, the laughter and chatter surrounding me morphed into a dissonant hum, a cacophony of whispers that wound their way into my thoughts like unwanted weeds.

As I approached the break room, the clinking of mugs and the soft rustle of papers gave way to hushed voices that dripped with disdain. Peering through the half-open door, I spotted Mrs. Duvall and Mr. Grant, two teachers who seemed to have a penchant for gossip that rivaled the town's gossip mill itself. Their expressions were a blend of shock and schadenfreude, as if they were dissecting a scandal rather than discussing a budding relationship.

"Isn't it inappropriate for her to date Cassie's brother?" Mrs. Duvall asked, her tone a cocktail of concern and moral superiority. The words hung in the air, heavy and suffocating, wrapping around my chest like a vice. I felt exposed, as if my heart had been laid bare for them to examine and judge.

I pulled back, the sting of their judgment gnawing at my confidence. Ethan and I had shared our fears about the town's prying eyes and judgmental tongues, but I hadn't expected the whispers to reach this far. What had started as stolen glances and shy smiles had morphed into a topic of conversation among those who wielded the power of influence. The thought that our love was fodder for gossip sent a wave of insecurity crashing over me.

Later that day, with the weight of the rumors weighing heavily on my heart, I found Ethan waiting by the entrance. His dark hair tousled by the breeze, he looked impossibly handsome, and for a moment, I forgot about the whispers swirling in my mind. The warmth of his smile beckoned me forward, a lighthouse in a stormy sea.

"Hey," he greeted, his eyes sparkling with mischief. "You ready for our epic escape?" He always had a way of turning mundane moments into adventures. But as I stepped closer, the joy faded. The shadows of doubt loomed, and I struggled to find the right words.

"I heard..." I hesitated, the words tasting bitter on my tongue. "I overheard Mrs. Duvall and Mr. Grant today."

His smile faltered, a flicker of concern crossing his face. "What did they say?"

"They were talking about us, about how it's 'inappropriate' for me to be with you. I didn't think it would get this bad, Ethan." The vulnerability in my voice was palpable, a crack in my armor.

Ethan's expression shifted from surprise to determination. He stepped closer, his presence grounding me. "Let them talk. They don't know us, what we have. We can't let their opinions dictate our happiness."

His words were a balm to my wounded heart, but the uncertainty still lingered. "What if it gets worse? What if we can't escape this town's whispers?"

He reached out, taking my hands in his, the warmth of his skin igniting a spark within me. "Then we face it together. I'm not going anywhere." There was an intensity in his gaze that made my heart race, filling me with a sense of bravery I hadn't felt moments before.

But as the words settled between us, I couldn't shake the feeling of impending doom. Living in a small town meant every action was magnified, scrutinized, and dissected. It wasn't just the whispers I feared; it was the judgment of those I had once considered friends, and the possibility of alienation from my own community.

"Together," I echoed, testing the weight of the promise. I wanted to believe him, to believe that we could carve out our own path amidst the chaos. "What if we take a trip? Just the two of us? Somewhere far away from here."

His brow furrowed in thought, the corners of his lips twitching up in a mischievous grin. "Are you suggesting a getaway to escape the gossips? I can get on board with that. But where do you want to go? The beach? A cabin in the mountains?"

"The mountains sound perfect. I've always wanted to hike those trails near Lake Serenity. Just us, nature, and no judgment." The idea ignited something deep within me, a yearning for freedom, a chance to explore not just the world but also the depths of our relationship without the weight of expectations.

"Then it's settled," Ethan declared, his voice infused with excitement. "A weekend in the mountains it is. We'll leave Friday after school. Just you and me against the world."

As we stood there, hands clasped and hearts beating in sync, I felt a renewed sense of purpose. This would be our rebellion against the shadows creeping in, a declaration that our love was real and worthy of celebration, not scrutiny.

But just as I was about to get lost in the daydream of our adventure, the school bell rang, pulling us back to reality. The moment shattered like glass, reminding me that the world outside was still buzzing with whispers and shadows. As we walked back inside, I felt a lingering tension in the air, the question of how to navigate this new landscape hanging between us like an unspoken challenge.

The following week crept along like molasses on a winter's day, each hour stretching longer than the last as rumors festered and morphed into something almost tangible. It felt as though the walls of our small town had ears, ears that listened and twisted our affection into something sinister. Walking through the halls of the school became a game of dodgeball, where whispers ricocheted off lockers and judgmental glances collided with my heart, leaving behind a bruise I couldn't quite shake.

Ethan and I were determined not to let the gossip cloud our newfound relationship. Every day after class, we escaped to our secret spot behind the old oak tree on the edge of the schoolyard. It was a sanctuary, its gnarled roots weaving into the earth like our intertwined lives, a place where we could breathe freely, far from the prying eyes of our peers. The sunlight filtered through the leaves, casting playful shadows on our faces as we shared stories, dreams, and the occasional slice of pizza from the corner shop.

"Are you sure we can trust the squirrels?" Ethan quipped one afternoon, leaning against the tree, arms crossed and a grin dancing on his lips. "They seem like they know more than they let on."

I laughed, the sound brightening the air around us. "If they start showing up with notes from Mrs. Duvall, I'll reconsider our hiding spot."

Our laughter faded as we settled into a more serious conversation, the weight of the rumors creeping back in like a chilling draft. "I can't help but feel like we're living in a soap opera," I confessed, tracing patterns in the dirt with my finger. "Every little thing we do is analyzed and scrutinized, like we're on display."

Ethan tilted his head, his expression softening. "You know what they say: when life gives you lemons, make lemonade. Or, in our case, let's just throw those lemons at the people who think they can define us."

His fierce determination ignited a spark within me. "Maybe we should hold a lemonade stand. Market it as 'Love Potion No. 9' and serve it with a side of eye-rolls."

"Now that's a business plan I can get behind," he replied, a teasing light in his eyes. "We'll charge a dollar for each cup and an extra fifty cents for every judgmental look we get from the teachers."

As we chuckled, I felt a swell of gratitude for this boy who turned mundane moments into magic. But just as I was beginning to feel invincible, a sudden rustle in the bushes nearby stole our attention. A moment later, Cassie emerged, her auburn hair bouncing like a warning flag. The air thickened with tension; her presence had a way of making even the sunniest days feel overcast.

"What are you two doing?" she asked, a hint of suspicion lacing her voice.

Ethan straightened, shifting slightly to put some distance between us. "Just catching up," he replied, though I could sense the unease in his tone.

Cassie's eyes narrowed, and I braced myself for what was sure to come. "You know, people are saying a lot of things about you two. Like, what even makes you think it's okay to date my brother?"

The question hung in the air, a dagger ready to plunge. I could feel my heart racing, adrenaline surging through my veins as I prepared for a defensive retort. "It's not like we're breaking any laws here," I shot back, my voice steady despite the tremor beneath the surface.

"But you're kind of breaking the girl code, don't you think?" Cassie countered, crossing her arms. "What if you two don't work out? It'll make things so awkward."

Ethan stepped forward, his voice firm. "You know what, Cassie? This isn't about you. This is our decision, and honestly, it's none of your business."

The words hung in the air, both surprising and electrifying. For a brief moment, I felt a rush of pride at Ethan's assertiveness, but Cassie's expression twisted into something dark, a flicker of betrayal.

"Fine. But don't say I didn't warn you," she said, before turning on her heel and storming off. I exhaled sharply, the tension in my shoulders easing slightly, but the unease lingered.

"Should we be worried?" I asked, looking after her, uncertainty creeping in.

"Nah, she'll come around. It's just her way of showing concern," Ethan replied, though I could see the flicker of doubt in his eyes. "She'll realize that we're good together, that it's not some juvenile fling."

We spent the rest of the afternoon exchanging plans for our upcoming trip, our laughter ringing out in the warm air, a protective bubble against the uncertainty that surrounded us. But as the sun dipped below the horizon, painting the sky in hues of orange and pink, the shadows of doubt loomed larger.

The day of our escape arrived, and I could barely contain my excitement. Ethan and I piled into his car, the engine rumbling to life like a beast awakening from slumber. The anticipation crackled in the air, a potent mixture of adrenaline and the promise of freedom.

"Are you ready for this?" he asked, a grin spreading across his face as we hit the open road. The wind whipped through the windows, carrying away the whispers of our small town, leaving behind the sweet scent of pine and adventure.

"Ready as I'll ever be," I replied, glancing at him with a mix of apprehension and thrill. "Just promise me we won't run into any surprise family reunions or exes."

Ethan chuckled, his eyes sparkling with mischief. "I can't promise anything, but I will ensure we have the best time possible. Just you, me, and a lot of questionable decisions."

As we drove further from the familiar streets, I felt the weight of the world lift off my shoulders, replaced by the exhilarating promise of new experiences. I knew there would be challenges ahead, but for now, we were free, hurtling toward the mountains and the unknown, with only the road beneath us and our dreams ahead.

The winding road beckoned like a siren song, each curve promising a glimpse of untouched beauty. Ethan's car hummed beneath us, the engine purring like a contented cat as we left the familiar behind. The trees grew taller, their branches arching like welcoming arms, and I couldn't help but lean my head out the window, feeling the cool breeze rush past me, wild and liberating. It was as if the weight of the world slipped away, replaced by the fresh scent of pine and adventure.

"Okay, you need to tell me your deepest, darkest secret," Ethan declared, breaking the comfortable silence. His eyes danced with mischief, and I turned to him, curiosity piqued.

"Deepest, darkest secret? Like 'I secretly wish to be a professional napper' level?" I shot back, my tone light.

He laughed, a rich sound that rolled through the air like music. "No, no. I mean the kind of secret that could ruin your reputation or land you in the gossip column."

I feigned contemplation, tapping my chin dramatically. "Hmm, does it count if I once staged an elaborate fake breakup with my childhood teddy bear to avoid my mom's relentless questions about why I was still single?"

Ethan's laughter echoed, and the tension of the past week began to evaporate. "I can see that going viral in our small town. 'Local Girl Engaged in Teddy Bear Drama!'"

"I can't help it! It was an elaborate performance. I had an audience of three cats and a neighbor who definitely thought I was losing it." I grinned at the memory, but as the road straightened out, my smile faltered slightly. "What about you? Any juicy secrets?"

"Hmm, my big secret is that I once tried to bake cookies for Cassie, and I may have accidentally used salt instead of sugar." His expression was comically serious, and I burst into laughter.

"Is that why she's so salty toward you?" I teased, but the joy of our banter faded when I caught a glimpse of the looming mountains in the distance. They rose majestically, dark and imposing, their peaks obscured by a curtain of mist. A flicker of apprehension danced in my stomach.

Ethan must have sensed my shift in mood. "Hey, it'll be fine. Just us, the wilderness, and nature. What could possibly go wrong?"

"Famous last words," I muttered, half-serious. But the truth was, the closer we got to our destination, the more I felt the pull of unease.

As we arrived at the lake, the sun hung high, reflecting off the water in dazzling patterns that sparkled like diamonds. It was breathtaking. Ethan pulled the car into a small clearing, and we stepped out, inhaling the crisp air that felt like a new beginning. The lake stretched before us, a canvas of blue, surrounded by lush greenery. I felt the stirrings of excitement mingling with the lingering anxiety, the world around us bursting with possibilities.

"Race you to the water!" Ethan called, his eyes twinkling with challenge before he sprinted off, leaving me in a cloud of dust and laughter.

"Not fair!" I shouted, running after him. My legs flew beneath me, and I felt free, alive in a way that made everything else fade into the background.

We reached the lake's edge, and I splashed him, the water shimmering in the sunlight as it cascaded off his shoulders. "Now you'll never get to bake cookies again!" I giggled.

"Never. I'll stick to the pre-made stuff," he replied, wiping water from his face, but the moment was short-lived. Just as I turned to enjoy the serenity of the lake, my heart dropped. A figure stood at the treeline, silhouetted against the trees.

I squinted, trying to make out the face, but the shadows hid their features. "Ethan?" I called, but he was too busy trying to shake off the water.

The figure moved closer, and I felt a chill sweep through the air. My heart raced, a thrumming in my chest that screamed something wasn't right. The moment I caught a glimpse of familiar auburn hair, my stomach twisted into knots.

"Cassie?" I asked incredulously, stepping back as she emerged from the shadows, her expression a mix of anger and hurt. "What are you doing here?"

"Nice to see you too, Emily," she said, her voice dripping with sarcasm. "I thought you might need a reality check."

Ethan turned, surprise washing over his face as he took in the scene. "Cassie, what's going on?"

"Oh, just making sure my brother knows what he's gotten himself into." She shot me a glare that could freeze fire. "You really think you can just waltz into our lives and take what's not yours?"

My pulse quickened, the tension in the air thickening like the fog rolling off the lake. "I'm not taking anything, Cassie. We care about each other. You don't get to dictate who he spends time with."

She stepped closer, her presence looming ominously. "You think it's that simple? You're just a distraction, and I won't let you mess with my family. You'll regret this."

The weight of her words landed heavily between us, and I felt my breath hitch. I turned to Ethan, searching for his reassurance, but the conflicted expression on his face made my stomach churn.

"Cassie, this isn't how we should handle this," he said, his voice steady but strained. "Emily means a lot to me. You can't just come here and—"

"Exactly. You're blinded by infatuation," Cassie interjected, her voice rising. "What do you really know about her? You think it's love? You're just kids playing at something you don't understand."

The moment hung in the air, thick with tension, the water lapping quietly at the shore, indifferent to our turmoil. I could feel the panic rising in my throat, the shadows of doubt creeping back in. "I thought we were past this," I managed, my voice barely a whisper.

Ethan stepped forward, his hand reaching for mine, but the moment he touched me, Cassie's eyes blazed with fury. "You think holding her hand will make her any more right for you?"

Then, just as the tension reached a breaking point, a loud crack echoed through the air. The ground trembled slightly beneath us, and I glanced at Ethan, fear pooling in my stomach. "What was that?"

Before I could fully process the sound, the trees beyond the lake began to sway violently, as if something was pushing through the underbrush. Ethan pulled me close, a protective instinct igniting within him, but Cassie stood frozen, eyes wide with a mix of fear and disbelief.

The underbrush parted, and the figure that emerged sent shockwaves through me. It wasn't just a wild animal or a harmless hiker; it was a man, tall and imposing, his face partially obscured by a dark hood. He stepped forward, and the world around us seemed to shrink, narrowing into this single, terrifying moment.

"Emily," he said, his voice low and menacing, sending a chill down my spine. "I've been looking for you."

As I stood there, caught between the man's piercing gaze and the chaotic emotions swirling around us, the realization hit me like a thunderbolt. Whatever was unfolding here was just the beginning, and I was standing on the edge of a storm that threatened to swallow us all whole.

# Chapter 17: "Cracks in the Facade"

The chill of autumn wrapped around me like a reminder of all the changes that had swept through Evergreen Creek, each gust of wind whispering secrets I wasn't ready to hear. The air was rich with the scent of damp earth and woodsmoke, an olfactory quilt stitched together by the season's decay. I paused for a moment, inhaling deeply, hoping the familiar aromas might ground me. As I resumed my walk, my sneakers crunched over a tapestry of leaves, their vibrant reds, yellows, and browns turning the ground into a patchwork of fading glory.

It was supposed to be one of those quintessential fall afternoons, the kind that made you want to drink apple cider while wrapped in a knitted blanket by the fire. Yet, as I turned the corner by the old mill, a knot formed in my stomach. Ahead of me, in the dappled sunlight filtering through the branches, stood Cassie. Her laughter rang out like wind chimes caught in a breeze, but it faltered when she caught sight of me, the spark dimming like a candle snuffed out too quickly. The small gathering of our mutual friends—familiar faces now marred by a palpable tension—shifted their attention, their chatter falling away like leaves from a tree.

Cassie's eyes, usually so warm and welcoming, flickered with an unrecognizable emotion. There was a moment when our gazes locked, a silent conversation hanging heavily in the air. Was it disappointment I saw there? Frustration? I swallowed hard, feeling like an intruder in a space that should have felt safe. The atmosphere was thick, each of them exchanging glances, the unspoken words swirling like the wind around us.

"Hey, Cass," I managed to say, forcing a smile that felt more like a grimace. It didn't reach my eyes, and I knew she could see that. "What's up?"

"Just talking about the Harvest Festival," she replied, her tone clipped. "You know how it is." The warmth that usually enveloped our exchanges was conspicuously absent, replaced by an awkward chill that made my skin prickle.

"Sounds fun," I said, my voice lacking its usual enthusiasm. I could sense the electric undercurrent of judgment radiating from the group. It was unsettling, like stepping into a room filled with static electricity, just waiting for the spark to ignite. I glanced at the others, faces painted with a mixture of sympathy and intrigue, their expressions flickering like candles in a draft.

One of our friends, Jenna, shifted her weight, her gaze darting between Cassie and me. "You two okay?" she asked, her voice dripping with that careful sweetness that often signaled trouble. The subtle concern in her tone made it clear that she felt the need to bridge a chasm that was widening by the second.

"Of course," I lied, the word tasting bitter on my tongue. "Why wouldn't we be?" I could almost hear the collective inhalation, the silence stretching, filling the space with tension.

Cassie glanced away, her brow furrowing as she kicked at a stray pebble. "Yeah, just... stuff, you know?" Her words were light, but the heaviness in her eyes told a different story. I felt my heart sink further, the cracks in our friendship becoming chasms.

As the awkwardness lingered, I wanted to shout, to make them understand that this wasn't just about a relationship gone sour. It was about all the threads of connection fraying at the seams, unraveling the very fabric of our community. But instead, I forced a laugh that echoed hollowly in the cool air. "Well, if you guys are busy, I won't interrupt." I turned on my heel, the heat of their stares burning into my back.

That evening, I lay in bed, the ceiling above me a blank canvas for my racing thoughts. My mind replayed the afternoon's encounter like a broken record, skipping over moments that stung and hurt. The laughter, the whispers, the sidelong glances—they all intertwined, each thread pulling tighter around my heart until it felt like I couldn't breathe. I was suffocating under the weight of expectations and unspoken words.

Outside, the wind howled, rattling the windowpanes like a ghost desperate to escape. I curled deeper into my blankets, trying to ward off the chill that seemed to seep through the walls. Every time I closed my eyes, I saw Cassie's face, twisted in a mixture of anger and confusion. I wanted to reach out, to mend the rift that had grown between us, but I was paralyzed by the fear of what it would take to confront the truth.

A soft knock on my door jolted me upright. "Tessa?" My mother's voice drifted through the wood, warm and soothing like the crackling fire I longed for. "Are you okay?"

I hesitated, weighing my options. Should I admit the truth, let her see the cracks in my carefully constructed facade? Or should I put on a brave face, the mask I had worn for too long? "I'm fine, Mom," I called out, the words tasting like ashes in my mouth.

"Alright, but if you need anything, I'm right here." She moved away, her footsteps retreating down the hallway. I stared at the door long after she left, the silence pressing in on me like a weight I couldn't shake.

Underneath the stillness, a slow burn of determination began to kindle. I had to face this, confront the whispers swirling in the small-town air. If I didn't, they would only grow louder, fracturing everything I held dear until there was nothing left but echoes of what used to be. It was time to gather my courage, time to step into the light and own my story. No more hiding. No more pretending.

The darkness of night outside mirrored the storm brewing within me, and as I lay back against my pillow, I made a silent vow. Tomorrow, I would find Cassie. Tomorrow, I would begin to piece together the fragments of my life.

Morning light spilled through my window, illuminating the dust motes dancing in the air like tiny stars. I blinked at the brightness, my heart still heavy from the previous day's encounter. The sunlight felt intrusive, a cheerful reminder that life went on outside my cocoon of anxiety. I rolled over, burying my face in the pillow, hoping to disappear into the depths of sleep. But the echoes of my friends' laughter haunted me, intertwining with my guilt, forming a melody I couldn't escape.

After a futile attempt to drift back to sleep, I reluctantly peeled myself from the sheets. The world outside was vibrant with the colors of fall, the leaves painted in shades of amber and crimson, inviting me to join the festivities of the season. Maybe I could start with a walk, a chance to gather my thoughts and summon the courage to face Cassie. Maybe I could pretend for just a little longer that everything was fine, that the cracks in my facade didn't extend deep into my very being.

I dressed quickly, pulling on a cozy sweater that smelled faintly of cinnamon—my mother's favorite autumn fragrance—and slipped into my well-loved boots. The crisp air outside wrapped around me, a sharp contrast to the warmth of my home, and I inhaled deeply, letting the fresh scent of pine and earth fill my lungs. Each step through the fallen leaves crunched with a satisfying crackle, the sound a small comfort amidst the chaos swirling in my heart.

As I strolled through the town square, I passed familiar shops with their welcoming window displays—floral arrangements spilling from crates, pumpkins lining the sidewalks. The café on the corner, usually filled with the rich aroma of freshly brewed coffee, was bustling with life. I considered stopping in, hoping to grab a hot chocolate and perhaps chat with a friend, but the idea felt daunting. I needed to confront Cassie; I couldn't let the shadows of yesterday linger over me like a cloud.

Instead, I headed toward the park where the Harvest Festival preparations were underway. Colorful banners flapped in the breeze, and laughter bubbled up from clusters of families setting up booths. Children raced about, their laughter blending with the crisp rustle of leaves. It was a scene of joy that should have lifted my spirits, but instead, it only amplified the weight on my shoulders.

I spotted a familiar face amidst the throng—Clara, my childhood friend, her bright red hair a beacon in the sea of autumn hues. She was balancing a stack of hay bales with a determined look, and I couldn't help but smile at her tenacity. As I approached, she straightened up, a grin spreading across her face.

"Tessa! You look like you've seen a ghost!" she teased, her blue eyes sparkling with mischief. "Or maybe you just need a coffee. Either way, you're too pale for this sunshine!"

I chuckled, but it felt strained. "More like I need a miracle," I replied, avoiding the weight of my truth. "What's with the hay? Planning to build a fort?"

"Only if you're joining me!" she exclaimed, her laughter infectious. "But seriously, I'm just helping set up for the festival. You know how it goes—the more hands, the less work. What about you? Are you going to hide in your room all day?"

"Uh, well, I was thinking of finding Cassie," I admitted, my voice dropping to a whisper as if her name alone could summon the storm clouds.

Clara's expression shifted, her teasing demeanor replaced with concern. "Ah, Cassie. Heard the grapevine's been buzzing about you two. You okay?"

"Not really." I hesitated, weighing whether I should share my turmoil. Clara had always been a good listener, a safe harbor in turbulent waters. "We had a bit of a fallout, and I don't know how to fix it. It's like... everything's broken."

"You mean she's not just mad at you; she's mad at everyone, right?" Clara nodded knowingly, as if she had faced similar storms. "She's like that sometimes, you know? Blaming everyone for her problems. You just have to remind her she's not alone."

"But what if she doesn't want to hear it?" I whispered, my voice thick with emotion. "What if I've messed everything up beyond repair?"

Clara reached out, squeezing my arm. "You're not that easy to get rid of, Tessa. If anyone can mend that bridge, it's you. Just be honest. That's all you need to do."

I appreciated her encouragement, but the fear still clung to me like a shroud. "Thanks, Clara. I'll give it a shot."

As we continued chatting, I noticed a flurry of movement at the edge of the park—Cassie, standing with a group of friends, her laughter echoing like shards of glass. The sight of her made my heart race, a mix of longing and dread coursing through me. I felt like a moth drawn to a flame, yet terrified of the burn.

"Go on. I'll finish up here," Clara urged, nudging me gently in Cassie's direction. I hesitated, my feet rooted to the ground as if the earth had decided to swallow me whole. But Clara's encouraging smile urged me forward, and I took a deep breath, steeling myself for whatever confrontation awaited.

I approached the group, each step heavy with uncertainty. Cassie caught sight of me, her laughter fading once again, replaced by that familiar flicker of annoyance. "Well, look who it is," she said, her voice laced with sarcasm that cut through the air like a knife.

"Cassie, can we talk?" The words tumbled out before I could second-guess myself. "Just us?"

She rolled her eyes, but the tension in her shoulders relaxed slightly. "Sure, if you want to make it even more awkward than it already is."

We stepped away from the group, the sounds of the festival fading into the background. The silence between us was charged, thick with unspoken words. I opened my mouth, but the right words evaded me, slipping through my fingers like sand.

"Look, Tessa," she began, her voice softer than I had anticipated. "I didn't mean to shut you out. It's just... everything feels out of control right now. I thought we were supposed to be in this together."

"We are, but you're shutting me out," I replied, the frustration spilling over. "I don't know how to help if you won't let me in."

Her expression softened, and for a moment, I saw a flicker of the Cassie I had always known—the friend who would drag me to movie marathons or sneak chocolate into late-night study sessions. "I'm sorry," she whispered, the apology hanging in the air like a fragile promise. "It's just... I feel like I've lost everything. And it scares me."

The vulnerability in her voice pulled at my heartstrings. "You haven't lost me, Cassie. We can work through this together. Just like we always have."

"I know," she said, her voice barely above a whisper. "But it's hard when everything feels like it's falling apart."

Before I could respond, a sudden shout erupted from the festival. Startled, we turned to see a group of kids chasing after a runaway balloon, laughter ringing out as it floated higher into the sky. The sight was absurd and beautiful, a reminder that even amidst chaos, there were still moments of joy.

"See?" I said, smiling despite the weight in my chest. "Life has a way of surprising us, doesn't it?"

Cassie nodded, a tentative smile breaking through her guarded expression. "Yeah, I guess it does." As we stood there, the tension between us began to melt, replaced by the warmth of our shared history and the hope that perhaps we could navigate the storm together.

The breeze shifted, sending a cascade of leaves swirling around us like confetti celebrating our fragile truce. As Cassie and I stood there, something shifted in the air, a tentative bridge forming between us, but the shadows of the past still loomed large. I felt a flicker of hope igniting within me, but it was quickly quelled by the weight of uncertainty that pressed down like a heavy fog.

"Maybe we could, I don't know, grab coffee later?" I suggested, my voice shaky but resolute. "Just us, like old times? We can talk through this. I miss that."

Cassie looked away, her gaze drifting towards the bustling crowd, where laughter danced on the breeze like an elusive melody. "I'd like that, but..." she trailed off, biting her lip, and I could see the gears turning in her mind. "I don't want to drag you into my mess."

"Too late for that, don't you think?" I shot back lightly, trying to mask the worry bubbling just beneath the surface. "We're all tangled up in this, whether we like it or not."

A fleeting smile crossed her face, but it was gone as quickly as it appeared. "You always did know how to talk me into things." She sighed, crossing her arms protectively. "Okay, let's do it. Just promise me it won't turn into a therapy session."

"I make no promises," I quipped, nudging her shoulder playfully. "But I'll bring the cookies. You know they make everything better."

As we rejoined the fray of festival-goers, the air buzzed with excitement. Kids darted around us, clutching bags of candy, their faces painted with joy. The aroma of caramel apples and roasted corn wafted through the air, wrapping around me like a nostalgic hug. It felt like a sliver of normalcy amid the chaos, but I couldn't shake the undercurrent of tension that still swirled between Cassie and me.

"Look!" Clara called, pointing toward a booth decked out with colorful streamers. "They have a pie-eating contest! Who's in?"

"I'll pass," I said, laughing. "I might just eat my way into a sugar coma." The sight of the pie-eating booth reminded me of our childhood antics, the two of us diving headfirst into whatever culinary disaster the festival had to offer.

"Why not? It's for fun!" Clara encouraged, already rushing toward the booth. Cassie hesitated, her brow furrowing as she glanced between the pies and me. "Come on, it'll lighten the mood!"

With a reluctant chuckle, Cassie joined in, her laughter finally warming the air between us. We approached the booth, where a jovial announcer in a bright blue apron called for contestants. The energy was infectious, and as Cassie and I shared conspiratorial glances, I felt the tension easing slightly.

"Okay, but if we do this, you have to promise to let loose for once," I challenged her playfully.

Cassie arched an eyebrow, a spark of mischief igniting in her eyes. "Let loose? You're on. But you better keep up."

Before I knew it, we were elbow-deep in whipped cream and laughter, our competitive spirits igniting old rivalries. We dove headfirst into the pies, face-first really, as the crowd cheered us on, their shouts blending with our giggles. With each mouthful, the weight of our earlier conversation began to lift, replaced by a sense of camaraderie that felt almost electric.

"Last one to finish buys coffee!" I shouted, wiping whipped cream from my cheek with a laugh.

"Not happening!" she shot back, her voice muffled by the pie. "I'll take you down!"

And in that moment, amidst the chaos of laughter and cheers, the cracks in our friendship began to heal, each shared smile a tiny stitch binding us back together. But just as I felt a wave of relief wash over me, I caught a glimpse of a familiar figure at the edge of the crowd—Ryan.

My heart dropped. He stood there, arms crossed, watching us with a look that was equal parts irritation and disbelief. The jovial atmosphere around us dimmed, the laughter fading into an uncomfortable silence. It felt as though the world had shifted, like stepping off a cliff into an abyss of uncertainty.

Cassie noticed my shift in demeanor and turned to see what had captured my attention. "Oh." Her voice barely above a whisper. "This is... not good."

"What is he doing here?" I murmured, my mind racing as I fought the urge to hide behind the nearest booth. The weight of his presence threatened to pull me back into the chaos I had fought so hard to escape.

"He probably heard the whispers," Cassie replied, her tone a mix of sympathy and frustration. "This isn't the time for him to show up, especially not here."

"Great. Just when I thought we were making progress." I could feel my heart racing as the unease settled back over us, the joy we had just shared seeming so fragile now.

"Let's just ignore him," Cassie suggested, but I could hear the hesitation in her voice.

"Easier said than done," I replied, my mind spinning. "He's the one who needs to talk, not me."

Just as I turned to walk away, Ryan approached, his expression shifting from irritation to something softer as he locked eyes with me. "Tessa," he said, his voice steady but laced with a tension that made my stomach knot.

"Ryan," I responded, trying to keep my tone neutral, though it felt as though we were standing on a tightrope, teetering dangerously close to the edge.

"I need to talk to you." His gaze flickered to Cassie, who had taken a step back, clearly caught in the crossfire of our unresolved issues. "In private."

"Not here," I insisted, the protective instinct flaring within me. "This is a festival. We're supposed to be having fun."

"Yeah, well, this isn't fun for me," he shot back, his voice rising slightly. "And it hasn't been for a while."

The tension crackled between us, an unspoken battle raging in the silence. I could feel Cassie's eyes on me, the weight of her concern adding to the heaviness in the air. "Can't this wait?" I asked, my voice firm but trembling beneath the surface. "We're trying to enjoy the festival."

"Is that really what you want?" he challenged, stepping closer, his voice low and intense. "To pretend everything is fine?"

A crowd of onlookers began to gather, their expressions a mix of curiosity and concern, and I felt my cheeks burn with embarrassment. The laughter of the festival faded into an echo, replaced by the weight of our unresolved issues pressing in like an impending storm.

"Can we just—" I began, but before I could finish, Ryan's phone buzzed violently in his pocket, interrupting the tension. He pulled it out, glancing at the screen with a frown that deepened the lines of worry on his forehead.

"Great. Just great," he muttered, his expression shifting again. "This isn't over, Tessa."

Without another word, he turned and stalked away, leaving me in a whirlwind of confusion and emotions, the festival's lively atmosphere suddenly feeling like a distant memory. Cassie stepped closer, concern etched on her face. "What just happened?"

"I don't know," I said, shaking my head as I struggled to process it all. "But I don't think this is the last I'll hear from him."

The sudden tension hung in the air like a storm cloud, and just as I opened my mouth to respond, the sky above us darkened ominously. A rumble of thunder rolled in the distance, echoing the turmoil within my heart. The wind picked up, whipping through the trees, scattering leaves like confetti at a funeral, and I couldn't shake the feeling that a storm was brewing—not just in the skies above, but within the fragile connections of my life.

Cassie's eyes widened as she glanced up at the darkening clouds. "Tessa, we should probably—"

But before she could finish, a blinding flash of lightning streaked across the sky, illuminating the crowd for just a heartbeat. The thunder cracked, loud and ominous, as raindrops began to fall, heavy and relentless. The festival's laughter morphed into a frantic buzz as people rushed for cover, and I felt the weight of the world crashing down around us.

"Let's get out of here," I urged, grabbing Cassie's arm, but even as we ran, I couldn't shake the feeling that this was only the beginning. The storm was coming, and it had nothing to do with the weather.

# Chapter 18: "The Storm Brews"

The chill of the autumn evening seeped through the windows of the town hall, curling around my ankles like a playful ghost. A line of weary townsfolk sat in the folding chairs, their eyes dull from too many discussions about funding and community outreach. I could almost taste the tension in the air, sharp and metallic, mingling with the scent of damp leaves that clung to the evening. As I shuffled my notes, ready to voice my ideas about the community center, I glanced up and met Cassie's gaze.

Cassie, my best friend since kindergarten, sat with her arms crossed, a fortress of resentment built high against her chest. The flickering overhead lights illuminated her face, accentuating the hard lines of anger etched into her features. I had always known Cassie as the sunniest of friends, the one who laughed until she snorted and could always pull me out of my darkest moods. But today, she was an unyielding storm cloud, and I was just a hapless traveler caught in her tempest.

Ethan, my boyfriend, sat beside me, his presence a comforting warmth. He was the rock I could lean on when the world felt too heavy. As I glanced at him, I found him fidgeting with his tie, the small gesture a telltale sign of his own anxiety. He caught my eye and offered a reassuring nod, his blue eyes filled with unwavering support. "You've got this," he whispered, his voice a low murmur that made my heart flutter.

When it was my turn to speak, I could feel Cassie's eyes boring into me, like daggers that threatened to slice right through my resolve. I cleared my throat, the sound echoing off the walls, reverberating in my chest. "Thank you all for being here," I began, trying to mask the tremor in my voice. "I believe that the community center has the potential to become a true hub for our town. We can create a space where everyone—young, old, families, and individuals—can come together, learn, and grow."

The audience shifted slightly, some nodding in agreement while others stared vacantly, lost in their own thoughts. I pressed on, my passion igniting a fire within me. "Imagine cooking classes for families, art workshops for kids, and a support group for the elderly. This center could bridge the gaps between us and foster a sense of belonging."

From the corner of my eye, I noticed Cassie rolling her eyes, the movement sharp and exaggerated. My stomach sank, a lead weight anchoring my hope. I forged ahead, determined not to let her cynicism deter me. "I know we face challenges—budget cuts, a lack of volunteers—but if we come together as a community, we can overcome anything."

Ethan stood to bolster my resolve, his voice resonant and clear. "I agree with Mia. This is an opportunity for us to redefine our community's future. We have the resources, the passion, and the desire to make this work. Let's not waste it."

A ripple of applause broke through the tension, but Cassie remained unmoved, her scowl unwavering. As the meeting droned on, I could sense her seething frustration, a simmering pot ready to boil over. I tried to catch her eye, to convey my sincerity, but she averted her gaze, as if my attempts were poison she refused to touch.

When the meeting finally concluded, an uneasy silence settled over the room, heavy as the clouds outside. I stepped down from the podium, my heart racing with the adrenaline of speaking out, but I was met with the storm that was Cassie. She surged toward the exit, her back straight, every step radiating disapproval.

"Cassie, wait!" I called, my voice cracking under the weight of her disdain. I hurried after her, dodging chairs and startled faces, my heart pounding in a chaotic rhythm. "Can we talk about this?"

Her response was a sharp laugh that echoed in the hallway, devoid of warmth. "Talk? You mean like you did up there? It's not a real conversation if you're only interested in putting on a show, Mia."

I flinched at her words, a defensive heat rising in my cheeks. "It wasn't a show. I care about this town, about our community center. I thought you did too."

Her eyes flashed with indignation, a stormy sea crashing against the rocky shores of my heart. "I did, once. But that was before you decided to turn everything into a competition. Since you started dating Ethan, it's like you've forgotten what really matters."

A part of me wanted to scream, to shake her and remind her of all the times we had dreamed together, painted vibrant futures with nothing but our hopes. But instead, I took a breath, grounding myself in the reality of our friendship. "I haven't forgotten anything, Cassie. But I'm not going to sit back and watch while we let this opportunity slip away. It's not a competition; it's about building something together."

She stepped closer, her voice a venomous whisper, cutting through the tense air between us. "Together? You mean you and Ethan. Don't you see? You've chosen him over everything else, even over our friendship."

The accusation stung like a bee, sharp and bitter. "That's not fair," I replied, the hurt in my voice undeniable. "You know it's not like that. I love you, but I'm trying to grow too. You can't hold me back just because you're scared of change."

Cassie's face twisted, emotions warring behind her stormy gaze. "Scared of change? Or scared of losing you? Because it feels like I'm watching you slip away, and I don't know how to stop it."

Her words hung between us, heavy and unyielding. I could see the glimmer of tears threatening to spill from her eyes, and for a moment, I felt the air thicken with the weight of our shared history.

"Cassie, I—" I began, but the words evaporated as the door swung open, and the townsfolk streamed out, their chatter cutting through our moment. Cassie turned on her heel, her expression a mask of defiance. "I can't do this right now," she said, her voice shaking slightly as she walked away, leaving me standing in the hallway, a swirl of emotions brewing within me.

I watched her go, my heart heavy with uncertainty. In that moment, I realized that the storm was not only brewing outside in the darkening sky but also within the fragile bonds of our friendship. I turned back toward the flickering lights of the town hall, my mind racing as I pondered how to mend what felt irrevocably broken.

The cold air whipped around me as I stepped outside, the fading light of the day casting long shadows across the pavement. I inhaled sharply, trying to ground myself amidst the chaos swirling in my heart. The air was thick with the scent of damp earth and impending rain, an atmospheric reminder of the turmoil that had just unfolded. I spotted Ethan leaning against the weathered stone wall, his hands shoved deep into his pockets, brows furrowed with concern. The warmth of his gaze brought a flicker of comfort, though it felt like trying to light a candle in a storm.

"Mia," he said, pushing himself off the wall and closing the distance between us. "Are you okay?"

His voice was soft, but the worry etched in his features was unmistakable. I couldn't help but chuckle, a sound tinged with both amusement and exasperation. "Well, considering I just got chewed out by my best friend and tried to rally the town behind a sinking ship, I'd say I'm a solid seven on the anxiety scale."

Ethan raised an eyebrow, the corners of his mouth twitching in an attempt to suppress a grin. "A seven? That's a surprisingly optimistic take. I would have gone for a solid ten."

I shrugged, trying to shake off the weight of Cassie's words, which felt like iron chains around my heart. "It's all relative, I suppose. Besides, I still have a bit of time before I drown in my own sorrows."

His laughter was a balm, cutting through the lingering tension. "True. But seriously, what's the plan? You can't let her just walk away like that."

I sighed, the sound escaping my lips like a deflating balloon. "I know, but every time I try to reach her, it's like she's built this fortress around herself. I don't know how to penetrate her defenses without sounding like I'm minimizing her feelings."

Ethan placed a hand on my shoulder, the gesture grounding and reassuring. "Maybe you need to show her that you're still in her corner. Why not invite her to dinner? A low-key gathering might break the ice."

Dinner. The thought was both comforting and terrifying. A shared meal had always been our way of reconnecting, an unspoken promise that we'd weather any storm together. "It could work," I mused, contemplating how to bridge the widening chasm between us. "But what if she refuses? What if she doesn't want to be friends anymore?"

"Then you keep inviting her," he replied, his tone steady and unwavering. "Friendships aren't always smooth sailing. Sometimes they need a little pushing to steer them back on course."

With that, a plan began to form in my mind, each thread weaving together into a tapestry of hope. "I'll invite her over tomorrow night. Just us and some comfort food. It's hard to argue when you're chewing on a slice of pizza."

Ethan laughed, and for a moment, the tension dissipated like fog under the sun. "I think you're onto something there. And if all else fails, you can always bribe her with dessert."

"Chocolate always wins her over," I agreed, the idea sparking a flicker of determination within me. "Thanks for always being my sounding board, you know? I don't know what I'd do without you."

He leaned down, pressing a gentle kiss to my forehead, his warmth enveloping me like a favorite blanket. "You'd manage, but I'm glad to be here, even if it's just to be your cheerleader. Just remember, you're not alone in this."

With a newfound sense of purpose, I made my way home, the streets dimly lit by the soft glow of lampposts. The wind picked up, rustling the leaves above me, whispering secrets of change and uncertainty. I was ready to face the tempest of my friendship head-on, to wade through the rising waters of emotion.

That evening, I prepared for the dinner, my heart thrumming with a mix of excitement and dread. I set the table with mismatched plates—a charmingly chaotic reflection of our friendship. Each plate carried memories of laughter-filled dinners, late-night confessions, and a bond that had been tested but never truly broken. As I slid the pizza into the oven, the rich aroma filled the kitchen, wrapping around me like a warm hug.

I paced the living room, my thoughts dancing between hope and anxiety, imagining Cassie's face when she walked through the door. Would she be willing to share a slice of pizza and put aside her anger, even for a moment? The doorbell rang, pulling me from my reverie, and my heart raced as I opened the door to find Cassie standing there, arms crossed defiantly, her expression a mix of skepticism and reluctance.

"Mia," she began, her voice steady but lacking the warmth I craved. "I didn't think you'd actually go through with it."

"Neither did I, honestly," I replied, trying to inject humor into the situation. "But I promise there's pizza, and I even dug up that tiramisu you love."

The mention of her favorite dessert made her lips twitch slightly, the tiniest sign of softening. "You know I can't resist dessert," she said, stepping inside. The moment she crossed the threshold, the air felt charged, thick with unspoken words and heavy emotions.

"Good. That was the plan," I said, closing the door behind her and leading her to the table. "I thought we could use a little comfort food."

Cassie hesitated before taking a seat, her posture rigid, the walls still firmly in place. I grabbed the pizza from the oven, the cheese bubbling and golden, and set it on the table, watching as she eyed it warily. "You're not going to check for spit or anything, are you?" I asked, a playful tone lacing my voice.

Her laugh was a sudden burst of warmth in the cool room, but it didn't last long. "You know I'd be too polite for that," she replied, her smile fading as she glanced away.

I took a deep breath, willing myself to dive into the depths of our fractured friendship. "Cassie, I know things have been strained between us. I miss you, and I'm really sorry if you feel like I've chosen Ethan over you. That's not how I see it."

She looked at me then, her defenses wavering, and I seized the moment. "You're my best friend. I want to grow and thrive in our friendship, but I also want to embrace new experiences. Can't we do both?"

For a long moment, she remained silent, and the air thickened with the weight of unspoken truths. "I don't want to lose you, Mia. I really don't. But sometimes it feels like you're moving on without me."

"Moving on? I'd never want to leave you behind. You're the one who knows all my secrets," I replied, a smile breaking through the tension. "You're stuck with me. I promise, pizza and all."

Cassie's shoulders relaxed just a fraction, a small but significant shift. "Okay, maybe pizza is a step in the right direction."

As we began to eat, I watched her take a bite, the tension in her shoulders softening just a bit more. We shared the kind of laughter that felt like a balm, healing old wounds and creating new ones in the process. The warmth of the food melted away the chill of the storm brewing outside, if only for a moment.

"See? Food really does solve everything," I teased, my heart swelling with hope. But even as I laughed, I felt the undercurrents of our conversation still waiting to be explored, ready to surface and reveal the layers beneath the surface.

The evening stretched out before us, filled with the comforting sounds of laughter and the occasional clink of plates. The pizza vanished quickly, but the real feast lay in the conversation that began to unfurl like a flower tentatively opening to the sun. I watched Cassie take a sip of her soda, the tension still visible in the slight furrow of her brow. I wanted to peel back the layers of her frustrations, to navigate through the thicket of emotions that had grown between us.

"Okay, so aside from pizza, how's life treating you?" I asked, my voice light, but the question weighed heavily on both of us.

She sighed, leaning back in her chair as if considering how much of her world she wanted to reveal. "It's just been... complicated. Between my job and everything else, I feel like I'm in a constant state of flux. I guess I've just been feeling a bit lost."

"Lost?" I echoed, nodding in understanding. "I get that. But you know, you're not in this alone. It's okay to ask for help, to lean on me. I'm still here."

Her eyes glistened momentarily, and I could see the inner battle she was fighting. "It's not just that, Mia. It's this feeling of being left behind. I thought we were in this together, but lately, it seems like you're moving forward while I'm stuck. It hurts, you know?"

The admission hung in the air, heavy and raw. I set my slice down, my appetite dwindling as the gravity of her words sank in. "Cassie, I promise, I'm not trying to leave you behind. I want us both to thrive. This isn't about moving ahead without you; it's about us finding a way to grow together."

She paused, her expression softening as the warmth of nostalgia flickered in her eyes. "Remember when we used to dream about taking that trip across the country? Just the two of us, with no responsibilities?"

"How could I forget?" I chuckled, the memories washing over me like a gentle wave. "We had our whole lives planned out—stopping in every quirky roadside diner and getting matching tattoos of pineapples because they were 'the universal symbol of hospitality.'"

Cassie laughed, the sound bright and unexpected. "I think we were just grasping for something that sounded cool at the time."

"Cool? Pineapples are the epitome of coolness. I mean, just look at them. They wear their spiky hair with confidence!"

As we exchanged memories and laughter, the heaviness began to lift, slowly melting the ice that had built between us. I could feel her walls cracking, just a little, enough for hope to seep in. "Mia, I really miss that connection we had," she said softly, her voice trembling with sincerity. "I want it back."

"I miss it too. And I promise, we'll figure this out together."

In that moment, a semblance of our former friendship blossomed back to life. The warmth of the pizza faded, and in its place, I sensed a new kind of energy beginning to spark. Just as I was about to suggest we plan that long-overdue adventure, my phone buzzed on the table, cutting through the warm glow of our reconnection.

I glanced at the screen, my heart stuttering in my chest. It was a message from Ethan: Emergency at the community center. Please come ASAP.

The smile slipped from my face, replaced by a wave of concern. "Ethan needs me," I said, my heart racing. "There's something going on at the center. I should—"

"Wait," Cassie interrupted, her brow furrowing. "What kind of emergency? Is everything okay?"

"I don't know. He didn't say," I replied, the uncertainty gnawing at me. "But I can't just ignore it."

She stood up abruptly, her chair scraping against the floor. "I'm coming with you."

I hesitated, torn between wanting her support and the need to keep this situation contained. "Cassie, I don't want to drag you into whatever mess is happening. You've had enough for one night."

She narrowed her eyes, determination sparking a fire in her gaze. "I'm not going to sit here wondering. If there's something going on, I want to be there with you. Besides, you might need backup."

Her fierce spirit was contagious, igniting my own resolve. "Okay, let's go then."

We hurried out of my apartment, the night air brisk against our skin, our footsteps quickening as we approached the community center. The streetlights flickered, casting an eerie glow on the pavement, creating shadows that seemed to dance with anticipation. I felt an undercurrent of anxiety pulse through me, twisting my stomach into knots as we neared the entrance.

Inside, the atmosphere was charged, thick with the murmur of voices and the rustle of movement. Ethan stood at the center of the room, surrounded by several concerned faces, all eyes focused on him. The air felt electric, charged with uncertainty as he caught my gaze and hurried over.

"Thank you for coming," he said, urgency lacing his tone. "We've got a situation."

"Situation?" I echoed, glancing around the room at the worried expressions of my neighbors, the community members who had once gathered to discuss building dreams together. "What happened?"

Ethan leaned closer, lowering his voice to a conspiratorial whisper. "It's the funding. The town council just announced a sudden freeze on all community projects, including ours. They're pulling support for the center effective immediately."

My heart sank, a lead weight in my chest. "But we've been working on this for months! How can they just shut it down?"

"Politics," he replied tersely, his frustration palpable. "There's been some backdoor dealing, and they're prioritizing other projects. We're collateral damage in their games."

Cassie, who had been listening quietly, stepped forward. "Is there anything we can do? Can we appeal, raise awareness? Surely, the community will rally behind us."

Ethan nodded, the spark of hope igniting in his eyes. "That's the plan. We need to mobilize, gather support, and show them that this community stands behind the center. If we can organize a meeting and get everyone involved, we might just turn this around."

As he spoke, I felt a mix of dread and determination swirling inside me. "Then let's do it. Let's gather the town, spread the word, and fight for our future."

Just as I finished speaking, the lights flickered ominously above us, plunging the room into darkness for a heartbeat before they sputtered back to life. A loud crash echoed from the back, followed by a series of panicked gasps.

"What was that?" Cassie exclaimed, her eyes wide with alarm.

Ethan's expression hardened. "Stay here."

But before he could move, the lights dimmed again, and a shadowy figure loomed at the entrance, the tension crackling in the air like static electricity.

"Looks like the real storm is just beginning," I whispered, my heart racing as the figure stepped forward, revealing a familiar face that sent shivers down my spine.

"Hope you're ready for some unexpected changes," said the newcomer, a smirk playing on their lips, eyes glinting with mischief as they crossed the threshold.

Panic surged through me as the weight of the moment settled heavily in the pit of my stomach. The night had transformed from a reunion of friends to a battlefield, and we were standing right in the eye of the storm.

# Chapter 19: "Facing the Music"

The air in my apartment was thick with the scent of rosemary and garlic, the promise of comfort wrapped in a warm embrace. I had transformed my modest space into a sanctuary, each detail meticulously arranged to soothe the soul: soft throw pillows, flickering candles casting gentle shadows, and a playlist of mellow tunes that danced lightly in the background. As I stood by the kitchen counter, arranging a colorful platter of Cassie's favorite snacks—golden-brown pastries nestled beside vibrant cherry tomatoes and creamy hummus—my heart drummed a nervous rhythm against my ribs.

When the doorbell chimed, it echoed like a whisper of fate, carrying with it the weight of the conversation I had rehearsed a thousand times in my mind. I opened the door to find Cassie standing there, her silhouette framed by the warm glow of the hallway light. She wore a light jacket, the collar turned up against the chill of the evening air. A hesitant smile flickered across her lips, yet I could see the apprehension lurking beneath her cheerful facade.

"Hey! Smells incredible in here," she said, stepping inside and shedding her coat, which fell like a shadow onto my couch. I motioned for her to take a seat at the small table in the corner, a cozy nook that had witnessed countless late-night conversations and shared secrets.

"Just trying to make it special," I replied, forcing a smile that felt slightly brittle. I didn't want to acknowledge the tension hanging between us, palpable like a thick fog. As I set the platter down, I felt the moment stretch, like the taut string of a bow, ready to snap at the slightest touch.

With her plate piled high, Cassie began nibbling on the pastries, but her eyes darted around the room, as if searching for something—maybe a sign that I wouldn't bring up the elephant in the room. It was a dance we had both perfected over the years, avoiding the things that gnawed at us, instead filling the silence with laughter and light-hearted banter. But tonight was different. I could no longer hide behind snacks and playlists; the heaviness in my chest demanded to be addressed.

"Cassie," I began, my voice steady despite the storm brewing inside me. "There's something I need to talk to you about."

She looked up, her gaze locking onto mine, vulnerability flickering in her eyes. "I figured as much," she murmured, her tone a mixture of curiosity and dread.

Taking a deep breath, I plunged in. "It's about Ethan."

Her expression shifted, shadows crossing her face as I spoke his name. "Oh," she said, her voice barely above a whisper. "I thought we were done with him."

"I thought so too," I admitted, feeling the warmth of embarrassment wash over me. "But he's back in town, and things... they've gotten complicated."

Cassie's brow furrowed, and she set her plate down, her appetite fading into the backdrop of our conversation. "Complicated how?"

I could feel the weight of every unspoken word hanging between us, as if the air had thickened with unacknowledged fears. "I like him, Cassie. More than I should."

There it was, my truth laid bare. I watched her process my confession, the delicate flicker of surprise dancing in her eyes. "You like him? After everything?"

"Yes, but it's not just that," I rushed to explain, my heart pounding in my ears. "I'm scared. Scared of what it means for us, for our friendship. I don't want to lose you."

Her silence stretched like a taut wire, and I could see the conflict play across her face. "I don't want to lose you either," she finally said, her voice soft, yet laced with uncertainty. "But I can't help feeling like... like he's come back and changed everything. I was getting used to my life without him, you know?"

A rush of empathy flooded me. "I understand, really. He's not the same guy he was before. And I'm not the same person I was when he left. But this feels different, like it could be something real."

Cassie blinked back tears, her walls crumbling just a little. "What if it is real? What if it's just another way to hurt each other?"

I reached across the table, taking her hand in mine, the warmth of her skin grounding me. "That's the risk we take, isn't it? In love and in friendship? I want to be honest with you, but I don't want you to feel pushed aside."

Tears glistened in her eyes, each droplet a testament to the heartache and confusion she carried. "You know, I've been feeling lost since Ethan returned. It's like I don't know where I fit in anymore. I used to be sure of my place, but now..." She trailed off, the vulnerability in her voice stark against the soft music playing in the background.

"I'm here, Cassie. No matter what happens with Ethan, you will always have a place with me. Always."

A small, fragile smile broke through her tears, and in that moment, I realized we were both facing our fears—my fear of losing her and her fear of losing herself. The evening stretched before us, an open canvas, ready to be painted with honesty, laughter, and a new understanding. We were at a crossroads, and the decisions we made could either strengthen our bond or create chasms we might never bridge.

As the conversation shifted, easing into lighter topics, I could feel the tension receding like a tide. But the uncertainty of the night lingered, a gentle reminder that while friendships could be rebuilt, the journey was fraught with unexpected twists, and I was ready to face whatever lay ahead.

The days drifted by, each one melding seamlessly into the next like watercolors bleeding together on a canvas, leaving me to navigate through a haze of lesson plans and lingering emotions. My classroom became a refuge, a space where I could immerse myself in the challenges of teaching. I poured my heart into each lecture, using every ounce of creativity I possessed to engage my students. Yet, behind the vibrant facade of interactive projects and enthusiastic discussions, an ache nested deep within me, its roots entwined with thoughts of Ethan and the unresolved tension with Cassie.

It was a Friday evening when the dull throb in my chest became too much to bear. The end of the week had left me feeling more fragmented than fulfilled. I flipped the "Closed" sign on my classroom door, the echo of the latch sounding like a small promise of solitude. After gathering my things, I returned home and sat in the silence, contemplating the delicate fabric of my life that seemed to unravel thread by thread.

A plan began to take shape—a heart-to-heart with Cassie, a chance to clear the air and maybe stitch our friendship back together. I pulled out my phone and sent her a message, suggesting a night in. The response was almost immediate, her enthusiasm spilling through the screen.

The next evening, I transformed my apartment into a cozy cocoon, filled with the warm scent of freshly baked cookies and the soft flicker of candles casting gentle shadows against the walls. I set the table with our favorite snacks: a spread of artisanal cheeses, succulent olives, and a vibrant fruit salad. Everything was in place, yet a sense of trepidation clung to me like a second skin.

When Cassie arrived, her usual bright smile seemed dimmed, and the air was thick with unspoken words. She took off her jacket, and as she settled into her seat, I felt a rush of nerves tightening my stomach. I gestured for her to dig in, but she merely picked at the fruit, her eyes wandering around the room.

"Hey, you okay?" I asked, my voice softer than I intended.

"Yeah, just... a lot on my mind," she replied, glancing down at the table as if the snacks held all the answers.

I steeled myself, letting the silence settle between us for a moment longer before diving in. "I need to talk to you about Ethan."

The name hung in the air, thick and heavy. Cassie's fork clinked against her plate, a small sound that felt monumental in the stillness. "What about him?"

Her guarded tone told me all I needed to know. This was it—the moment of truth. "I think I might have feelings for him again."

The confession slipped out like a sudden gust of wind, raw and unfiltered. Cassie's expression shifted, her eyes widening with a mix of surprise and something darker, a flicker of hurt that sliced through me like glass.

"I thought we agreed—"

"I know," I interrupted, my heart racing. "But things are different now. He's different, and I can't pretend I don't feel this way. It's just... complicated."

Cassie's brow furrowed as she tried to process my words. "Complicated how? You think this won't end up in disaster?"

"Cassie, I'm scared too," I said, leaning forward, willing her to understand. "But I can't ignore it. Not anymore. I don't want to lose you in the process."

Her silence was an unwelcome companion, and I could feel the tension crackling like static electricity. Finally, she took a deep breath, her voice trembling. "What if this is just a way to hurt each other again? You know he can't just waltz back into our lives and fix everything."

"I know he can't," I said, my voice earnest. "But what if he can help us heal? What if—"

"Stop," Cassie interjected, her voice sharp, cutting through the air like a blade. "You sound just like him. What if he's not the answer? What if he's just going to hurt you? Or worse, what if he hurts me again?"

The frustration bubbled within me, and I felt my pulse quicken. "I'm not trying to hurt you! I thought we were past this."

"Past what?" she snapped back, her eyes flashing. "You mean your infatuation with a guy who left without a word? You think that's healthy?"

For a moment, we locked eyes, the tension thick enough to slice with a knife. I could see the conflict swirling within her, battling her insecurities and the remnants of their past.

"I'm not asking for permission," I said, my tone sharper than intended. "I'm just asking for honesty."

The moment hung heavy as we both leaned back, the air filled with unspoken thoughts. Cassie's features softened slightly, her defenses crumbling. "I don't want to lose you. I don't want this to come between us."

"And I don't want to lose you either," I said, the heat of the argument dissipating like morning fog. "But pretending this isn't happening isn't going to help either of us."

"Okay, fine," she sighed, her shoulders slumping. "What do you want to do? Just dive back in and hope for the best?"

"Honestly? I'm not sure. But I know I can't keep this bottled up. I want to see where it goes, but I need you by my side, no matter what happens."

As the conversation shifted into softer tones, we began to weave our fears and hopes together, like threads in a complex tapestry. We talked about our past, the heartbreaks that had shaped us, and the reasons we had chosen to forge ahead without Ethan. With each confession, the walls between us began to crumble, revealing a foundation built on trust and vulnerability.

Just as the mood lightened and we shared laughter over old memories, Cassie's phone buzzed on the table, breaking the moment. She glanced down and her face blanched. "It's Ethan."

The room froze. I felt the weight of that name loom large again, pressing against the fragile truce we had just established. Cassie's finger hovered over the screen, and I could see her heart race in the tightening of her jaw.

"Answer it," I urged, my voice barely above a whisper.

"I can't," she said, her face a mask of conflict.

But something shifted in me, a surge of courage, as I realized that this was not just about Ethan; it was about us. "You need to. If you're going to be honest with me, you have to be honest with him too."

Her eyes searched mine, a mixture of fear and determination swirling within her. As the phone continued to vibrate on the table, I knew this moment could change everything once more, the fabric of our friendship now woven tightly with a new, unpredictable thread.

As Cassie's phone buzzed insistently, the atmosphere in my cozy apartment shifted palpably, tension coiling like a spring between us. Her eyes darted between the screen and my face, a silent battle waging behind those usually bright eyes. I could almost hear her thoughts, echoing in the silence—should she answer, or would it unleash the very chaos we had been trying to navigate?

"Cassie, you have to pick it up," I urged, feeling the urgency crackling in the air. "This is your chance to set things straight. You owe it to yourself."

Her lips pressed into a thin line as she weighed the options. "But what if he tries to sweep me back into his world? What if he thinks it's all forgiven?"

"Then you tell him it's not," I said, leaning forward, my hands clasped tightly together. "You've got the strength for this. Just remember, you're in control now."

After a moment of tense deliberation, she inhaled deeply and reached for the phone, her fingers trembling slightly. As she accepted the call, I held my breath, the room suspended in anticipation.

"Ethan," she said, her voice surprisingly steady, although a quaver lurked beneath the surface. "What do you want?"

His voice crackled through the speaker, muffled yet unmistakable, filling the room with an intensity that made the air feel charged. "Cassie, I need to see you. I know things have been complicated, but we need to talk."

She glanced at me, her expression a mix of determination and apprehension. "Why now? After all this time? You just show up and expect me to drop everything?"

"Because I've realized something," he replied, his tone earnest. "I made a mistake when I left, and I want to make it right."

The words hung in the air, potent and heavy, igniting a flicker of hope in Cassie's eyes. My heart raced, unsure whether this was a turning point or the beginning of another tumultuous cycle.

"I don't know, Ethan," she said, her voice quivering slightly. "Things have changed. I've changed."

"Can we just talk?" he pressed. "I need to explain. Please, give me a chance to show you."

Cassie hesitated, her thumb hovering over the end call button. "Where?"

"Same place as always," he said, a hint of nostalgia coloring his voice. "The coffee shop downtown, our spot."

She looked at me again, and in that moment, I understood that this wasn't just a decision for her. It was a choice that could shift the balance of everything we had rebuilt together.

"Go," I said softly, my heart aching with mixed emotions. "You have to see him. You need closure, and maybe I do too."

With a reluctant nod, she ended the call, her fingers trembling as she placed the phone back on the table. "I don't know if I'm ready for this."

"Ready or not, you've got to do it," I encouraged. "For yourself. You deserve the chance to voice your feelings."

Cassie took a deep breath, a spark of resolve igniting within her. "You're right. I'll go. But you have to promise me something."

"Anything."

"Promise me you won't let this affect us," she implored, her voice laced with vulnerability. "No matter what happens, we stay friends."

"I promise," I assured her, though my stomach twisted with uncertainty.

With that, she stood up, smoothing her clothes nervously as she prepared to leave. "I'll call you afterward," she said, her voice steadying.

"Take your time," I replied, a mix of pride and anxiety swelling within me.

As she stepped out into the crisp night air, I sank back into my chair, the weight of our conversation settling around me. I flicked off the candles, the soft glow extinguishing, leaving my apartment in shadowy silence. My thoughts raced—about Ethan, about Cassie, about what this meant for us all.

The minutes ticked by, each second stretching into eternity. I busied myself with cleaning up, but my mind was a whirlpool of worry and anticipation. What if this meeting opened old wounds? What if Cassie came back heartbroken, or worse, disillusioned?

Just as I was about to lose myself in those thoughts, my phone buzzed. I grabbed it, hoping for a message from Cassie, but it was a notification from social media. A video of Ethan had been shared, showcasing his return to town—interviews, laughter, and all the charisma that had drawn me to him in the first place.

I watched, my heart twisting as I saw him speak animatedly about his plans for the future. He seemed so alive, so vibrant, and it struck me hard how much he had changed, how his absence had left a void that felt impossible to fill. And now, here he was, inching back into our lives, creating ripples in the pond of our shared history.

I quickly exited the app, shaking my head as if to dispel the visions of him that crowded my mind. This wasn't about him anymore; it was about Cassie. It had to be.

Suddenly, my phone buzzed again. A message from Cassie popped up on the screen, and my heart leaped. I clicked it open, my breath hitching as I read her words:

He's here. I can't believe it. He looks... different. I don't know what to say.

My fingers hesitated over the keyboard as I struggled to find the right words, to offer support and reassurance through the screen. Just as I started to type, a sharp knock at my door startled me, reverberating through the quiet space.

"Who could that be?" I muttered, standing up and moving toward the door with a mix of curiosity and dread.

I opened it slowly, revealing a figure silhouetted against the dim light of the hallway. My breath caught in my throat as recognition washed over me, an unexpected wave of emotions crashing through me.

"Ethan," I breathed, stunned into silence, his familiar smile tinged with a vulnerability I hadn't seen before.

"I need to talk to you," he said, his voice steady but urgent, as if he had just stepped off a precipice and into my world again.

The ground shifted beneath me, the world narrowing to just the two of us, the tension electric in the air. And just like that, everything I had tried to keep at bay surged forward, threatening to engulf us both in a tide of emotions I had never anticipated.

"Right now?" I asked, a mix of disbelief and excitement swirling within me.

"Yes," he replied, taking a small step closer. "It's important. Can I come in?"

Before I could respond, the weight of the moment crashed down, the uncertainty of Cassie's decision and the complexity of our intertwined lives colliding in a way I never expected. The air crackled with unspoken words, and as I stepped aside to let him in, I realized this conversation might change everything—not just for me, but for all of us.

# Chapter 20: "Ethan's Dilemma"

The office was a masterpiece of design, every corner whispering tales of ambition and artistry. Sunlight streamed through vast, floor-to-ceiling windows, casting playful patterns on the polished hardwood floor. I couldn't help but admire the blend of modern flair with rustic charm—a sleek, black metal desk was paired with a reclaimed barnwood shelf lined with books on architecture, family histories, and a smattering of travel guides. It was like stepping into the mind of a man who was torn between the past and the future, where dreams collided with the weight of reality.

Ethan leaned against his desk, hands shoved deep into his pockets, a posture that betrayed his inner turmoil. His dark hair, tousled in a way that somehow managed to look both effortless and deliberate, caught the light, emphasizing the sharp angles of his face. I could see the flicker of determination in his hazel eyes, yet it was quickly eclipsed by the cloud of uncertainty that had been hanging over him like an uninvited storm.

"I've been thinking about expanding the office," he began, his voice steady but laced with an underlying tension. "We could incorporate more collaborative spaces, maybe even a coffee corner. You know, somewhere people can gather and share ideas." He gestured vaguely, as if envisioning the transformation in his mind, but I could tell that his heart wasn't in it.

"Sounds great, but—" I started, cautious not to derail his enthusiasm, "are you sure that's what you want? Or is it what you think you should want?"

He met my gaze, a flicker of surprise dancing in those hazel depths. "It's just... everyone expects so much from me. My family, the community." He sighed deeply, running a hand through his hair. "Cassie's been putting pressure on me to settle down, to think about starting a family of my own. I know I should want that, but..."

"But it doesn't feel right," I finished for him, my heart aching as I spoke. "You've always had this fire, Ethan. The kind that can't be extinguished by expectations."

He nodded slowly, his expression a mixture of gratitude and confusion. "I want to build something that lasts, but at the same time, I feel like I'm being pulled in two directions. Every time I think I've made a decision, I second-guess myself."

The air in the room grew thick with unspoken words, each one heavy with the weight of our uncharted territory. My chest tightened as I considered the implications of his dilemma. It was easy to see how his struggles reflected my own; we were both standing at the crossroads of our lives, unsure of which path would lead us to happiness.

"You've always dreamed of more, Ethan. This town may love you, but it can also stifle you. You're meant for bigger things." My words hung between us, charged with an urgency that felt almost palpable. "But what about us? Where do we fit into all of this?"

The question lingered in the air, unacknowledged yet echoing louder than any answer. He glanced down, avoiding my gaze, and in that moment, I felt the tension crackle like a live wire. I could sense the turmoil within him, as if he were standing on the precipice of a decision that could change everything.

"I don't want to hurt you," he said, finally breaking the silence. The honesty in his voice was both comforting and disheartening. "But I don't know how to reconcile my responsibilities with what I want."

A soft chuckle escaped my lips, lightening the mood momentarily. "Welcome to adulthood. It's all one giant mess of wanting things you can't have and trying to balance expectations."

Ethan's eyes met mine, the ghost of a smile breaking through the tension. "You make it sound so appealing."

"It is, in a way. It's messy, but it's real," I replied, warmth spreading through me despite the heaviness of the conversation. "You've just got to find your way through the chaos."

He stepped closer, the distance between us shrinking as he considered my words. "And what if I lose myself in the process? What if I make the wrong choice and it costs me everything?"

"Then you take a breath, and you start again," I said, my voice firm. "You're not alone in this, Ethan. No matter what decision you make, we'll figure it out together."

For a moment, the uncertainty in his eyes softened, replaced by a flicker of hope. He reached for my hand, the warmth of his skin grounding me amidst the swirling emotions.

"I wish I could see the future," he admitted quietly, his thumb brushing against my knuckles, sending a shiver up my spine. "But I guess it's more about the journey, right?"

"Exactly. Life's an unpredictable journey filled with choices and consequences. You've got to trust yourself."

The vulnerability between us was palpable, a delicate thread binding our fates together as we faced the unknown. Yet even in that moment of connection, I could feel the weight of Cassie's discontent looming like a storm cloud over our heads.

"I just... I need to find clarity. Before I make any big decisions," he said, pulling his hand away reluctantly, as if fearing that the warmth might fade away with it.

"Clarity takes time," I reassured him, reluctant to let go of that connection. "But remember, it's okay to take a step back. You don't have to have all the answers right now."

He nodded, though the doubt still lingered in his eyes, casting shadows over his resolve. I could sense the gravity of the situation and the toll it was taking on him. The clock on the wall ticked away the moments, reminding us that time was both a friend and foe in this precarious dance we were engaged in.

And as the afternoon sun dipped lower in the sky, casting a golden glow over the office, I knew that whatever decisions lay ahead, we would have to face them head-on. Together, we would navigate the labyrinth of our dreams and expectations, hoping to find a way to emerge not just intact, but stronger.

The air in the office felt thick with unspoken words, as if the walls themselves held their breath. Ethan shifted his weight, one foot tapping restlessly against the floor, and I could almost see the gears turning in his mind. The sunlight had softened into a warm glow, casting golden rays across the room, but it didn't quite manage to dispel the shadows creeping into our conversation.

"I've thought about moving," he blurted suddenly, the words tumbling out as if he had been holding them back for far too long. "Maybe to the city. It's just... it feels like everyone expects me to stay here, to take over the family business, but my heart... it's somewhere else."

A flash of disbelief darted through me. "The city? That's a big leap, Ethan. What about your family? What about Cassie?"

"Exactly!" he exclaimed, throwing his hands up in exasperation. "Everyone wants something different from me. Cassie's been talking about wedding plans, kids, all while I'm sitting here sketching blueprints of my dream office in a city I can't even afford to live in."

His honesty was like a jolt, sharp and electrifying. I admired his passion for architecture, the way his eyes lit up when he spoke about designing spaces that breathed life into dull buildings. Yet the weight of expectation dimmed that spark, forcing him to mold himself into someone he didn't recognize.

"Have you told Cassie how you feel?" I asked gently, mindful of the delicate nature of the topic.

He raked a hand through his hair, frustration radiating off him like heat from a summer pavement. "I can't! What would I even say? 'Hey, Cassie, I know you want a white picket fence and two-point-five kids, but I'm having a quarter-life crisis and dreaming of urban landscapes instead'?"

Laughter bubbled up in my throat, unexpected but welcomed, momentarily cutting through the tension. "You make it sound like you're trying to escape from a rom-com cliché."

"Maybe I am," he muttered, a ghost of a smile touching his lips. "But you have to admit, it's a pretty strong genre. High stakes, romantic tension, and a confused protagonist who can't quite figure out what he wants."

"You're definitely the confused protagonist," I teased, leaning against the desk, relishing the warmth of our banter. "But you know what? The best stories usually start with someone stepping out of their comfort zone."

Ethan's gaze softened, and for a moment, the lightness lingered between us, buoyed by our shared humor. But it quickly dimmed again as he pressed his lips together, grappling with his thoughts. "You're right, but what if I step out and fall flat? What if I make a mistake?"

"Then you pick yourself up and try again. It's not like you haven't faced challenges before." I could feel the weight of his worry pushing down on me, heavy like an anvil. "You've built this incredible office, and that took guts. This isn't any different; it's just a bigger canvas."

His eyes locked onto mine, a mixture of hope and uncertainty swirling in their depths. "What if I fail and it hurts everyone? What if I end up hurting you?"

"Ethan," I said, softening my tone. "You won't hurt me by being true to yourself. If anything, I'd rather see you chase your dreams than live a life for someone else. And Cassie... well, she deserves the same honesty from you. If you don't want that life, it's better to tell her now."

He sighed, the sound heavy with the weight of a thousand thoughts. "It's just... hard to imagine my life without her, yet it's harder to imagine a life where I'm unhappy."

"Sometimes you have to choose the discomfort of honesty over the comfort of a lie," I replied, my heart aching for the conflict he was navigating. "It might hurt in the short term, but it's far better than lingering in a relationship out of obligation."

He looked out the window, his expression contemplative. The sun was dipping low in the sky, its golden hue turning the world outside into a dreamscape. "What if I end up alone?"

I stepped closer, the space between us shrinking as the quiet of the office settled around us. "You won't be alone. You'll have your dreams, and if you're lucky, the right people will find you along the way."

Ethan turned to face me fully, his eyes searching mine for something, perhaps reassurance or a sign that he wasn't as lost as he felt. "You're really something, you know that?"

"Flattery will get you everywhere," I replied with a playful smile, but my heart raced under the weight of his gaze. "Just don't make me the reason you stay put. I'll be fine, I promise."

"But I want you to be more than fine," he said, his voice dropping to a whisper, the intensity in his eyes igniting a spark of something deep and complicated between us. "I want us to be good."

The words hung in the air, raw and honest, making my pulse quicken. "Then you have to decide what 'good' looks like for you."

A moment of silence stretched between us, thick with possibilities and unspoken dreams. I could see the wheels turning in Ethan's mind, his shoulders shifting as if he were preparing for a monumental decision. It was a moment of reckoning, a crossroads where everything could change.

"Maybe it's time I had that talk with Cassie," he murmured, more to himself than to me. "I've been holding back for too long."

"Good," I encouraged, my heart swelling with admiration for his courage. "It's the first step, and it's the hardest one. Just remember to be kind to yourself, okay? This isn't about tearing anyone down."

He nodded, a resolute look settling over his features as he pulled his phone from his pocket, the screen lighting up with a barrage of notifications. "Right after I send this text, I'll plan a time to meet her."

"Smart. Clear communication. It's how adults operate," I joked lightly, hoping to ease the tension again.

"Adulthood is overrated," he said with a mock grimace, but I could see a flicker of relief in his eyes. "But I guess we're in it whether we like it or not."

"Welcome to the club," I said, laughter bubbling up again. "We've got snacks."

As he thumbed the screen of his phone, the shadows in his expression began to lift, replaced by a glimmer of hope and determination. For the first time that afternoon, the weight of uncertainty didn't seem quite so heavy.

"I appreciate you being here," he said softly, his voice wrapping around me like a warm embrace. "It's nice to have someone who understands."

"Always," I replied, my heart thrumming in my chest as I leaned closer, caught in the moment between friendship and something more. The light was fading outside, but in that office, we were both shining, ready to face whatever came next.

The atmosphere shifted in the office, charged with unspoken tensions as Ethan sent his text, the soft tap-tap of his fingers barely breaking the silence. I watched him, my heart fluttering with anticipation and apprehension. Each ping of his phone echoed like the ticking of a clock, counting down to a moment of truth.

"Just one more," he murmured, glancing at me with an expression that was both anxious and determined. The light from the window illuminated the lines of worry etched on his forehead, revealing the weight of his decisions as he typed. "I can't keep dancing around it. I need to be honest with Cassie."

"Exactly," I replied, my voice steady, though my own heart raced. "You can't build a future on half-truths. Trust me, she'll respect you for it."

Ethan paused, a deep breath escaping his lips. "What if she doesn't take it well? I mean, we've been together for so long. What if she decides she can't handle it?"

"That's a risk you have to be willing to take," I said gently. "You deserve to be with someone who understands your dreams, not someone who confines you to theirs."

He nodded, the corners of his mouth twitching into a fleeting smile. "You really are wise beyond your years."

"Flattery won't save you when the conversation gets tough," I teased, trying to lighten the mood. "But seriously, this isn't about what anyone else wants. It's about your happiness."

He fell silent again, the gravity of the moment pulling us both into deep contemplation. The office, once a bright haven of creativity, felt stifling under the weight of impending revelations. The sunlight began to fade, shadows creeping into the corners of the room like whispers of doubt.

Finally, Ethan placed his phone on the desk and turned to face me, vulnerability etched in every line of his face. "What if I lose my connection with her? Or worse, what if she feels betrayed?"

"She might feel hurt, but that doesn't mean she'll stop caring for you," I assured him. "This is about being honest. Relationships built on honesty have a much stronger foundation than those built on pretense."

He let out a long breath, a mix of resignation and resolve. "You're right. It's time to take that leap. But, um..." He hesitated, glancing at the door. "Can you stay for moral support? I might need a cheerleader."

"I can manage that," I replied, crossing my arms and leaning back against the desk. "But I can't promise pom-poms."

He chuckled, the tension in the room easing just a fraction. "Well, I'll take what I can get."

As he prepared to make the call, I couldn't help but feel a swell of pride for him. The man standing before me was ready to face his fears head-on, and I admired his bravery. But even as I cheered for him, a nagging sense of foreboding settled in my stomach.

"Okay, here goes nothing," Ethan said, reaching for his phone again. He hesitated for a brief moment before pressing the call button.

The phone rang, each tone echoing in the silence, amplifying the weight of the moment. I held my breath, heart racing as I imagined the conversation that was about to unfold. Would Cassie understand? Would she fight for what they had, or would she dismiss him, angry and hurt?

"Hey, Cassie," Ethan began, his voice steady despite the fluttering in his chest. "Can we talk? It's important."

I leaned against the desk, listening intently, my pulse quickening as I tried to read his expression. The frown that settled on his features didn't bode well, and I felt a knot tighten in my stomach.

"Yeah, I know we've been busy...," he continued, his brow furrowing deeper. "But it's something I need to discuss face-to-face."

A tense silence stretched out as he listened, his eyes darting to mine, silently pleading for reassurance. I offered a supportive nod, though I felt the weight of uncertainty hanging heavily between us.

"I understand, but please... just give me a chance to explain," he urged, desperation creeping into his tone. "I care about you, but I've been feeling like I'm living a life I didn't choose."

The line crackled, and the tension ratcheted up as he took a deep breath, preparing to lay his heart bare. But just as he opened his mouth to continue, the door swung open with a loud bang, causing us both to jump.

Cassie stood in the doorway, her face a mask of confusion and anger. "Ethan, what's going on? I thought we were supposed to—"

The words died on her lips as she took in the scene before her. Ethan's phone still pressed against his ear, and me standing uncomfortably close, tension radiating from both of us like heat from an open flame.

"What is this?" she demanded, her eyes narrowing as she crossed her arms defiantly. "What are you two talking about?"

I could see the shift in Ethan's expression, a mixture of fear and determination flickering across his face. In that instant, it felt as if the air had been sucked from the room, leaving behind a palpable tension that crackled with unresolved feelings.

"Cassie, I was just about to tell you—" Ethan started, but she cut him off.

"I don't want to hear excuses," she snapped, her voice sharp. "You're being weird, and I don't like it. Are you hiding something from me?"

Ethan's gaze darted between Cassie and me, and I could feel the weight of the world resting on his shoulders as he struggled to find the right words. "No, it's not like that—"

But Cassie wasn't having any of it. "Then what is it?"

The tension in the room surged, my heart racing as I realized we were standing on the precipice of something monumental, something that could change the course of all our lives. I felt like an intruder in a scene that was spiraling out of control.

"Cassie, please," Ethan said, his voice calm but firm. "Let me explain."

"Explain what? That you're having secret meetings with her?" she shot back, gesturing between us.

"Cassie, it's not like that at all! You have to believe me!"

The fight was in her eyes, and I sensed the storm brewing as her emotions shifted, the air thickening with unspoken accusations. I wanted to intervene, to soothe the chaos spiraling around us, but I knew this was Ethan's moment.

He took a step closer to her, vulnerability etched into his features. "I need you to understand that I care about you, but I also have to be honest with myself. I don't want to pretend anymore."

The silence that followed was deafening, each second stretching out like an eternity. I could see Cassie's expression falter as reality sank in, her defenses momentarily crumbling.

"What do you mean?" she whispered, confusion creeping into her voice.

"Cassie, I'm torn between what you want and what I want. And I've realized that I can't keep living for someone else," Ethan confessed, his voice filled with raw honesty.

As her expression shifted, I felt a rush of emotions surge through me—fear for Ethan, sympathy for Cassie, and a profound sense of uncertainty about what would happen next. Would Cassie lash out in anger, or would she surprise us both with understanding?

But just as the tension seemed to reach a breaking point, Ethan's phone buzzed loudly, drawing all eyes to the screen. A message flashed across the display, and I could see Ethan's face drain of color.

"I... I need to take this," he stammered, stepping back from Cassie, panic flickering in his eyes.

The room seemed to tilt as I held my breath, realizing that this unexpected interruption could very well change everything. The air crackled with unspoken words and unresolved feelings, and as Ethan turned away to read the message, I knew we were all standing on the brink of something monumental.

The moment hung in the balance, and I had no idea how it would all unfold.

# Chapter 21: "The Breaking Point"

The air was thick with the scent of caramel apples and cinnamon, wafting through the town square like a sweet embrace. Strings of twinkling lights crisscrossed above us, illuminating the jubilant faces of friends and families gathered to celebrate the annual Harvest Festival. Laughter echoed against the backdrop of a folk band strumming cheerful melodies, yet my heart was ensnared by a somber thread that tugged insistently, reminding me of the void where Cassie should have stood.

I scanned the crowd, feeling like a ghost wandering among the living. Couples twirled under the star-studded sky, their movements fluid and carefree, while I stood at the edge, my feet rooted in a disconcerting reality that dulled the colors of the celebration. Each peal of laughter felt like a staccato note in a symphony, harsh against the longing that blossomed in my chest. Cassie had opted out of the festivities, citing exhaustion and a desire for solitude, but I suspected there was more—an unspoken chasm growing between us, fraught with jealousy and unaddressed grievances.

As I stood there, a glass of apple cider clutched in my hand, I felt a familiar warmth envelop me. Ethan appeared, his smile as bright as the lights overhead, and for a moment, the world seemed to realign. "You look like you need rescuing," he said, his eyes sparkling with mischief. He extended his hand, and I found myself slipping my fingers into his, the connection igniting a flicker of hope amidst the uncertainty.

We moved to the center of the square, where couples danced with abandon, spinning under the soft glow of lanterns. I let Ethan guide me, our bodies swaying in unison, and for the first time that night, I allowed myself to indulge in the moment. The music wrapped around us like a cozy blanket, momentarily soothing the unease that lingered just beneath the surface. "Isn't this magical?" I asked, trying to infuse enthusiasm into my voice.

Ethan nodded, his gaze unwavering. "It's perfect, just like you." His words floated between us, heavy with implications I wasn't ready to confront. I caught a glimpse of the townsfolk enjoying the festivities, their laughter a stark reminder of what I was missing. A part of me longed to dissolve into that happiness, to forget the weight of unspoken words that clung to me like a second skin.

But then, amidst the melody of joy, a voice cut through the ambiance, sharper than any knife. "Homewrecker." The term lingered in the air, swirling around me like a cloud of smoke. I turned, searching for the source, my heart pounding in my chest. My mind raced with the implications of that single word, the accusation that held the power to unravel everything.

Ethan must have noticed the shift in my demeanor. "What's wrong?" he asked, concern etching lines across his forehead. I swallowed hard, feeling the sting of tears threatening to spill. The laughter around us faded into a distant hum, replaced by the relentless drum of my heartbeat.

"Did you hear that?" I whispered, not sure if I was more shocked by the insult or the recognition that it struck a chord. "What are they even talking about?"

He paused, searching my face for answers. "Ignore them," he said, squeezing my hand gently. "People will say anything to create drama."

But the reassurance fell flat. I felt the walls of my resolve start to crumble, the foundation of my courage cracking beneath the weight of scrutiny. I had tried to be strong, to weather the storm of gossip that had swirled around me since Cassie had pulled away, but now, I felt exposed, raw, as if everyone was watching me unravel.

The music shifted, and the couples around us twirled with renewed vigor. I wanted to join them, to lose myself in the moment and forget the world beyond this square, but the laughter felt hollow now, a bitter reminder of what I had lost. I glanced at Ethan, hoping for something—understanding, support, maybe even a distraction. Instead, I saw concern etched deeply on his features.

"Why don't we step away for a minute?" he suggested, his voice low and soothing, as if he could sense the turmoil churning within me. I nodded, grateful for the escape, and together we slipped away from the dance floor, seeking refuge beneath the protective canopy of an oak tree that had stood sentinel over the festival for decades.

Once we were out of the crowd's gaze, the atmosphere shifted. The laughter became a muffled echo, and the warmth of the lights above felt like a cocoon. I leaned against the tree, my fingers tracing the rough bark as I struggled to articulate the whirlwind of emotions roiling inside me. "I didn't choose this, you know," I said, my voice barely a whisper, thick with the weight of my frustration. "I didn't ask for this mess."

Ethan stepped closer, his presence both comforting and confounding. "I know," he said gently, his tone laced with empathy. "But you can't let their words define you. You're more than what they say."

"Am I?" I retorted, my voice rising as I felt the anger bubble to the surface. "Because it feels like I'm just a plot twist in someone else's story. Cassie's my best friend, and now everyone thinks I'm the villain."

His eyes softened, and I could see the battle raging behind them. "You're not a villain, you're... complicated. We all are." He stepped closer, the space between us shrinking as he captured my gaze. "And it's okay to be messy. It's okay to feel lost."

But as those words hung between us, the tension crackled like electricity, igniting something deep within me. I took a deep breath, trying to steady myself against the tumult of emotions. "But it doesn't feel okay, Ethan. It feels like I'm standing on a precipice, and any misstep could send me tumbling over the edge."

His expression shifted, a mix of resolve and something unnamable flickering in his eyes. "Then let's find our footing together. You don't have to face this alone." The sincerity in his voice sent a shiver down my spine, and for a moment, I allowed myself to believe him. Yet, doubt gnawed at the edges of my hope.

And just like that, the air was charged with an unspoken promise, the space between us trembling with possibilities. But before I could voice my thoughts, the distant sound of laughter morphed into a shout, pulling our attention back to the festival. The atmosphere was shifting once more, the carefree joy replaced by a tangible tension that crackled in the air. My heart sank, realizing that whatever we had just begun to explore was about to be tested.

A sudden burst of laughter echoed from the festival as a group of children dashed past us, their arms laden with sticky candy and glittering trinkets, oblivious to the undercurrents of tension swirling around. I glanced at Ethan, whose face was a mixture of concern and determination. "You know, I'd never take you for the type to let a couple of whispers get to you," he remarked, trying to inject a lightness into the moment. But the playful tone felt strained, almost as if we were both acting out roles in a drama we hadn't agreed to perform.

"Let's just say my patience is wearing thin," I replied, folding my arms tightly across my chest, hoping to shield my vulnerability. The swirling lights above seemed to mock me, twinkling with a joy that felt out of reach. "Maybe I'm just not cut out for this small-town drama."

Ethan studied me for a moment, the corners of his mouth curling in a hint of a smile. "Oh, come on. You're made for this. You're like the lead in a rom-com who doesn't realize she's in a rom-com until the last act." He leaned against the rough bark of the oak tree, his posture relaxed, a stark contrast to the tumult in my heart.

"Maybe I don't want to be the lead," I shot back, a smirk tugging at my lips despite the heaviness in my chest. "What if I just want to be the quirky best friend who gives sage advice and then rides off into the sunset on her own?"

"Trust me, you're far too compelling for that role. Besides," he said, his voice dipping conspiratorially, "you know how that goes—quirky best friends often end up with someone unexpectedly charming."

My heart raced, but the thought of Cassie's potential response to our interaction sent a chill through me. "We both know that unexpected charm leads to complications," I murmured, trying to steer the conversation away from the electric tension between us.

Before he could respond, a ruckus erupted from the festival. A shrill voice cut through the music, slicing the evening air like a serrated knife. "I can't believe you'd even show your face here!" A woman stood a few yards away, hands on her hips, glaring at someone I couldn't quite see. The crowd around her began to shift, curiosity piqued, the atmosphere thickening with anticipation.

Ethan stiffened beside me. "Is that Jenna?" he asked, his tone low and guarded. I squinted through the mass of bodies, spotting a figure that could only be Cassie's ex-boyfriend. A sense of dread coiled in my stomach, and I wondered if Cassie was about to step into the spotlight for an impromptu scene that promised no happy ending.

"I thought he was in another town," I whispered, my heart sinking. "This isn't good."

Ethan's jaw tightened as he caught my gaze, determination etched into his features. "Whatever happens, stay close to me." His grip on my hand tightened, and I nodded, even though the very idea of confronting a potential showdown filled me with trepidation.

As the crowd parted, Jenna's voice rang out again, sharper this time. "Do you think you can just waltz back into town after everything? You think you have any right to be here, knowing what you did?" The weight of her words struck me like a physical blow, leaving me reeling.

I glanced up at Ethan, who looked as if he were grappling with a storm inside him. "This isn't about you," he murmured, barely audible over the noise. "Just breathe."

But it was hard to breathe when the air crackled with accusations and the specter of Cassie loomed large. I had tried to stay out of her drama, but here I was, smack in the middle of it, feeling the heat of judgment searing into my skin. What if Cassie heard Jenna's words? What if the fragile thread of our friendship frayed beyond repair?

"Hey!" I shouted, the adrenaline igniting a flicker of bravery. Jenna's eyes narrowed, surprised by my interjection. "This isn't about any of us. Why don't you take your anger and drama elsewhere?" I felt Ethan's hand tighten around mine, but it wasn't enough to drown out the rush of blood pounding in my ears.

"You think you can defend her?" Jenna sneered, stepping closer. "You really think you're some knight in shining armor? News flash—she doesn't deserve it. You don't know what she's done."

"Neither do you," I shot back, my voice steadier than I felt. "So why don't you try listening for a change instead of assuming the worst?" The crowd murmured, eyes darting between us like spectators at a tennis match.

"Really? You're going to defend her?" Jenna laughed, a sound devoid of humor. "That's rich coming from someone who's played the part of the best friend. What's next? Are you going to take the fall for her, too?"

Before I could reply, the familiar figure of Cassie materialized at the edge of the crowd, her eyes wide, reflecting the chaos unfolding before her. "What's going on?" she called out, her voice cutting through the tension like a lifeline.

I felt a rush of conflicting emotions. Relief flooded me at her arrival, but dread followed closely behind. She approached us slowly, and for a moment, time hung suspended in the air, heavy with unspoken words. The festival lights glimmered around us, but they felt distant, as if they were part of another world.

"Cassie," I said, my voice softer now. "I—"

"Just stop," she interrupted, stepping forward, her gaze darting between Jenna and me. "What did I miss?"

Jenna seized the moment, her eyes gleaming with malicious delight. "Oh, just your best friend sticking up for you while I remind everyone of the truth," she spat, arms flailing dramatically. "She's the homewrecker here, not me. Or have you forgotten?"

Cassie's expression shifted, confusion morphing into something deeper. "What do you mean?" Her tone was tinged with disbelief, and I felt my heart plummet as her gaze locked onto mine, searching for reassurance. "Is this true?"

"It's not like that," I said, struggling to find the right words, but each syllable felt like it weighed a ton. "I swear I didn't mean to—"

"Enough!" Cassie snapped, her voice breaking through the tumult. "You don't get to twist this into something it's not, Jenna." The firmness in her voice surprised me, a spark of the fierce friend I had known rising to the surface. "You don't get to dictate our stories."

Jenna faltered, clearly unprepared for Cassie's sudden defiance. "But everyone thinks—"

"I don't care what everyone thinks!" Cassie shot back, her eyes blazing. "What matters is what I know, and I'm not about to let you rewrite my life for your drama. I've had enough."

Ethan's grip on my hand relaxed slightly, and I could see the pride gleaming in his gaze. My heart swelled, filled with a mixture of hope and dread. Perhaps this was the turning point we all needed—a chance to reclaim our narrative.

As Jenna opened her mouth, clearly ready to launch another attack, I stepped forward. "No more. This stops now. We're not going to let you tear us apart, Jenna. We're stronger than your words."

The words were a declaration, a promise made not just to Cassie but to myself. The evening might be rife with conflict, but in this moment, I felt an undeniable sense of unity forming between us, a thread connecting our hearts and reminding us that we could confront the storm together.

"Let's get out of here," Cassie said, her voice steadier now, resolving to break free from the chaos. "We can't let this define us."

Ethan nodded in agreement, pulling me closer as if to fortify our connection. The lights above twinkled like stars, but the world around us felt brightening, igniting a flicker of hope in the dim shadows that had threatened to engulf us. Together, we turned our backs on the turmoil, stepping away from the whirlwind of whispers and accusations, ready to carve our own path, one that would lead us back to the light.

As we moved away from the chaos, the festival's laughter faded into a muffled backdrop, leaving behind a tenuous peace that felt both liberating and fragile. Cassie walked beside me, her brow furrowed, the sparkle in her eyes dimmed by the confrontation that had just unfolded. I could see the internal battle she was fighting—a mix of hurt and defiance battling for dominance.

"Did I hear Jenna correctly?" she asked, her voice low, laced with disbelief. "Did she really just say that about you?"

"I didn't want you to find out like this," I confessed, guilt seeping into my voice. "I was trying to protect you."

Her eyes softened, and for a moment, the weight of our shared history hovered between us like a fragile thread. "Protect me? Or yourself? Because it feels like we've been tiptoeing around this for too long. I deserve to know what people are saying, even if it's painful."

I sighed, the truth heavy on my chest. "I thought if I kept my head down, maybe it would blow over. I didn't want to add fuel to the fire."

Cassie chuckled dryly, shaking her head as if dismissing the absurdity of our situation. "Fuel? We're practically dousing ourselves in gasoline at this point. Do you really think avoiding the truth is going to fix anything?"

The fiery determination in her tone ignited something in me. "You're right. I shouldn't have tried to shield you. But it's not just about us anymore. It's about Ethan, too. He didn't ask for any of this."

Her gaze flicked to where Ethan lingered at the edge of the crowd, his expression a mix of concern and frustration. "And what about you? Are you ready to be part of this drama, or do you want to step back?"

"I don't know," I admitted, running a hand through my hair, feeling the weight of uncertainty settle like a thick fog. "But I do know that I care about you, and I care about him. I just wish we could find a way to be honest without tearing everything apart."

Cassie studied me for a moment, her eyes searching mine for something—reassurance, perhaps. "Honesty doesn't have to mean destruction. It can mean healing, too."

Before I could respond, Ethan approached us, his brow knitted with worry. "Hey, is everything okay?" His voice was steady, but the way he looked at me told a different story; it was a mix of concern and urgency, as if he sensed the tension that still lingered like smoke in the air.

"Just a little chat about... everything," I said, my voice faltering slightly. "Jenna made it clear that people have opinions, and we're all caught in the crossfire."

He nodded, his expression resolute. "Then let's face it together. We can't let them dictate our lives. Whatever this is, we need to decide what we want." His eyes darted between Cassie and me, and I could see the gears turning in his mind. "We can't keep pretending we're okay if we're not."

I wanted to believe that facing our problems together would bring clarity, but the doubts danced just beneath the surface. "But what if that only makes things worse? What if it costs us everything?"

"Sometimes you have to risk it all to gain what you truly want," Ethan replied, his voice firm. "And right now, we're all on the brink of something. Let's not step back into the shadows."

His words hung in the air, a challenge wrapped in a plea. I felt a flicker of resolve igniting within me. "Okay. But we need to do this the right way. No drama, just honesty."

As I spoke, I could see Cassie processing the weight of our choices, the ramifications swirling like a tempest in her mind. "Are we really ready for this?" she finally asked, her voice small yet steady. "Because once we confront the truth, there's no turning back."

I glanced at Ethan, who nodded, his eyes resolute. "We're ready. Together."

With that agreement, we moved through the festival, the sounds of celebration now more like a distant memory than a present reality. The air was thick with the scents of roasted corn and freshly baked pies, but the sweetness was overshadowed by the uncertainty we carried.

"Let's find a quieter spot," I suggested, hoping to escape the prying eyes of the crowd and the relentless gossip that seemed to lurk behind every corner. Cassie and Ethan fell in step beside me, and as we walked, I could feel the weight of our intentions settling around us like a cloak, wrapping us in a shared resolve.

We made our way to the edge of the festival, where the twinkling lights faded into the shadows of the trees lining the park. The distant music was muffled now, replaced by the soft rustling of leaves in the gentle breeze. Here, surrounded by nature, we paused, allowing the serenity to settle our nerves.

"Okay," I began, taking a deep breath to steady myself. "We need to lay everything on the table. No secrets, no half-truths."

Cassie nodded, her expression serious. "I'll go first, then. I've felt like I've been losing control of my life ever since the breakup. Everyone expects me to just bounce back, but I'm not sure how to move forward." Her voice wavered, the vulnerability cracking through her usual bravado. "And now with you and Ethan... I just—"

"Cassie, stop." I stepped closer, placing a hand on her shoulder. "You don't have to feel pressured to move on just because everyone else expects it. We're all dealing with this in our own ways."

Ethan cleared his throat, drawing our attention. "I've been trying to be there for both of you, but I feel like I'm being pulled in two directions. I care about you both, but it's hard when the stakes keep rising."

A tension hung in the air, thick and palpable. "You can't be the glue holding us together," I reminded him gently. "We need to support each other without relying on you as our crutch."

"Agreed," Cassie added, a hint of relief breaking through her serious facade. "We need to lean on one another but also figure out who we are without each other's influences clouding our judgment."

"Right," I said, the weight of our conversation settling heavily on my shoulders. "So what do we do now? How do we face the world without letting it tear us apart?"

Before anyone could respond, a sudden commotion erupted from the festival, the laughter and music drowning out our carefully constructed moment. I turned, scanning the crowd to see what had sparked the sudden shift in energy.

A crowd had gathered near the center of the square, and shouts echoed through the night air, rising in volume. "Get back! Call the police!" someone shouted, panic threading through the words.

My heart raced as I exchanged worried glances with Ethan and Cassie. "What's happening?" I asked, my voice barely above a whisper, an unsettling fear creeping into my chest.

"I don't know," Ethan replied, urgency lining his features. "But it can't be good."

Without a second thought, we rushed toward the crowd, adrenaline surging as we wove our way through the throngs of people. As we drew closer, I could see faces filled with shock, eyes wide as they gaped at the scene unfolding before us.

And then, as we broke through the last line of spectators, my breath caught in my throat. There, at the center of the chaos, was Jenna, her face pale, pointing frantically at a figure sprawled on the ground. "Someone call an ambulance!" she screamed, the fear in her voice slicing through the air like a knife.

In that moment, everything shifted—the laughter, the lights, the festival itself became a blur. My heart raced, and a new reality began to take shape around us. I felt Cassie grip my arm tightly, her expression a mix of disbelief and horror.

As the crowd surged, I could barely make out the figure lying motionless beneath the stars, but the dread pooling in my stomach told me all I needed to know. We were no longer just facing whispers and judgment; we were staring into the abyss, the consequences of our choices spilling out before us, and it was clear—nothing would ever be the same again.

# Chapter 22: "Rebuilding Trust"

The air was thick with the scent of fresh paint and laughter as I entered the community center, a place that had transformed into my sanctuary over the past few weeks. Each morning, the sun spilled through the large windows, illuminating the vibrant murals painted by local artists—children's drawings of fantastical creatures and landscapes of dreams. The laughter of kids echoed in the hallways, a melodious reminder of the joy I had yearned to feel again. I volunteered not just to keep busy, but to rebuild the fragments of my life that felt scattered, like autumn leaves caught in a gust of wind.

As I maneuvered through the bustling crowd, a sense of purpose ignited within me. I had always been the planner, the one with a perfectly curated schedule, but life had shifted so dramatically since the festival. Now, I welcomed the unpredictability, savoring the spontaneous bursts of creativity that filled each day. I spent hours organizing activities, setting up art stations, and helping with the younger children, their faces lighting up with excitement as they smeared paint across canvas like they were magicians casting spells.

It was during one of these afternoons that I spotted Cassie, standing on the edge of the playground, her silhouette framed by the golden rays of the sun. She watched the children with a softness in her eyes that reminded me of the girl I had once known—full of dreams and laughter, unguarded and open. My heart twisted with the memories of our friendship, the bond we had forged through late-night talks and shared secrets. Yet, I felt a chasm between us, an invisible wall built from misunderstandings and unspoken words.

Taking a deep breath, I approached her. "Hey," I said, my voice barely above a whisper. She turned, her surprise evident, and for a heartbeat, we stood there, two lost souls on either side of a vast ocean of unresolved tension.

"Hi," she replied, a hint of uncertainty dancing in her tone. "I didn't expect to see you here."

"I've been volunteering," I offered, hoping to ease the atmosphere. "Trying to help out where I can. I figured it might help me, too."

Cassie studied me for a moment, her gaze piercing yet cautious. "That's great. The kids love having you around."

"Do you need help with the charity event next month?" I ventured, sensing the opportunity to bridge the gap between us. "I'd love to pitch in."

A flicker of warmth crossed her features, but she quickly masked it. "I guess we could use more hands. It's going to be a big one."

The prospect of working together felt like an olive branch, and as we began to plan, I could feel the walls slowly crumbling. Each idea we exchanged, each laugh shared, felt like a step toward rebuilding a trust that had been shattered. Cassie's laughter, though tinged with hesitance, began to weave itself into the tapestry of my days, wrapping me in a comfort I had sorely missed.

In the evenings, I'd return home, heart lighter but mind still heavy with reflection. Ethan was often absorbed in his architectural sketches, the lines and angles spilling across the paper like rivers of thought. His focus was both a comfort and a reminder of the distance between us. The walls of our shared home held their own memories—echoes of arguments and silences that hung in the air like thick fog.

One evening, I plopped down beside him, glancing at the intricate designs sprawled before us. "You're really good at this," I said, nudging his shoulder. "These buildings could change the skyline."

He looked at me, surprise flickering in his deep-set eyes. "You think so?"

"Absolutely," I replied, my sincerity weaving warmth between us. "Your vision can uplift this community."

Ethan's expression softened, the lines of worry easing from his brow. "Thanks. I've been trying to focus on that. It feels good to put my energy into something positive."

Our conversation meandered into the night, a gentle easing of the tension that had clouded our interactions. I shared my experiences at the community center, and in return, he opened up about his aspirations, his dreams entwined with the hopes of those around him.

But beneath the surface of our discussions lay a current of unresolved feelings. Each time I felt a sense of closeness, a flicker of intimacy, the memory of our past mistakes loomed over us like a specter, reminding me that trust wasn't easily rebuilt. It required time, patience, and an unyielding commitment to forge ahead, together.

The weeks slid by like the changing seasons, and I found myself looking forward to every moment spent with Cassie. We shared laughter over paint splatters, strategized over event planning, and conspired with the kids to create a surprise for the charity event. Each shared secret was a brick in the bridge we were reconstructing, but it wasn't without its obstacles.

One afternoon, as we were setting up a crafts station, Cassie turned serious, her expression shifting like shadows in the late afternoon sun. "Can I ask you something?"

"Of course," I replied, my heart racing.

"Do you think we can really fix what happened between us?"

Her question hung in the air, heavy with the weight of our history. I could feel the ache in my chest, the fear of losing her all over again. "I believe we can," I answered, my voice steady. "But it's going to take time and honesty. No more hiding."

She nodded, a soft smile breaking through the tension. "I want that, too."

As the sun dipped below the horizon, casting a golden hue across the playground, I knew we were on the brink of something beautiful, a new beginning woven from the threads of our past. Together, we would learn to trust again, to laugh freely, and to rediscover the magic that had once connected us. With each moment, we moved closer to healing the wounds of yesterday, building a future filled with possibility.

The rhythm of the community center had become a comforting soundtrack to my days, each burst of laughter from the children, each squeal of delight at a newly crafted project, weaving a tapestry of hope. I found solace in this vibrant chaos, a welcome distraction from the uncertainty of my own life. With Cassie, our tentative reconnection blossomed into something more profound, a fragile yet resilient friendship slowly taking root like the spring flowers that dared to bloom in defiance of a lingering winter.

As we worked side by side, our shared tasks transformed into something akin to a dance—an easy back-and-forth that reminded me of the old days. While organizing supplies for the upcoming charity event, I often caught Cassie's eye, and the corners of her lips would lift in a smile, sparking something warm inside me. There was a lightness in the air, an unspoken understanding that we were both invested in rebuilding not just our friendship, but also ourselves.

"Did you ever think about what we could do with the kids for the talent show?" Cassie asked one afternoon, her hands busy threading beads onto a colorful bracelet.

"Absolutely!" I replied, excitement bubbling up as I contemplated the possibilities. "What if we got them to perform a group dance? Kids love to show off their moves."

Cassie laughed, her voice a melodic chime that danced through the air. "I can just picture them—chaotic little whirlwinds on stage, leaving a trail of glitter and confetti in their wake."

I grinned, envisioning a whirlwind of tiny feet, all competing for attention and joy. "And the inevitable chaos of parents trying to catch it all on their phones. It'll be beautiful."

We tossed around ideas like children trading marbles, each suggestion building upon the last, and for the first time in a long while, I felt the shadows of our past begin to dissipate, replaced by the glow of potential.

As the weeks rolled on, the charity event loomed closer, and with it, the challenge of reconciling the remnants of the past. One evening, Cassie and I huddled over a table scattered with flyers and colorful markers. The scent of fresh ink filled the air, mixing with the faint aroma of the takeout we'd ordered from our favorite local diner.

"Okay, Miss Artistic Genius, what do you think of this slogan?" I said, holding up a flyer adorned with vibrant colors and overly ambitious lettering. "Let's get together for a cause!"

Cassie squinted, her lips pursed in mock contemplation. "Well, it sounds like we're inviting people to a barbecue, not a charity event."

I burst out laughing, and it felt like the weight of the world lifted off my shoulders. "Fair point! How about, 'Join Us in Changing Lives!'"

She considered this, tapping her finger against her chin. "Still a bit too formal. How about 'Let's Spark Some Joy!'? It feels more... us."

"Us?" I echoed, raising an eyebrow. "Since when do we spark joy? I thought we were all about the emotional rollercoaster."

Cassie smirked, the mischief dancing in her eyes. "Maybe we can combine the two. 'Join Us to Spark Joy and Navigate the Emotional Rollercoaster of Life!'"

"Now that's a slogan," I replied, chuckling. "We'll either draw in a crowd or scare everyone away. Either way, it'll be memorable."

With laughter ringing in our ears, the evening transformed into one of those moments that clings to your heart. We worked late into the night, sharing stories, hopes, and fears like we were stitching a patchwork quilt of our lives. I spoke of my childhood dreams, the ones that seemed foolish in hindsight, and she shared her own, tinged with a bittersweet longing for the paths not taken.

Amidst the laughter and warmth, a moment of silence fell over us. Cassie's gaze turned introspective, the weight of our past evident in the shadows that flickered across her face. "Do you think we can ever really put everything behind us?"

I considered her question, the sincerity in her eyes pulling at my heart. "I want to believe we can," I said carefully, choosing my words as if they were precious gems. "But it won't be easy. Trust is delicate, like glass. It takes time to build back, but once it's cracked..."

"...it's hard to repair," she finished softly, her voice barely above a whisper.

Just then, Ethan entered the community center, his presence instantly grounding me. He carried a stack of papers, a look of determination etched across his face. "I thought I'd find you two here," he said, glancing at the chaos we'd created. "What's the theme for this shindig? 'Desperation'?"

I rolled my eyes, but couldn't suppress the grin that tugged at my lips. "We're working on something much more sophisticated. Right, Cassie?"

"Absolutely! We're going for 'Joyful Chaos,'" she declared, a mischievous spark igniting in her eyes.

Ethan raised an eyebrow, a smirk playing on his lips. "Sounds like you've got your work cut out for you."

As he leaned against the doorframe, arms crossed, I felt a familiar flutter of connection, yet the air between us was thick with unspoken words. I appreciated his playful banter, but there was something heavier lurking beneath the surface. A tension that whispered of the conversations we hadn't had, of the truths we were still dancing around.

"Actually, we could use your help," I said, tilting my head toward the papers in his hands. "You're an architect. Think you could design the layout for the event?"

Ethan's expression shifted, the teasing glimmer replaced by genuine interest. "You want me to build a stage for a bunch of kids to dance on? Challenge accepted."

Our eyes locked, and in that moment, I felt the familiar pull of the past weaving through my heart, reminding me of everything we had shared. But the specter of what we had lost lingered like smoke in the air, and I wondered if this collaboration was a step toward healing or merely a distraction from the deeper issues that simmered beneath the surface.

As the night wore on, laughter and creativity swirled around us like confetti in the wind, yet the uncertainty loomed, an uninvited guest at our table. I couldn't shake the feeling that while we were making progress with Cassie, the road ahead with Ethan would require navigating some treacherous terrain. Each moment was a reminder that we were all still learning to trust again, each other and ourselves.

The days melted into a rhythm of purpose, and the charity event was quickly becoming a whirlwind of excitement and creativity. Cassie and I were immersed in planning, her laughter blending seamlessly with the sound of children's voices. The playground buzzed with energy, and each little project we tackled together felt like adding another colorful stitch to a patchwork quilt of our mending friendship.

One evening, as we fine-tuned the details of the talent show, Cassie suggested we host a bake sale alongside it. "I mean, what's a community event without cookies? They're practically the currency of childhood," she said, wiggling her eyebrows in mock seriousness.

I couldn't help but laugh. "True! What if we turned the bake sale into a contest? The kids could compete for the best recipe, and we'd have a panel of judges."

"Oh, like a reality show!" Cassie's eyes sparkled with delight. "Imagine the drama—'The Great Bake Off: Playground Edition!'"

"Complete with secret ingredients and sabotage," I added with a grin. "I can see the headlines now: 'Cookie Wars at the Community Center!'"

As we shared a laugh, I couldn't shake the feeling that Cassie was starting to let her guard down. The barriers between us were fading like morning mist, and it felt exhilarating yet terrifying. We were rediscovering not just our friendship but also the essence of who we were before everything had turned upside down.

The day of the event arrived, and the community center was transformed into a festival of color and laughter. Banners waved in the light breeze, and the aroma of freshly baked goods wafted through the air like an inviting hug. Kids dashed around, their faces smeared with frosting and joy, and the atmosphere crackled with a tangible excitement that felt electric.

Ethan had designed a small stage in the center, a beautifully crafted platform where the children could perform their dances and skits. I marveled at his handiwork, the way he had managed to create a sense of warmth and support through his designs. He stood nearby, overseeing the setup, a proud smile lighting up his face as he watched the children prepare.

"Not bad for a bunch of cookie-crazed kids, huh?" he called out to me, his voice laced with playful challenge.

"Not bad at all! If I didn't know better, I'd say you were trying to steal the spotlight," I shot back, teasing him.

"Only if it means you'll join me up there to perform a duet," he countered, crossing his arms and raising an eyebrow, a charming smirk playing on his lips.

"Only if you promise not to step on my toes," I quipped, my heart racing at the thought of being so close to him again, our playful banter creating a delightful tension that hung in the air like a well-timed pause in a song.

As the event unfolded, Cassie and I moved through the crowd, helping kids prepare for their performances and cheering them on. The laughter was infectious, and with each passing moment, it felt as if we were weaving the threads of our friendship back together, tighter and stronger than before.

The first act began—two little girls, clad in glittery costumes, who launched into a dance routine that was a delightful blend of chaos and creativity. They twirled and stumbled, giggling through their missteps, and the audience erupted into applause. It was beautiful, an imperfect perfection that reminded me of the joy in embracing life's unpredictable moments.

I caught a glimpse of Cassie watching with pride, her eyes shining as she clapped along with the crowd. "They're incredible!" she shouted over the noise, her enthusiasm infectious.

"They remind me of us!" I replied, my heart swelling with warmth.

After a series of performances, it was time for the bake sale contest. The air buzzed with anticipation as the judges—Cassie, Ethan, and I—took our places at a makeshift table piled high with colorful pastries. The children lined up, each proudly presenting their creations with the kind of enthusiasm only kids could muster.

Cassie held up a lopsided cupcake, adorned with a precarious tower of sprinkles. "And what do we have here?" she asked, her voice playful.

"A masterpiece," the little girl declared, puffing out her chest, and I couldn't help but grin at her confidence.

I leaned in, "So, is there a secret ingredient, or is it just pure ambition?"

"Both!" she exclaimed, beaming at us. "And love!"

"Love? That's the most important ingredient!" Ethan chimed in, pretending to jot down notes. "I might have to borrow that for my next architectural project."

The children's laughter filled the air, a sweet melody of innocence and joy that enveloped us. As we tasted each entry, the competition grew fierce but friendly, the kids delighting in the praise and constructive critiques.

When it was time to announce the winners, I felt a swell of happiness, the kind that fills you to the brim and spills over. As we stood before the crowd, Cassie turned to me, her expression earnest. "I couldn't have done this without you. Thank you for being here."

My heart skipped a beat, the sincerity of her words hanging between us like a promise. "You've been the best part of this, Cassie. I'm so glad we're back together."

But just as we began to announce the winners, a commotion erupted from the side of the crowd. A shout rang out, sharp and piercing, cutting through the joy like a knife. "Stop! You can't do this!"

We turned to see a figure pushing through the throng, a familiar face marred by anger. It was my ex, Alex, his eyes wild, and I felt the ground shift beneath me. The laughter and applause faded into a dull roar as he stepped forward, the confrontation looming like a storm cloud.

"What are you doing here?" I asked, my heart racing as I took a step back, uncertainty flooding my veins.

"I came to talk to you," he snapped, his gaze darting around the scene. "This isn't what you think it is."

Cassie stepped beside me, a protective stance forming as she glared at him. "You shouldn't be here, Alex. Not now."

His eyes narrowed, scanning the crowd as if looking for something—or someone. "You're all just playing pretend. You don't know what you're getting into."

The air thickened with tension, and I felt the blood rush in my ears, a mix of confusion and fear swirling inside me. I had been rebuilding my life, piece by piece, and now, just as things felt like they were coming together, the ground shifted beneath my feet once more.

"Leave. Just leave," I demanded, my voice shaking but resolute.

But he took another step closer, the intensity of his presence suffocating, a reminder of everything I had tried to escape. "You need to listen to me. This isn't over."

As my heart raced, I glanced at Cassie and Ethan, their faces a blend of concern and determination. The laughter around us faded, the vibrant atmosphere dissolving into a tense silence, all eyes on the unfolding drama. In that moment, I knew I had a choice to make—a choice that could redefine everything.

"Stop it!" I shouted, my voice rising above the tension, the truth of my heart spilling out. "I'm not going back. Not now, not ever."

But even as the words left my mouth, I felt the weight of the moment, the uncertainty of what lay ahead. With every beat of my heart, I sensed the precariousness of my newfound strength. I was ready to fight for my future, but as Alex's presence loomed large, the question hung in the air: Would it be enough?

# Chapter 23: "The Heart of the Matter"

With each footfall echoing against the polished linoleum of the community center, I felt the weight of anticipation pressing against my chest. This place had seen countless meetings, events, and moments of laughter, yet today, the atmosphere crackled with a different kind of electricity. The scent of freshly brewed coffee hung in the air, mingling with the faint aroma of paint from the art classes taking place in the adjacent room. I could almost taste the bittersweet tang of our shared past, a potent reminder of everything that had led us to this point.

Cassie arrived first, her expression a mix of determination and uncertainty. Her fiery auburn hair, usually a symbol of her vivacity, fell loosely around her shoulders, framing her face like a halo that, on this day, seemed to obscure her usual radiance. She glanced at me, and I offered a reassuring nod, hoping it would anchor her in the storm of emotions swirling around us.

"Are you ready for this?" she asked, her voice barely above a whisper, yet it resonated with the gravity of her fears.

"Ready as I'll ever be," I replied, my own heart thumping a frantic rhythm in my chest.

Cassie shifted in her seat, her fingers playing with the edge of the tablecloth, tracing patterns as if trying to weave together a safety net. The door swung open with a creak, revealing Ethan, his tall frame silhouetted against the bright hallway lights. He stepped inside, a hesitant smile playing on his lips, but the warmth of it never reached his eyes. There was a lingering tension in the air, a chasm that felt insurmountable, yet here we were, determined to bridge it.

"Hey, sorry I'm late," he said, his voice casual, almost too casual for the weight of the moment. "Traffic was a nightmare."

I could see the slight tremor in his hands, the way his fingers fidgeted with the edge of his jacket as if it were a lifeline. "No problem," I said, gesturing for him to join us at the round table. "We've got some things to discuss."

Ethan settled into the chair opposite us, his gaze shifting between Cassie and me, the weight of unspoken words hanging heavily in the air. The fluorescent lights overhead buzzed, adding an unsettling backdrop to our fragile atmosphere.

Cassie broke the silence, her voice quivering with emotion. "Ethan, I've been feeling... lost. I'm scared of losing you both. I don't want to fight anymore."

Her words struck a chord deep within me. I shared her fears, but it was crucial we said them aloud, like casting away shadows with light. "We're a family, Ethan. We've always been more than just friends. We've built something real, something worth fighting for," I interjected, hoping my voice carried the conviction I felt.

Ethan's brows knitted together, his expression pensive. "I know, and that's why this is so hard. I don't want to hurt either of you. But I feel like I've been caught in the middle, like I'm losing you both at once."

"None of us wants that," I said, frustration creeping into my tone. "But we can't keep avoiding the heart of the matter. We need to face what's tearing us apart."

The air between us thickened, charged with unspoken grievances and long-held hopes. It was as if we were three lost souls stranded on a desert island, each of us clutching onto our fears like driftwood, afraid to let go and find a way home.

Cassie leaned in, her eyes glistening with unshed tears. "I want us to be honest. I need to know if you still care about us, Ethan. Because I do."

"Of course I care!" he blurted, the heat of his words a stark contrast to the coolness enveloping the room. "But caring doesn't solve anything. It doesn't make this any easier."

"Then let's make it easier," I urged, my heart racing. "Let's be vulnerable. Let's admit that we've all made mistakes. We can't rebuild if we're not willing to acknowledge what's broken."

A flicker of something—fear? Hope?—crossed Ethan's face, and for the first time, he looked truly uncertain. "I've never wanted to lose you both. I don't want to pick sides."

Cassie squeezed her hands together, her knuckles white against the table's surface. "It's not about picking sides. It's about finding a way to be together again. To heal."

I leaned forward, drawing the three of us into a tighter circle. "We can redefine our relationships, our expectations. But we have to be honest about what we want."

The honesty of the moment hung in the air, raw and unfiltered, and I felt the weight of our fears lifting just a little. As the minutes ticked by, we spoke—truly spoke—for the first time in what felt like ages. Each revelation, each shared laugh and tear, became a brick in the foundation we desperately needed to rebuild.

A warmth spread through me as we began to rediscover each other, the laughter weaving through our conversation like a vibrant thread. The path forward was not clear, but it was ours to navigate together. I felt the love between us rekindling, and for the first time in a long while, hope shimmered on the horizon, inviting us to step toward it.

The warmth in the room gradually transformed the charged atmosphere into something more akin to a sanctuary. The sun dipped low in the sky outside, casting a golden glow that danced through the windows, illuminating the flecks of dust swirling in the air like tiny stars caught in a cosmic embrace. The mood shifted subtly, and I could feel a fragile thread of connection weaving its way among us, binding our hearts in shared understanding.

Cassie took a deep breath, her exhale laced with a sense of newfound resolve. "Ethan, what do you want?" The question hung between us, a heavy yet necessary anchor. She leaned forward, her fingers now tracing intricate designs on the table. "Because I think we need to stop skirting around the truth. I don't want to waste time if you're not in this with us."

Ethan shifted in his chair, the wood creaking beneath him, and I could almost see the gears turning in his mind, wrestling with an answer. "It's not that simple," he replied, his voice low and contemplative. "I care about both of you, but sometimes I feel like I'm trying to keep two boats afloat while I'm drowning."

I exchanged a glance with Cassie, who looked like she was weighing her next words with the delicacy of a tightrope walker. "We can help you with that," I urged. "But we have to be honest about how we feel."

A flicker of doubt crossed Ethan's face, but he leaned back slightly, visibly contemplating our words. "I suppose… I just don't want to hurt you."

"Then don't," Cassie said firmly, her voice resolute. "We can only be hurt if we keep pretending everything is okay when it's not."

The truth of her statement hung in the air, a silent agreement between us, fragile yet electrifying. I could feel my heart racing, not out of fear, but exhilaration—this was the turning point we had desperately needed. The moment hung suspended, and for a heartbeat, the world outside ceased to exist, the petty troubles of life fading into the background as our conversation took center stage.

"You're right," Ethan finally admitted, his gaze dropping to the table. "I've been trying to keep the peace, but I'm tired of tiptoeing around everything."

"Then let's not tiptoe anymore," I encouraged, feeling a surge of hope rising within me. "Let's lay it all out on the table. What scares you the most?"

Ethan looked up, meeting my eyes with a mixture of vulnerability and determination. "What if we can't come back from this? What if I can't make you both happy?"

"Ethan, happiness is a team sport," I said with a wry smile. "It's not something you have to shoulder alone. We need each other to lift us up. Just like when we were kids, building that treehouse. It took all of us to get it done."

Cassie chuckled softly, the tension in her shoulders easing slightly. "You mean the one that collapsed under the weight of our dreams?"

"Exactly! But we rebuilt it, didn't we? We just learned to add a bit more support along the way."

Ethan chuckled, a genuine smile breaking through the cloud of anxiety that had shrouded his features. "Okay, okay. I see your point. But what happens when the dream shifts, when we start wanting different things?"

A ripple of silence enveloped us, each lost in thoughts of our individual dreams, the uncharted territories of our futures. I broke the silence, wanting to steer the conversation back toward the connection we had. "We adapt. We compromise. Life is fluid, after all, and so are our feelings."

Cassie nodded, her eyes sparkling with the embers of hope. "If we can embrace those changes together, then maybe it's not so daunting. It's just a new adventure."

"An adventure?" Ethan raised an eyebrow, skepticism etched on his face. "Are we really comparing our emotional turmoil to an amusement park ride?"

"Why not?" I leaned in, my enthusiasm bubbling over. "Life is full of twists and turns, unexpected drops that make your stomach lurch and your heart race. The key is to keep your hands up and scream together!"

With that, a laugh erupted from Ethan, a genuine sound that filled the space between us with warmth. "You know, you two are ridiculous."

Cassie chimed in, a playful smirk on her lips. "And yet, somehow, it's working."

The atmosphere transformed, our shared laughter breaking through the remaining tension. It felt like we were peeling back layers of fear, exposing something vibrant and raw beneath. I realized how much I had missed this—our connection, the laughter, the undeniable spark that ignited when we were all together.

As the conversation flowed, we began to share not only our fears but also our dreams. Cassie talked about her desire to start a community garden, a place where people could come together, share their stories, and grow something beautiful. "Imagine it," she said, her eyes lighting up. "A place filled with flowers and vegetables, a sanctuary of life amid the chaos."

"I can already see it," I chimed in. "Children running around, laughter echoing off the walls of the community center. It could become a hub for us."

Ethan smiled, his earlier worries momentarily forgotten. "You two really have a way of seeing the silver lining. I like that."

"Life's too short to dwell on the shadows," Cassie added, a new lightness in her voice. "We need to chase the sun, not hide from the clouds."

The conversation shifted back and forth, weaving through our lives, desires, and even some long-held grudges. We unearthed old memories, laughing about the time Ethan accidentally set fire to the BBQ or when Cassie dared me to jump into the lake in the dead of winter. Each story was a thread, stitching us closer together, weaving a fabric rich with history and shared experiences.

As we delved deeper, I felt the walls we had erected start to crumble. With each confession and shared laugh, the bond between us grew stronger, more resilient. The room, once thick with uncertainty, now pulsed with an undeniable energy—a promise of new beginnings.

With laughter and stories swirling around us like dandelion seeds caught in the wind, the atmosphere transformed into something lighter, filled with the promise of renewal. The warmth of the late afternoon sun streamed through the windows, bathing us in golden light that seemed to amplify our shared connection. I leaned back in my chair, a grin stretching across my face, savoring this moment of rediscovery. It felt as though we were all shedding our skin, each layer revealing a deeper understanding of one another.

But as the laughter faded, I sensed an undercurrent of tension still lurking beneath the surface. Ethan's brow furrowed again, the joviality that had briefly lit his eyes dimming slightly. "I appreciate what you both are saying," he began, his voice lowering, "but we're not out of the woods yet. We've only just scratched the surface of what's been festering."

"Fester sounds so...unpleasant," I replied, attempting to inject humor into the moment. "Can't we call it 'the blossoming of emotions' instead?"

Cassie rolled her eyes, a smile still tugging at her lips. "You know, I think we need to dig deeper. There are things we haven't addressed, wounds that still need healing."

"Agreed," I nodded, my tone shifting to match the seriousness of the conversation. "But how do we approach that without setting off fireworks?"

Ethan leaned forward, his hands clasped together as if in prayer. "I think we need to be brave enough to confront the real issues, even if it hurts. The longer we dance around them, the more explosive they become."

Cassie nodded, her expression earnest. "Like that time at the Fourth of July barbecue when you accidentally launched the fireworks straight at my mom's car?"

"Still sorry about that!" Ethan chuckled sheepishly, his humor returning for a moment. "I promise, no more dangerous pyrotechnics today."

"Let's hope!" I quipped, but I could feel a weight pressing against my chest. The laughter faded again as the reality of our conversation settled in.

Ethan cleared his throat, the levity dissolving into a serious tone. "Okay, let's talk about the elephant in the room. What about the feelings we've all been tiptoeing around?"

I exchanged a glance with Cassie, and I could see her concern mirrored in my expression. "You mean the love triangle?" I offered, attempting to mask my own uncertainty with humor.

"The tangled web of affection, more like it," Ethan replied, the seriousness in his eyes palpable. "I care about you both, and it's been weighing heavily on me. I don't want to hurt either of you, but I also can't ignore my feelings."

The words hung between us, heavy and charged, and a chill ran down my spine. This was the crux of our struggle, the truth that had been hiding beneath our laughter and stories. "What do you want, Ethan?" I asked, my voice steady yet trembling with the weight of my own question.

His gaze was piercing, the air thick with unspoken truths. "I want to find a way for all of us to be happy. But right now, I feel like I'm being torn in two. I need to know how you both feel about what's been happening between us."

Cassie inhaled sharply, her blue eyes sparkling with unspoken emotions. "I think we all feel the pull, Ethan. But can we make this work? Can we navigate a relationship that isn't confined to the boundaries we've always known?"

Ethan shifted in his seat, considering her words. "I don't know if there's a blueprint for this, but I'm willing to figure it out if you both are. But we need to communicate. No more hiding behind laughter."

"Agreed," I said, heart racing. "But there's also the fear that if we open this Pandora's box, we may unleash something we can't control."

Cassie nodded, her expression pensive. "That's true. But is it worse to never know what could be?"

Ethan's gaze softened. "What's the alternative? Living a lie? Just coasting along while pretending everything is fine? We're already too far into this to turn back now."

I felt the pull of the moment, the weight of our shared histories pressing down on me. "Then let's be brave," I said, feeling an unfamiliar surge of courage. "Let's dive into those emotions, raw and real. But if we're doing this, we need to promise each other to be honest about our feelings. No matter how difficult."

"Okay," Cassie said, her voice strong. "But we need ground rules. No assumptions. If something's bothering us, we say it, even if it's uncomfortable."

"Agreed," Ethan affirmed, the fire in his eyes igniting once more. "And no matter what, we remember our bond. It's what brought us together in the first place."

The moment settled, a tangible weight of commitment swirling in the air around us. With newfound resolve, we delved into the depths of our feelings, peeling back layers of uncertainty. We shared fears, dreams, and insecurities, our words weaving a rich tapestry of connection that felt both terrifying and exhilarating.

But just as the conversation began to settle into a rhythm, a loud bang reverberated through the community center, startling us. The sound echoed ominously, jolting our hearts into a frenzied beat.

"What was that?" Cassie exclaimed, her eyes wide with alarm.

"I don't know," I replied, rising from my seat. The echo of the noise bounced around the walls, mingling with our heightened emotions, sending a jolt of adrenaline coursing through me.

Ethan stood, too, his brow furrowed in concern. "Let's check it out."

We moved cautiously toward the door, our earlier discussions momentarily forgotten as curiosity and unease took hold. The world outside seemed eerily still, the vibrant life of the community center abruptly muted. I pushed the door open slowly, and a gust of wind swept in, carrying with it the unmistakable scent of smoke.

"What's happening?" Cassie whispered, her voice barely above a breath.

As we stepped into the hallway, the lights flickered ominously, plunging us into a half-light that felt unsettling. Just ahead, shadows danced against the walls, and a distant shout echoed through the corridor, sending a chill racing down my spine.

"Stay close," Ethan said, gripping my hand tightly as we pressed forward.

The air thickened with anticipation as we moved cautiously toward the source of the commotion. I could feel the pounding of my heart against my ribcage, a wild rhythm that mirrored the tension coiling within me.

Suddenly, a figure appeared at the far end of the hallway, silhouetted against the flickering lights. "Help! Someone's trapped!"

Our hearts raced in unison, the weight of the moment crashing down on us as we exchanged panicked glances. It was time to face not only the chaos unfolding around us but also the deeper complexities of our entangled lives.

# Chapter 24: "Embracing New Beginnings"

Winter settled over Evergreen Creek like a soft, white blanket, transforming the quaint town into a landscape straight from a storybook. The air, crisp and invigorating, was laced with the scent of pine and woodsmoke, while delicate flakes of snow danced lazily from the sky, settling upon the rooftops and covering the ground in a silvery sheen. It was as if nature itself had conspired to create a magical backdrop for our community's annual charity event at the center, where laughter and cheer floated through the air, mingling with the aroma of hot cocoa and spiced apple cider.

Inside the bustling hall, warm golden lights twinkled like stars, illuminating tables adorned with handcrafted decorations and gleaming with an array of baked goods that tempted every passerby. The hum of conversation was punctuated by bursts of laughter as neighbors mingled, their faces flushed with excitement and the kind of camaraderie that can only be fostered through shared efforts and mutual goodwill. Each corner of the room radiated joy, from the colorful banners strung overhead to the cheerful carolers harmonizing softly in the background, their voices weaving through the air like a gentle lullaby.

I stood near a table laden with gingerbread cookies, each one a tiny masterpiece of frosting and candy, when a familiar figure caught my eye. Ethan moved through the crowd with an easy grace, his dark hair tousled and his smile wide enough to brighten the dullest winter day. My heart fluttered, a wild bird trapped within a cage, and I felt an undeniable pull toward him. Our eyes met across the room, and in that instant, the noise faded into a soothing hum, allowing the warmth of our connection to fill the space between us.

As the evening unfolded, we worked side by side, organizing the donated gifts that would soon find their way to families in need. There was an effortless rhythm to our movements, a dance we had perfected over the months. Cassie, with her unquenchable energy and infectious laughter, flitted around us, her small hands busy wrapping gifts and teasing Ethan about his terrible knack for bow-tying. I couldn't help but chuckle at their playful banter, the dynamic that had grown between us forming a trio unlike any I had known.

With every shared smile and soft touch, the tension that had once hung heavy in the air began to dissolve. It was as if we had finally acknowledged the truth of our intertwined lives—the past struggles, the misunderstandings, and the heartache—allowing us to bask in the warmth of acceptance. And so, as the clock neared the hour for the final raffle drawing, Ethan took my hand, pulling me gently aside.

In the glow of twinkling lights, away from the laughter and chaos, he gazed deeply into my eyes, his expression serious yet tender. My heart raced as he spoke, each word spilling out like a whispered secret. "I love you," he confessed, his voice low and earnest, "and I promise to prioritize both you and Cassie. I want us to be a family, to navigate this life together, no matter what storms may come."

Tears brimmed in my eyes, blurring the festive lights into a kaleidoscope of colors. I had anticipated this moment, hoped for it in the quiet corners of my mind, but hearing it spoken aloud ignited a flame of joy within me that I thought had long since extinguished. "Ethan," I murmured, my voice trembling with emotion, "you have no idea how much that means to me."

Just then, Cassie appeared at our side, her cheeks rosy and her smile wide. She had been busy winning hearts at the cookie table, and her excitement was palpable. "What's going on over here?" she chirped, looking between us with innocent curiosity.

With a swift glance exchanged between Ethan and me, we both knew we could no longer hide the truth from her. "We were just talking about how much we love you, Cassie," Ethan replied, his tone light yet sincere.

She beamed, wrapping her small arms around us both, and the warmth of our embrace spread through me like a comforting blanket. "I love you guys too! We're the best team!" she declared, her joy radiating into the chilly air around us.

In that moment, with laughter bubbling up and intertwining with the fragrant scent of pine and cinnamon, I felt the weight of the world lifting from my shoulders. We were no longer merely individuals navigating through the complexities of life; we had become something greater—a family bound by love, laughter, and the unyielding spirit of togetherness.

The evening continued, filled with games and a sense of purpose that wrapped around us like a thick quilt. As the clock struck nine, the hall erupted in cheers and applause, the last raffle ticket being drawn. My heart swelled as I watched Ethan and Cassie celebrate, their laughter a melody that danced through the air, wrapping around me like a hug. I realized then that this was our moment—a testament to the resilience of the human spirit and the beauty of new beginnings.

As the event wound down and the last of the guests began to leave, I felt an overwhelming sense of gratitude. Evergreen Creek had embraced us, held us through the darkest nights, and now, it was a place of hope and new possibilities. Together, we would navigate whatever lay ahead, hand in hand, with love as our guiding star, ready to embrace the adventures that awaited us.

As the last echoes of laughter faded from the community center, the reality of the evening settled in like the fresh layer of snow outside. I stood amidst the remnants of our charity event, the tables now strewn with colorful paper and leftover treats, feeling a bittersweet pang at the thought of returning to the quiet of my home. Ethan and Cassie had momentarily disappeared into the bustling crowd, and the warmth of our earlier embrace lingered in the air like a cherished melody.

I took a moment to breathe in the vibrant atmosphere around me, the scent of pine and freshly baked goods mingling with the crispness of the winter night. The glow of fairy lights illuminated familiar faces, each one alight with joy and the satisfaction of having contributed to something greater than themselves. Yet, amid this warmth, a flicker of unease stirred within me. Change was afoot, and I wasn't entirely sure I was ready for it.

"Hey, what's this?" a teasing voice cut through my thoughts, pulling me back into the present. It was Claire, my closest friend, her auburn hair catching the light in a way that seemed almost ethereal. She approached with her usual exuberance, balancing a plate of cookies in one hand and a steaming cup of cider in the other.

"Just contemplating life," I replied with a wry smile, pretending to be more philosophical than I felt. "You know, the usual."

Claire chuckled, her eyes sparkling with mischief. "Right, because that's what you do at festive charity events—ponder the universe over half-eaten cookies." She nudged me playfully, and for a moment, the weight on my shoulders lightened.

"Okay, you caught me. I was thinking about Ethan and Cassie," I confessed, the names slipping from my lips like a secret. "Things feel different now. Good, but different."

"Ah, love and family—two things that can turn a perfectly good brain into a mushy puddle." Claire raised her cup in mock salute. "But you're in it, and you're glowing, my friend. Embrace it! You've earned the right to be happy."

"I know, I know," I said, feeling the corners of my mouth lift. "It's just... what if I mess it up?"

She rolled her eyes dramatically. "You? Mess things up? Never. Look, you've already survived the apocalypse of your past. What's a little love and family compared to that?" Her voice was light, but I could sense the genuine affection beneath her playful ribbing.

I laughed, the sound easing the tightness in my chest. "You're right. I just need to trust that I can handle it."

"Exactly! Now, enough moping. Let's go find your man and that adorable daughter of his. They're probably plotting their next adventure without you."

With a gentle nudge from Claire, I found my way back into the throng of cheerful townsfolk. The lively chatter enveloped me, a comforting reminder of the community I had come to cherish. It was here, among these familiar faces, that I felt grounded, despite the swirling uncertainties of my heart.

We weaved through the crowd, finally spotting Ethan and Cassie near the cookie table, both grinning ear to ear. Cassie was triumphantly clutching a candy cane like a trophy, while Ethan held a plate of what appeared to be every flavor of cookie ever baked. My heart swelled at the sight—the two of them together embodied everything I had hoped for.

"Look who decided to join the party!" Cassie exclaimed, her eyes sparkling with joy. "I won the cookie competition! I told them my secret ingredient was love."

"Was that before or after you dipped them in half a jar of sprinkles?" I shot back, earning a playful glare from Ethan.

"Hey, a little sparkle never hurt anyone," he replied, chuckling as he placed an arm around Cassie. "What's a cookie without some pizzazz?"

As the three of us shared in the playful banter, a sense of normalcy began to weave itself back into the fabric of our lives. We were still figuring things out, still adjusting to this new reality, but in that moment, surrounded by laughter and sweetness, it felt like the weight of the world had lifted.

But just as I began to relax, the doors of the community center swung open, and a chill swept through the room. A newcomer stepped inside, shaking off the snow that clung to their coat. It was a man, tall and imposing, with an air of authority that instantly commanded attention. I could feel the room quiet as eyes turned to him, murmurs rippling like a stone thrown into still water.

"Who is that?" I whispered to Claire, who stood beside me, her brow furrowing with curiosity.

"I don't know, but he's definitely not from around here," she replied, her tone cautious. "Something about him feels... off."

The man surveyed the crowd with an intensity that sent a shiver down my spine, his gaze lingering for just a moment too long on Ethan and Cassie. My heart raced. What could he want?

Just as I opened my mouth to voice my concerns, he stepped forward, cutting through the murmur of voices. "Ladies and gentlemen," he said, his voice deep and resonant, "I'm here to speak about a matter of great importance to this community."

An uneasy silence fell over the room, the warmth of our earlier festivities overshadowed by a palpable tension. I exchanged a glance with Ethan, whose expression had shifted from joy to concern in an instant. Cassie, blissfully unaware of the growing unease, continued to clutch her candy cane like a shield.

The man cleared his throat, his eyes now locking onto mine. "I believe we need to talk about the future of Evergreen Creek, and the legacy we leave for our children."

With each word, a knot tightened in my stomach. I was prepared for change, but I hadn't expected it to come crashing in like this. And as the evening shifted around us, I sensed that this was just the beginning of something far more complex than a simple charity event.

The man's voice echoed through the hall, punctuating the warmth of our earlier celebration with an unexpected chill. I felt the collective breath of the room hitch, curiosity morphing into something akin to dread. Ethan shifted beside me, his arm tightening around Cassie, while Claire's eyes darted around as if searching for a way to defuse the mounting tension.

"Who are you?" someone from the back called out, the question heavy with skepticism. The crowd murmured in agreement, shifting uneasily as they scrutinized this stranger in their midst.

The man took a measured step forward, his features illuminated by the soft glow of the string lights, casting shadows that seemed to flicker with menace. "My name is Thomas Grayson. I'm here to discuss the future of this community—its very survival, in fact."

Survival? The word hung in the air like a storm cloud, darkening the festive atmosphere. I exchanged a glance with Ethan, whose brow was furrowed with concern, the warmth from earlier dissipating like the last remnants of daylight.

"What do you mean, survival?" Claire asked, her voice steady, but I could see the uncertainty flickering in her eyes.

Grayson's gaze swept over the crowd again, and I felt as if he were sizing us up, assessing our worth. "Evergreen Creek has faced challenges before, but none like what is looming ahead. There are plans in motion that could drastically alter the landscape of our town, and if we don't band together, we may lose everything we hold dear."

A ripple of whispers surged through the crowd. I could see the fear in their eyes mirrored in my own heart. Questions piled up in my mind like snowdrifts—what plans? Who was behind them? And why was this man so intent on instilling panic?

Ethan stepped forward, a protective instinct shining through his usually easygoing demeanor. "What exactly are you talking about? Is this some kind of threat?"

Grayson's expression softened, but his resolve remained. "Not a threat, but a warning. Development plans are being discussed at the county level that could pave over our parks, disrupt the river, and push out the very people who've made this town a home. It's not just about land; it's about community and our way of life."

The room fell silent, the festive air thick with the weight of his words. I could feel Cassie fidget beside me, sensing the tension that had settled like a dense fog. Her innocence, so vibrant just moments before, now felt like a fragile candle flickering in the wind.

"What can we do?" I found myself asking, my voice stronger than I felt. "How can we fight this?"

Grayson nodded, appreciation flickering in his eyes. "We need a united front. A rallying of the community to voice our concerns and put pressure on the decision-makers. I've already begun organizing meetings, and I would like you all to be a part of it."

Just then, the door swung open again, this time with a force that made everyone turn. A tall woman strode in, her expression a mix of determination and indignation. Her name came to me like a whisper on the wind—Megan, the town's former mayor, known for her fiery speeches and unwavering commitment to preserving Evergreen Creek.

"I heard someone was stirring up trouble," she declared, her voice strong and unyielding. "What's this about development? You know I won't stand for it."

Grayson's eyes lit up, his demeanor shifting slightly. "Megan! Glad you're here. We need your voice. There are plans to develop the old mill site and turn it into a commercial complex. If we don't act quickly, we'll lose not just that land but the soul of Evergreen Creek."

Megan's jaw tightened, and I saw a flicker of fear in her eyes, quickly masked by resolve. "Then we need to rally the people. We've fought for this town before, and we'll do it again. The heart of this community beats strong, and it's time we show them just how strong we can be."

A murmur of agreement rippled through the crowd, sparking a flicker of hope in my chest. Perhaps we could do something; perhaps we could make our voices heard. But beneath the surface, uncertainty churned like a winter storm, threatening to engulf the flickering light of optimism.

"We'll hold a meeting," Megan continued, her voice steadying the crowd. "We'll spread the word and mobilize everyone. But it'll take more than just talk; we need action."

Ethan turned to me, his eyes searching mine. "Are you with us?" he asked, his tone serious yet filled with warmth.

"Absolutely," I replied without hesitation, but my heart raced with the weight of what lay ahead.

As the meeting began to take shape, ideas bounced around like snowflakes in the wind—petitions, community forums, strategies for outreach. The atmosphere buzzed with energy, and I could feel the collective determination growing, yet beneath it all lurked a shadow of doubt.

Just as we began to formulate a plan, Cassie tugged at my sleeve, her wide eyes reflecting a mix of confusion and fear. "Mommy, what's happening? Is our home in danger?"

I knelt to her level, forcing a smile despite the knot tightening in my stomach. "No, sweetie, we're just talking about how to keep our town safe and happy. Nothing's going to change without us fighting for it."

But as I spoke the reassuring words, an icy finger of dread trailed down my spine. I could see the worry etched in Ethan's face, mirroring my own fears. What if this was just the beginning?

As the evening wore on, voices rose and fell like the tide, momentum building in the room. Yet, amidst the passion and resolve, I couldn't shake the feeling that we were on the brink of something far larger than a mere town meeting.

Just when I thought I could finally breathe again, the door swung open once more, and a chilling gust of wind swept through the hall. This time, a figure stood silhouetted in the doorway—a man clad in a dark coat, his face obscured by shadows.

He stepped forward, revealing sharp features and an air of authority that sent a jolt of recognition through me. It was someone I never expected to see again, a remnant of my past that threatened to resurface like a specter from the depths.

"Hello, everyone," he said, his voice smooth and commanding. "I believe we have some unfinished business to discuss."

A gasp rippled through the crowd, and my heart dropped. Just when I thought we had a handle on our lives and futures, the past came knocking, and this time, it didn't look like it was going to be easy to shut the door.

Milton Keynes UK
Ingram Content Group UK Ltd.
UKHW020013061124
450708UK00001B/133